PROSE BEFORE BROS

GREEN VALLEY LIBRARY BOOK #3

CATHY YARDLEY

WWW.SMARTYPANTSROMANCE.COM

COPYRIGHT

This book is a work of fiction. Names, characters, places, rants, facts, contrivances, and incidents are either the product of the author's questionable imagination or are used factitiously. Any resemblance to actual persons, living or dead or undead, events, locales is entirely coincidental if not somewhat disturbing/concerning.

Made in the United States of America

Print Edition
ISBN: 978-1-949202-09-0

CHAPTER ONE

Thuy Nguyen had never seen so many casseroles in her life.

She'd seen plenty of food before, of course. She'd gone to too many large gatherings and block parties and Lunar New Year's to avoid seeing stacks of food presented for the delectation of the masses, but she'd never seen quite so many of the quintessential American food.

Squares, rectangles, circles of plastic storage ware covered every inch of the large oak dining room table. There were things she recognized, specifically salads: green, potato, macaroni. She guessed the pinkish stuff with cherries and marshmallows was ambrosia, since she'd remembered Maddy making that at the apartment. But the more food the throng of people brought in, the less recognizable it became. There was what looked like something with green beans, smothered in… gravy? With… almonds, maybe? Or mushrooms? Or — gah — *both?*

And then there was a dish that was just sort of smushy and… well, gray. Honest to God, *gray*. Like a vat full of spackle. She had to look away, gaining fortitude from the dark chocolate cake a nice woman named Jennifer Winston had dropped by, along with sincere condolences. Jennifer had mentioned that Mr. Blount had helped her when her roses developed a pernicious blight. Jennifer's husband, Cletus, said that the man "was a wizard with manure" as well.

This place is so weird.

The funeral service had been that morning. She'd stood by her best friend Madison "Maddy" Blount's side as they'd buried Maddy's father. There was now a small reception for those who wanted to pay their respects to the family of Edward Blount.

Thuy wasn't quite sure if the same number of people would've shown up if they just wanted to pay their respects, or because they were curious about Maddy's situation. Maddy hadn't been back to Tennessee since she'd left to go to college, which is how Thuy had met her — they'd been roomies in the dorms, and best friends ever since. Now, people saw that Maddy had returned seven months pregnant, with a woman in tow and no man in sight. Thuy had never lived in a small town, much less one in Tennessee, but she got the feeling it was the sort of thing that got tongues wagging. She could feel the curious stares crawling over her skin as she refilled the iced tea pitcher and made sure that Maddy wasn't on her feet too much.

She'd been to funerals before, obviously. With her family's history, funerals came a little too often, although the crowd was noticeably different. It was the town element that was really throwing her for a loop.

"So, you're a friend of Madison's, are you?" a woman's voice asked behind her.

Thuy turned to see an older woman looking at her critically. She vaguely remembered this one — Mrs. Simmons, maybe? — because she'd been making less-than-veiled comments about Maddy's pregnancy after the service. Thuy felt her protective instincts kick in, but knew this wasn't the time for a scene. It wasn't going to help Maddy at all to have her call this woman a nosy bitch in her living room.

Thuy pasted on her "can I help you?" smile, the one she'd perfected at the library. "Maddy's my best friend. We roomed together at Cal."

"Cal...?"

"University of California. Berkeley," Thuy supplied, since Mrs. Simmons still looked confused.

The woman curled her lip a bit. "Going off to that hippie school," she muttered.

"And how did you know Maddy's father?" Thuy asked, trying to change the subject from Maddy's supposed "hippie" ways.

The woman waved her hand. "Oh, everybody knew Edward Blount. How he managed to keep the farm going was a miracle, all by himself, with both of his kids going off and doing whatever they wanted..."

Thuy gripped her temper, feeling her smile sharpen on her face.

"... but the man had God's own green thumb, and he managed to grow anything, as well as keep those cattle," Mrs. Simmons continued. Her expression turned shrewd. "I suppose Maddy'll sell the place now? No need for forty acres, especially in her condition." Mrs. Simmons made a little gesture in front of her stomach, like she was rubbing a bowling ball.

"I have no idea," Thuy answered, keeping her voice even.

"Really?" Mrs. Simmons paused, then said, "Well, if Maddy's *husband* comes, maybe they could make a go of the farm, I suppose."

It was bait, the cheapest kind. This woman wanted confirmation or denial about Maddy's marital status. Maddy had warned her: *small towns turn gossip into blood sport. Just smile and nod.*

Fortunately, handling aggressive library patrons was something Thuy had some practice in. She could take some passive-aggressive nosiness. She smiled at Mrs. Simmons' comment, nodding silently.

Mrs. Simmons' expression turned irritated. "I said, if Maddy's *husband*... or boyfriend...?"

"Oh! We are out of iced tea," Thuy said, ignoring the implied question entirely. "Thank you for coming and being so supportive." With that, she deliberately turned her back on the woman, who gasped at the rudeness of the brush-off — but couldn't really reply, because of the complimentary statement at the end.

Thuy retreated to the kitchen where Maddy was leaning against a counter, dressed in black, rubbing her back. At seven months along, her stomach was prominent. "How're you holding up?" Thuy asked in a low voice, as she pulled more iced tea from the fridge, mixing in the sugar syrup solution. She then mixed up another batch of lemonade iced tea. She didn't want Maddy to worry about anything food related, not today. And she certainly didn't want Maddy to try lifting anything.

"I'm hanging in there," Maddy replied in a low voice. "I'd had a chance to make my peace with Dad, at least, over the past few years. Or as close to it as we were going to get."

She noticed Maddy kept staring at the door. "You're waiting for your brother, aren't you?"

Maddy nodded sadly. "I don't think he's coming."

"Why don't you describe him? So I know what to look for."

Maddy shrugged. "I've barely seen him since I was... what, twelve," she said. "He's big. Tall, I mean, and muscular. Or at least, he used to be. Maybe he got fat by now. It's been sixteen years."

"Maybe he just doesn't want to get caught in the crush," Thuy muttered, her eyes flicking to the doorway and the crowd of people beyond.

Maddy laughed. "Yeah, there are a lot of people. Dad would've been surprised at the turnout.

He was well known, but he wasn't exactly *popular*."

No, from what she'd gathered, Edward Blount Sr. was an asshole, to the world in general and to his kids in particular. A hell of a farmer or rancher or whatever, but an asshole.

"This morning at church, I had a woman ask me flat out where the father of my baby was," Maddy said in a whisper, making a face.

Thuy grimaced. "What'd you say?"

"That it wasn't her business." Maddy shrugged. "Hey, I figured, if she was going to be rude, then I could be rude, right? But she kept on going. Said that there was no way that I could take care of a baby all by myself."

Thuy stared. "Does she not realize how many single moms there are in the United States? What, does she live under a rock?"

"I told her that I wasn't alone. I had you." Maddy started giggling. "So, don't be surprised if people start making comments about us being lesbians."

Thuy grinned. "If I swung that way, I'd be all over you," she admitted. "And I don't care what these people think. It's not like we're going to be here that long anyway."

Maddy looked uncomfortable. "Still have the will reading," she said. "Dad set up some lawyer as the executor. I guess I'll see Teddy then if nothing else." She frowned. "If Dad left him anything in the will. He did basically disown Teddy. And ever since Teddy joined that gang, he wrote us off, too."

Thuy felt pain for Maddy. She of all people could understand how complicated feelings for family could be. She gave Maddy a hug, stroking her hair. "It'll be all right," she crooned, wishing fiercely that she could make everything all right for her friend.

Of course, that was the exact moment that Mrs. Nosy Simmons came in. She goggled at the sight of them hugging.

"I didn't mean to interrupt anything," she said, her eyes wide.

Thuy fought the urge to laugh, instead cuddling Maddy closer. "Yes?"

She felt Maddy's body shaking with suppressed chuckles.

"Oh. Uh..." The woman turned on her heel and retreated quickly.

"By the time that gets to her hairdresser, she's going to say we were full-on making out by the sink," Thuy observed, letting Maddy go.

"In front of God and everybody," Maddy agreed with a giggle.

Thuy glanced at her phone. It was eight-thirty, and it was going to take time to Tetris all the food into the fridge and freezer. Besides, Maddy needed her rest. "Let me know if you want me to clear the house," Thuy said.

"I'll take you up on that," Maddy said, grimacing a little and rubbing her back again. "Let's give it another hour, and then you can go all 'closing time' on people and kick them out. Nobody does it better than a librarian."

Thuy chuckled and knuckle-bumped Maddy, then went out to refill the pitchers of drinks. She loved Maddy like the sister she never had, and she owed Maddy more than she could ever repay. She could put up with a bunch of small-minded small-town people for a week or two if it meant making things easier for her bestie.

If only she could track down Maddy's brother, she thought with a grimace, and went back to work cleaning.

CHAPTER TWO

Drill sat at a low table at the Dragon Biker Bar, taking lazy pulls off a long-necked bottle of beer, feeling numb.

Part of it might be exhaustion. The club had been in a state of freefall since their president Razor St. Claire had gone to jail as a result of their vice president, Darrell Winston, going states' evidence against him. Their trusted lieutenant Repo had gone on the road — on the run, if rumors were to be believed. Even Razor's psycho wife had gone missing, under even more dire circumstances and rumors that were only whispered. The resulting power vacuum had meant a lot of infighting, a lot of desertion. The crew was a shadow of its former self. But the results were Drill's old friend Catfish landing on top, running the show. Of course, he'd leaned plenty on Drill as his muscle, and Drill had spent the past six months kicking a lot of asses to get people in line.

Now, Catfish was off in the back rooms somewhere with Dirty Dave, trying to brainstorm some way to build the crew back to its former glory. Their finances were a mess, their income significantly reduced. Drill didn't care about that so much. He felt tired just thinking about it.

But that wasn't the only reason for his numbness.

He'd seen his father's obituary almost by accident. He'd been eating breakfast over at Daisy's Nut House, and he'd picked up a newspaper someone had left behind out of sheer boredom. To see his father's stern face staring at him in inky newsprint had been like a blow to the sternum.

Edward Blount. Dead at age sixty-six, leaving behind a son and a daughter.

He didn't know who'd written up the notice. Obviously, someone who was good at putting things politely and succinctly. Whoever it was had mentioned that the elder Edward Blount had been predeceased by his wife, Maisey. It also said that he was the fifth generation of Blounts to run the farm that still sat on the outskirts of Green Valley.

They say if you can't say anything nice, don't say anything at all, so the obituary ended rather abruptly from there, only listing the funeral and burial, with family and friends gathering at the farmhouse after.

He figured his sister Maddy must be setting up the reception or whatever afterward, at his father's home. His father had no other kin to speak of, being an only child, to the constant disappointment of Drill's grandparents. Drill wondered absently how his sister was faring. Last he'd heard, she'd headed out to California, and as far as he knew, hadn't been back since.

Don't think about it. He took another pull of beer from the bottle. He was too tired to think about the past, anyway.

"Want some company?" one of the biker groupies — Tish? Misha? — asked, sliding onto his lap and reaching to stroke his shaved-bald head. He hated when they did that. He sighed, stopping her hands. Her closeness gave him a good look into her eyes. Even in the dim lighting, he could see her pupils were the size of dimes. Squinting, he saw that she was starting to get the tell-tale scabs and itchy rash of a meth head.

He sighed again, turning grim as she struggled harder, brushing her tits against his chest. "Not interested."

She pressed harder, until he gently shoved her off, turning back to his beer.

"What the hell, Drill?" the girl snapped, her voice high pitched enough to compete with the blaring music. "You think you're too good for me or something?"

Jesus be a fence, he thought with irritation, then blinked. He hadn't thought of that particular saying in years, not since he was...

Nope. Wasn't gonna accidentally wander down that Memory Lane. He shook his head. "I'm just not interested."

"Aw, lay off him, Alice," a young guy said. The kid was dressed in all black, his blond hair cut short at the sides but flopping at the top. Drill recognized him as Pete Lundy, son of the local bank manager, recent college drop-out, and low-level weed dealer. He was also a tentative Wraith recruit. *Man, we must be desperate,* Drill thought derisively. "Drill's father just died. That's bound to mess a guy up."

Alice's eyes were confused. "Who's his Dad?"

Drill stared at them as they continued their conversation. *Like I'm not even here.*

"Old man Blount," Pete continued easily. "Or Old Man Blunt, if the rumors were true. Said that he could grow anything, and just before he died, he pretty much did. Like some of the highest-grade pot in the world — for 'medicinal' purposes."

Drill gritted his teeth. He knew better. His father could probably grow roses out of granite — the man was God's own farmer — but Drill knew his father would sooner burn down all forty acres of land than break the law.

No, his stupid thug of a son was the only one capable of that.

"D'you know, I tried to sneak into his greenhouse one night to find out if it was true?" Pete went on conversationally to Drill, as Alice watched eagerly. "Guy went after me with his twelve-gauge."

Now, that *sounds like him,* Drill thought.

"So, did you go to the memorial service earlier?" Pete pressed, getting on Drill's nerves. "Or are you going later? I'm guessing later, when it's not so damned crowded."

Drill didn't even grunt. He watched as a stripper, with more enthusiasm than skill, shook her naked rack and then turned to flash her ass, swinging around the pole. He shook his head, sighing again.

She was obviously new, and needed practice, he thought clinically. His body didn't stir at all.

What is wrong *with you?*

It wasn't his father's death. As far as he was concerned, his father had died the day he'd joined the Wraiths. Maybe even earlier, when his mother had died. But this empty feeling had been growing for a while, and this numbness was starting to get alarming.

The meth girl interrupted, straddling him this time. "Poor baby," she crooned, leaning forward and licking his earlobe. "I can make you feel better. Just take me to one of the back rooms, and you'll forget all about it."

He got to his feet, picking her up easily. Then he handed her to Pete like she was a feral cat. "Not interested," he repeated.

Pete laughed as Alice shoved him away, cursing. "Not interested in the funeral," Pete clarified, "or in Alice here?"

"Either." Drill sat back down. "Both."

Unfortunately, Pete decided he was Drill's new best friend and sat down beside him, motioning to a waitress. "I hear your sister's back in town," he said.

Drill frowned. He hadn't seen Maddy in sixteen years, not really. Not since he'd joined the Wraiths. He felt his chest tug a little. He found himself wondering how she was. When he left all those years ago, he hadn't worried that his father would beat her — the man's old school sensibilities meant he'd never strike a woman, although Drill had inconspicuously kept tabs to make sure that his instincts weren't wrong. His sister hadn't gotten the whippings Drill himself had received. That said, he imagined that living with "Old Man Blount" hadn't been easy for her, since his old-fashioned take on life probably kept her pretty constrained. When he'd heard she went off to school, he was amazed — and cheered.

Of course, if Maddy was so smart… what the hell was she doing back in Green Valley?

Pete hunkered down, leaning across the table conspiratorially. "You know, there are some rumors going on around your sister. Like, deviant shit."

Drill finally focused on the kid. He might not have been in his sister's life, might have cut off that part of his family — but by God, he wasn't going to sit here and listen to Pete fucking Lundy talk smack about his kid sister.

"Like what?" Drill asked, his voice deceptively calm.

Pete perked up, as if thrilled that Drill was finally participating in the conversation. "I hear she's knocked up, and there's no husband. Just some Chinese chick," he said. "A *chick*. I heard that your sister told my Mom's friend that she doesn't need a man, she's got her woman." He looked like he was drooling over that tidbit of gossip.

Drill blinked. His sister was gay? That was news. Not that he cared one way or another. He knew some people in the Wraiths might not share his opinion, but he just didn't give a damn about who decided to sleep with who, if they weren't sleeping with him.

Obviously, Pete here cared.

What *was* more concerning was the fact that she was pregnant. He tried to imagine it, and couldn't. In his head, she was still the twelve-year-old kid, her hair in braids, her head bent studiously over books. Or she was playing softball, with the kind of easy grace that made winning plays look like a walk in the park.

Now, she was supposedly pregnant, with no man in the picture. How was she managing?

He found the numbness retreating, pierced by Pete's missive.

Was she all right?

"What the hell are you talking about?" a new voice chimed in.

Pete and Drill looked up to see Catfish standing in front of them, his arms crossed. He looked imposing, and irritated.

Pete saw that he had a new audience, and quickly crowed out, "Drill's sister here is *gay*! And pregnant! She brought her girlfriend to his Dad's funeral, and…"

"Drill doesn't have a sister."

Catfish's words were like a hammer striking an anvil, and Pete winced back. "Wha…what?"

"Drill doesn't have a sister. Or a father." Catfish's eyes gleamed. "You join the Wraiths, then *we are your family*. Period."

Pete looked abashed. "Uh..."

"If you have trouble cutting ties, if you want to sit around like it's a fucking sewing circle exchanging gossip, then maybe Drill here should kick your ass out, huh?"

"No, sir!" Pete was visibly trembling by now.

"Goddamn recruits," Catfish said, shaking his head. He gestured for Drill to follow him. Drill got up, abandoning his beer, following him to the back rooms. "I wanted to go over last week's take, and talk about some loans we've got to get collected. Okay?"

Drill nodded, following Catfish down the hallway. But the numbness had retreated, followed by a sense of curiosity, and concern. Not for his father — it was too late for that, even if he'd had a better relationship with the son of a bitch.

But Maddy...

What had happened to Maddy?

CHAPTER THREE

It was ten o'clock before the last of the mourners and well-wishers and neighbors left the Blount homestead. Getting all that food tucked away had taken some creativity, but at least they wouldn't go hungry in the next week. *Or possibly month,* she thought, as she crammed the last plastic container in and shut the fridge door firmly. Maddy had been yawning since nine, so Thuy had sent her off to sleep.

"You sure you don't need help?" Maddy had asked, rubbing at her eyes.

"You sure you're okay sleeping in your Dad's room?" Thuy had asked in return.

"Yeah. I mean, he had his heart attack in the field, not here in the house. Besides, this belly needs more room than my old twin bed." She'd disappeared up the stairs, saying goodnight.

Thuy felt a little freaked out. She was on a farm. She'd never been on a farm before. That probably came off as totally snobbish, but damn it, she'd lived in some of the sketchiest neighborhoods in Oakland, so it wasn't like she felt she was "above" it. She'd gotten used to the quick popping sounds of drive-by shootings, the wail of sirens, the screech of tires on asphalt. The loud braying laughter of drunks, usually from some of her family.

This? The weird silence and nature sounds? Downright eerie.

So was the total abundance of space and darkness. She was used to skies that glowed an unhealthy orange from light pollution, thank you very much. Not this vast threatening *void*. The stars were pretty, she thought, but it was November. The temperature wasn't too different from the Bay Area, but still, fifty degrees was a little nippy to be hanging out on the creaky porch, staring at the stars.

Besides, there was stuff to do.

She wandered around the small house, making a mental to-do list. When Madison called her in tears, saying her father had died, Thuy had immediately taken time off to help her. Fortunately, her boss at the bioscience library had been very understanding, and she'd found people to cover her shifts. They'd gotten to Tennessee, and she'd helped Maddy through the mundane details of taking care of death.

They'd need to get rid of everything, Thuy thought. Put the house on the market. She'd heard and seen some cattle on the way in (and wasn't *that* a trip — all those cows, *right there*)… one of the neighbors had said they were feeding them that week, to help out, but the cattle would need to be taken care of. And of course, there was the will reading.

So many details.

The brother, Teddy, had never shown up. Maddy didn't like talking about him, but Thuy knew how much Maddy missed him. Apparently, they'd been close as kids, probably as a united front against their asshole Dad. Thuy had heard only a little about how strict the man was, and how unhappy he'd been when Maddy had chosen Berkeley for college. He never visited. Of course, given Thuy's own family history, she wasn't going to throw stones.

She sat down at the sturdy oak dining room table, rubbing its surface. It looked like an antique. Most of the things in the house looked old, but in a good way. Again, it was a far cry from the way she'd grown up.

Because of the stillness of the night, she heard the buzz of an engine before she fully put together what the sound was. Then her body went on full alert.

That's not nature.

That was a motorcycle, something loud and growly.

She waited by the door, listening as the sound got louder. Whoever it was, was coming up the long-ass driveway that led to the farmhouse, the barn, and the little guest cabin. They were headed there deliberately. That driveway was nearly a half-mile, at least, to the main road.

Who would be coming here at this time of night? On a bike, no less?

She felt a prickle of fear. Maddy had mentioned a biker gang in town. If a member of a motorcycle crew were headed out at this time of night, to a deserted farmhouse, they would probably be there to rob the place. Not the most subtle of hits, admittedly. But they were out in the middle of nowhere. How sneaky did someone have to be when the nearest neighbor was miles away?

And anyone could've found out about the funeral, she thought, panic rising. Easier still to find out that the old man was dead, and in a town this small, they'd hear that the only people staying on this desolate property were two women. Off in a farmhouse so far from the main drag, no one would ever hear the screams. Two vulnerable women. One of them pregnant.

With that, she thought of Maddy, sleeping upstairs. She set her jaw.

Vulnerable, my ass.

She went to the hall closet, grabbing the shotgun Maddy had mentioned when they arrived. She opened it quickly, making sure it was loaded. Then she snapped it closed and turned on the porch light as the motorcycle roared to a stop in front of the house.

She waited until the figure on the bike looked at her. The gun was at her hip, tip down, ready to be tilted up at a moment's notice.

"Evening," she said, feeling a bit like one of those gunslingers in *The Magnificent Seven.* "Can I help you?"

It took her eyes a second to adjust to the darkness. He took his helmet off, and she couldn't help it. She gaped a little.

Whoever the guy was, he was tall and yoked. He had muscles that bulged the motorcycle leathers he was wearing. He had a shaved head that gleamed and a face that was carved out of marble, with piercing blue eyes that took her in with a lazy perusal that didn't seem terribly threatened. He looked like an octagon fighter. His full, sensual mouth was quirked up in a smile.

"You must be the girlfriend." His voice was deep, rumbling.

It took her a second to process his words because she was too busy processing his looks. She frowned. "What girlfriend?"

"Maddy's girlfriend."

She rolled her eyes. "Okay, whatever. Who are you, and what do you want?"

"I'm here to see Maddy." Now he looked a little more determined. "So you can put the gun down."

Instead, she held it tighter. "It's ten o'clock at night," she pointed out. "She's asleep."

"So wake her up." His expression turned irritated. "I need to talk to her."

"You can talk to her in the morning." She didn't feel scared of him, necessarily, but she got the feeling he was very determined when he wanted to be.

"Can't. Now's the only time I have." He started to walk towards the door.

She lifted the barrel of the gun up, and he paused. "I said she's asleep," she said carefully, her heart beating fast. "Get on the bike, and beat it. We're not available for visitors right now."

He stared at her, then took a step forward. "Or what? What happens if I don't leave?" He sounded genuinely curious.

She took a deep breath, and held the shotgun steady, holding the butt off to one side as the barrel edged closer to where he was standing. "That is a very good question."

He studied her for a moment. "You're holding it all wrong. Haven't you ever held a gun before? What are you going to do, toss it at me?"

For a second, she felt like shooting him out of sheer principle. She was holding it that way because it was how her father had taught her:

she was too tiny for the recoil of most guns, and if she braced it against herself, she'd dislocate her shoulder. She didn't feel like telling this stranger that, though.

"I've already called the cops," she lied, wishing now that she had. She'd gotten so used to avoiding the police, it wasn't second nature. And besides, what was she going to say? He hadn't done anything.

Yet.

Her muscles tensed.

He smiled lazily. "Darlin', I'm not trying to scare you, but this farm is a ways away from town — it takes easily half an hour for anybody from the station to get here. And even if it's a big county police station, they've only got three people assigned to our area. The police are usually too busy to pay much attention to a sleepy little backwater like Green Valley."

It was disconcerting, how well he knew the police situation in the area. The reason he was so well versed with the police set up couldn't be good — he hardly looked like the neighborhood watch type.

"Then I'll take care of it myself. Step *back,*" she growled, as he fearlessly put another foot forward. She prayed she didn't have to shoot this man. It had been years since she'd been in this position. "Who *are* you?"

He smiled, easily… a teeny little bit sexy, she thought traitorously, then grimaced at herself, surprised. Yeah, he was good looking, and he was dangerous. But didn't she of all people know that "bad boys" were just bad news?

"I'm Drill," he said, as if that cleared things up. "And I'm here to talk to Maddy… and get some answers."

Get some answers?

Just like that, the gun went up to point at his head. Her protective instincts roared. "Listen, *Drill.* Maddy's my best friend in the world. The only family I've got left. I don't know who you are, or what kind of answers you want, but I'll say this. If you hurt her, or scare her, or do *anything* that makes her uncomfortable," Thuy said, her voice a deadly calm, "Satan's gonna flinch when he sees what I do to you. Got it?"

They stood like that, staring at each other, for a long minute. Then Drill's smile grew wide.

"Little fireball, aren't you," he said, sounding surprised. "I like that."

"Thuy? What's going on?" Maddy's voice emerged from the doorway, sounding nervous.

Thuy panicked. "Maddy, go back to..."

But it was too late. Maddy stepped out on the porch, then took one look at the bald stranger and clapped her hands to her face.

"Teddy!"

With surprising speed for a pregnant woman, she flew down the stairs, hurling herself at the biker and throwing her arms around him, to Thuy's shock.

"Drill," he corrected her, with surprising gentleness, hugging her back. "Sweetie, you know it's Drill now."

"Thuy," Maddy said, ignoring his statement, "this is my brother."

Thuy stared at him, putting the gun down and blinking. "This? *This* is your brother?"

The guy winked at her. Actually *winked.*

Thuy groaned. Well. This promised to be awkward.

CHAPTER FOUR

She had a gun on me.

Drill stared at the little woman with a sense of bemusement, unsure of whether to feel insulted or intrigued. She obviously saw him as some kind of thug. And, considering how late he was showing up on their doorstep — and the fact that he was in a biker gang — it wasn't like she was *wrong*.

She was five-foot-nothing, with shoulder-length glossy black hair and eyes so dark they shone like obsidian. Her heart-shaped face was set in a frown. At least she no longer had the shotgun trained in his direction. There was a flush spreading over her pale skin. Embarrassed, he thought, as he helped his sister back up the stairs.

"Girl, you are huge," he couldn't help but notice, earning himself a swat as Maddy laughed. "How far along are you?"

"Only seven months," she said with a sigh, walking through the front door. "By the time I'm nine months, I think I'll be the size of a tour bus."

He turned back to the other woman, who was putting the gun back in the hall closet. "What's your name?"

She cleared her throat, saying something quickly. He frowned, unsure he caught it.

"Your name is... Tweet?"

"*Thuy*." She enunciated more clearly. "It sounds like 'twee', but it's spelled T-H-U-Y."

"Chinese?" he guessed, remembering Pete's announcement at the Dragon Bar.

She shook her head. "Vietnamese."

"And you're my sister's bodyguard?" he asked, with a small smile.

She reddened a little more. "If she needs it, yeah."

"And trust me, I'd be in good hands," Maddy said with feeling, rubbing at the small of her back. "Can I get you anything? We have a ton of food. The Casserole Brigade showed up for the funeral."

Right. The funeral. He'd been so intent on seeing his sister, he'd managed to push that out of his mind. Which brought the fact that he was standing here, in his father's house, after all these years, crashing to the forefront of his mind.

The place hadn't changed at all, he noticed. Well, not at the heart of it. It had gotten older, more weathered, but nothing had been deliberately altered — which would've been just like his old man. The same battered maple cabinets. Same oak table, with its mismatched chairs. Same light gold linoleum, only worn in some spots. Same old beige fridge and matching stove. He could still remember his mother pulling bread out of that beige oven, cinnamon bread, rolled in a tight spiral with plenty of cinnamon sugar and raisins.

He shook his head, trying to shake off the sensations. "I'm not hungry. Coffee's great, if you've got it."

"I'll make up a pot," Maddy said.

Thuy looked from one to the other, then took a deep breath. "I'll leave you two to talk, I'm sure you've got a lot of catching up to do," she said. "I'll be upstairs if you need anything, Maddy."

Maddy rolled her eyes. "Okay, Mom," she said, with obvious affection.

Thuy shook a small fist at her, with equal fondness, then gave Drill a look that clearly said *don't upset her.* He nodded, then winked. For all her small stature, he got the feeling she was the type that would probably fight until she was a bloody pulp, and not surrender.

He knew some guys like that, in the club. Or at least, he had before everything went sideways and club members started peeling off in droves.

He watched as she ascended the staircase. She was wearing jeans and a sweater. For such a slight figure, she didn't have a bad ass, he noticed.

"Still don't have a girlfriend, huh?" Maddy asked.

He turned back to see his sister studying him, a wry grin on her face. He shrugged. "Nobody serious," he found himself saying.

"Have you ever had anybody serious?"

He frowned, turning one of the chairs around and straddling it, propping his arms along the high back. His father had always hated it when he did that, but with his long legs, this was the most comfortable position in the damned things. "I don't do serious. No time, no interest." Which was true. Some of the guys in the club had old ladies, but most just hooked up with whatever biker groupies or strippers were available. He'd done that, from time to time, always careful to wrap up. They said share everything with your brothers in the Wraiths, but VD wasn't exactly one of the things he felt like sharing. And honestly, he hadn't done much with the groupies because he felt, well, like a commodity. Like he could've been any of the bikers there, and the girl wouldn't have given a shit.

Probably because they *didn't* give a shit.

"No time for a girlfriend," Maddy mused, shuffling across the Linoleum, reaching for the can of coffee their father kept on a shelf. "What's been keeping you so busy?"

He was on his feet immediately, smiling a little as he reached for the can that was just out of her grasp. "Go sit down. I'll make the coffee," he said. "You probably shouldn't be on your feet."

"Now you sound like Thuy." Still, she took his advice, sitting down with a low groan. "They tell you pregnancy is rough, but you don't really get it until you're there, you know? And don't change the subject. Busy with what?"

"Club business. You know I can't talk about it," he chided gently. He measured coffee into his father's old coffee maker, got water from the tap and filled the pot, setting it to percolate. "Speaking of pregnancy — what's the deal there? Where's the father?"

He leaned against the counter, crossing his arms, staring her down. In that minute, she looked like the stubborn tween he remembered. She might have a bob haircut instead of braids, and the freckles might've faded somewhat, but she still had the strong square jaw, and she crossed her arms in a movement that mirrored his.

"The father was my boyfriend," she said.

"Was?" Drill felt his muscles tense, his jacket sleeves getting tighter around his arms as his biceps bunched. "Why isn't he here, taking care of you?"

"Because I don't need a man taking care of me," she snapped.

"If you're having a baby, you damned well do!"

"Oh, really? Because we all know what great caretakers' men are?" Maddy snarled sarcastically.

"He should provide for you," Drill said, hating that Maddy was being deliberately thick about this. "What happened between you two, anyway?"

"We'd been together for a few years. The baby was an accident," Maddy said, with a sigh. "I was on the Pill, but apparently shit happens. So, I told him. And he freaked out." Her blue eyes watered, and she brushed the tears away with her fingertips. "Anyway, he said he'd stay for the baby, and I… God. I didn't want someone to stay just because of an accident. If he wasn't all in, I didn't want him. So I kicked him out. He was scheduled to go on a research trip to Australia anyway, so I haven't seen him since."

"You… Jesus, Maddy," Drill said, rubbing his hand over his head as the pot bubbled behind him. "You have got to be kidding me. You're just being stubborn."

"I'm not being stubborn," Maddy growled. "Would *you* want to be saddled to some woman out of obligation? If you knew she was just staying because she felt she had to?"

He winced. "Well, I'm really careful…"

"Oh, God, look who I'm talking to," she said, rolling her eyes.

"Hey, what's that supposed to mean?"

"You've probably never been in a relationship that's lasted longer than cottage cheese. So maybe you giving me crap about my relationship choices—"

"I'm not the one knocked up, though," he interrupted. "You've got a baby to think about. When I heard about it... you know how hard it's going to be, doing this all by yourself?"

She smiled a little at that. "But I'm not by myself. Thuy's going to help me."

He wanted to throttle her. "That little girl looks like she's a hundred pounds soaking wet," he said.

"What does her size have to do with anything?"

Drill's eyes narrowed. "Is she just your best friend? Or is there something else going on there?"

She looked at him, then chuckled, shaking her head. "She really is my best friend. She's like my sister. We were roommate's freshman year in college, in the dorms... both of us scared and out of our depths."

"She doesn't have family of her own?"

"It's a long story. And not my story to tell," Maddy said. "Bottom line: we bonded like family. I'd give a kidney for her. And she's moved in with me, and she's promised to help me. I'm not saying it'll be easy, but I'm not going to be completely alone."

Drill rubbed his head again, then the back of his neck, pressing at the tension headache that was forming at the base of his skull. "I don't know what it's like where you are, but I'm betting it's not like Green Valley," he said slowly. "Is that how you want to raise your kid? Do you have any kind of... I dunno, support system out there?"

"We never had support systems here," she said, with a bitter chuckle. "Dad made sure of that."

"I had the Wraiths."

Her blue eyes flashed at him. "Yeah. And I lost you — so maybe you don't get to talk to me about support systems, either."

He sighed. "I couldn't stay here. Not with Dad. You know that." He cleared his throat. "I kept tabs on you, though."

"Yeah?"

"Yeah." He paused a beat. "I had a friend take pictures of your high school graduation. Didn't want the guys to know — Razor would've skinned me — but I was really proud of you."

Tears filled up her eyes again, and she rubbed them away. "Are you happy with those assholes?"

"They gave me a place to belong when Dad kicked me out," he said. "They're my brothers."

She sighed, then rubbed her eyes with the backs of her hands. "They wouldn't want you here now, would they?"

He turned to the coffee pot, pouring himself a cup. "No."

"So why'd you come?"

He let out a huff. "Because I heard you were here, and pregnant with no father in sight." He paused. "I wanted to make sure you were okay."

"That's sweet. Marginally fucked up, but sweet." She sighed. "I am okay. I'll be okay."

They stayed there for a second, silent, surveying each other.

"There's a will reading Thursday," she said finally. "I'll text you the address. It's at one. You should be there."

He laughed mirthlessly. "Do you really think he would've left anything to me? He hated me."

She shrugged. "The lawyer said we both should be there."

He checked the coffee pot, then poured himself a cup and looked at his sister, grabbing an empty mug. "Can you even…?" He gestured at her pregnant belly with the cup.

"I'm not thirsty," she said, and nodded at the empty chair. "Come on, sit down. If I can only hang out with you tonight, we've got a lot to catch up on."

CHAPTER FIVE

Thuy woke up to laughter, a sharp burst of it that was quickly shushed to quiet. She turned over in the twin bed, immediately alert. She was a light sleeper, especially when she was somewhere unfamiliar, but she'd been lulled by the voices of Maddy and her brother downstairs. There wasn't a clock, so she fumbled her hand over the nightstand until she found her phone. Wincing at the light from the display, she saw it said 3:30 in the morning.

Feeling thirsty, she hopped out of bed, shivering a little. She was wearing sweatpants and a long-sleeved sleep shirt, as well as a pair of thick fuzzy socks. She padded down the stairs, peering at the two. "Everything okay?"

"Damn it, I was afraid we'd wake you," Maddy said. She looked happy, happier than she had in months. Drill was smiling at Maddy fondly.

"It's okay. I wanted some water, anyway." Thuy walked past them, grabbing a glass and turning on the tap.

"I should go," Drill said, his voice sounding reluctant. "It's late, and you need sleep."

"But I don't know when I'm going to get to see you again." Maddy's smile faltered. "I've really, really missed you, Teddy."

"Please don't call me Teddy," he countered, but without any bite to it. "It's not like you're going to be around anyway, Mads. Maybe I can call you more, okay?"

"I'd like that." Maddy sounded so wistful, it broke Thuy's heart.

They both got up, Maddy with obvious discomfort, and Thuy watched as the larger man gave his sister a long hug and a kiss on the top of her head. "You take care, sweetie."

"Love you, Te...*Drill*."

"Love you too." He patted her shoulder. "Now, go on. Go get some sleep."

"I'll see you out," Thuy said.

Drill looked surprised. Maddy had already started up the stairs to the bedroom. He nodded. She stepped into some slippers and grabbed a thick sweater, putting it on as she stepped out onto the porch with him and shut the door behind her. The early morning air was brisk. She stood on the top of the porch while he went down a few steps, to the ground.

"Something you wanted to say?" Drill asked immediately, and from the porch light, she could see the wry grin on his face. "Or did you just find me so irresistible that you wanted a few more minutes with me?"

She shook her head, smirking. "Tempting as that is, no."

"Because I could arrange for more time with you," he said, his grin turning ever so slightly sharper. "In fact, I'd love a chance to get to know you better."

"Why can't you spend more time with your sister?" she asked instead. "She doesn't talk about you much, or your family, but I know that she misses you. I mean, it's *obvious* that she misses you."

He sighed. "It's complicated."

She crossed her arms, both in irritation and against the chill. "Just give me the basics. I'm a smart woman, I'm fairly certain I can figure it out."

"I'm part of the Iron Wraiths. They're a motorcycle club." He paused. "Let's just say they're my family now."

She grimaced. "No family but the club, right?"

"Well, yeah."

"Not that complicated." She shrugged. "It's like a cult. They reel you in, then cut off all outside sources of support, making you completely reliant on them for all of your needs… emotional, financial, whatever."

He frowned. "They aren't that bad."

"You're one-percenter then, yeah?" One-percenters being the "one percent" of motorcycle clubs that were actually criminal.

"What do you know about one-percenters?" He was looking at her like she'd grown another head.

She thought of her brother, her parents, then shook her head. "It's complicated," she shot back at him.

He grinned broadly. "Thanks. For looking out for Maddy."

"She's my best friend. Trust me, it's not a hardship."

"She's pregnant and alone, and that's not easy." He frowned. "What the hell happened to the guy?"

She let out a deep huff, seeing her own breath in the cold air. "Also complicated," she muttered. "I think he really loves her, but everything happened too fast. He's a 'by the plan' kinda guy, and this was definitely not in his plan this soon. And Maddy didn't want to get into a marriage where the guy felt trapped."

"He set the damned trap himself," Drill pointed out.

She shook her head. "Maddy's got a point. She couldn't trust him to stick. What's the point in having him stay, only to cut and run later?"

They were quiet for a minute.

"She could really use your help," Thuy said. "This house is going to need to be emptied, and sold. And like I said, she'd like to stay in touch with you, even when she's in California."

He sighed. "I can't help with the house. But I'll try to come to the will reading. She gave me the address. Maybe from there, I can see about calling her sometimes. Okay? Best I can do."

"All right." She got the feeling it really was.

He took a step closer to her, zipping up his leather jacket. He was smiling at her, his blue eyes warm. "You never answered my question."

She felt her heart beat a little faster, and immediately felt annoyed with herself. "What question?"

"Want to spend a little more time together while you're here?"

She blinked at him. "You can't be serious."

He was crowding her. Not in a bad way, necessarily. But he was slowly moving towards her, where she stood on the porch. His hand went up to the post, and he leaned towards her, his eyes at her level. They really were a startling shade of blue.

"Why can't I be serious?" He sounded amused. "Hard to believe guys aren't all over you, sugar. Those dark eyes of yours, that hair… that tight little body."

She rolled her eyes. "And, amazingly enough, I have a mind, too."

"I'll bet you're smart," he said, surprising her. "You're my sister's friend, went to that fancy school. You probably are used to hipster jackasses hitting on you with their fucking micro craft beers and their 'aren't I bored' talk."

She bit her lip, fighting back a smirk. The damned thing was, he wasn't wrong. Her last two boyfriends had fallen perilously close to the "hipster" mold, and it seemed like all she found these days were guys who waxed their mustaches and were better able to pick out an antique typewriter at a flea market than find her G-spot. So that was disappointing.

Drill's eyes were mesmerizing. "I'm not like them. You're not here for that long. I'm just saying I could make the time you're here… *memorable.*"

She could smell his cologne, as well as leather and motorcycle oil or whatever it was that made him smell unbearably *male.* Maybe it was primitive, or chemistry, or pheromones. It was definitely stupid. But that handsome face, the intensity of his eyes, the sheer presence of that utterly built body of his, made her hormones bounce around like bingo balls.

He's Maddy's brother.

She leaned forward, just a little. Surely one stupid kiss wouldn't kill anyone? And Maddy wasn't squeamish…

He's a criminal.

Hadn't she had enough of that for one lifetime?

Just before her lips could touch his, she yanked back. "Yeah, that's not gonna happen," she said, hating how breathless she sounded.

His eyes blazed. "Teasing me, sugar?"

She shrugged. Let him believe that, if he wanted. She didn't owe him anything, not even an explanation. "Just come to the will reading."

"Are you going to be there?"

"Maybe. If Maddy wants me there, or needs my help."

His smile was slow and sensual and *damn* if it didn't make her body just melt. "Then I'll be there," he said. "Just to see you again."

"This isn't going to go anywhere," she warned him.

"You keep telling yourself that," he replied, his grin kicking up on one side. "Not going to kiss me goodbye?"

"Don't make me get the shotgun again."

He laughed, then stepped down from the porch step, moving away from her. For a second her knees felt like buckling just from the release of tension. *Good grief, what the hell was that?*

He walked over to his bike, getting his helmet off the back. "See you soon, pretty girl," he promised.

She watched as he strapped the helmet on and climbed on the bike, kick starting it easily. He drove down the driveway, kicking up dirt in his wake. She wrapped her arms around herself, shivering as the cold she'd barely been aware of seemed to crash in on her all at once. She walked back inside, locking the door carefully behind her. Then she kicked off her slippers and went back upstairs, stripping off the sweater and climbing back into bed.

Still, even as late as it was and as tired as she was, she found sleep hard to find. All she could picture was Drill's blue eyes, and the sheer heat of his gaze. Her shivers had nothing to do with the cold.

Damn man, she thought, and pulled the covers over her head. An inappropriate attraction was the last thing she needed. Please God, they wouldn't be here long enough for her to do something truly stupid.

CHAPTER SIX

On Wednesday afternoon, Drill found himself in the back room of the Dragon, sitting across a desk from Catfish as Dirty Dave fidgeted and leaned against a wall. Even after all this time, it still felt weird to be in what was essentially their war room, only without their president Razor, or vice president Darrell, or top lieutenant Repo. Catfish sat behind the desk now, frowning as he glanced over handwritten ledgers, looking like the world's toughest accountant. Drill smothered a smile.

"You wouldn't be smiling if you looked at these fucking numbers," Catfish said, sparing him a small, annoyed glance. "We're bleeding money like a gunshot wound. How the hell did things get this bad? Dammit, Dave, you're supposed to be bringing in cash."

"It's not my fault Monty blew up his house making meth," Dave said. Whined, more like. "It's going to take time to find a new supplier. We'll just have to make it up with weed, but it's not the same kind of money."

"What about car parts?"

"My best car thief took off for Vegas." Dave shook his head, scowling. "And a few others who showed promise are joining other clubs. No loyalty."

Catfish grimaced. "That brings up our other problem. We're losing members. Too many of them. Drill, where the hell are my new recruits?"

Now it was Drill's turn to frown. "Hey, I'm muscle, not hospitality," he protested. "What do I look like, the welcome wagon? I'm not on a recruitment drive."

"We're *all* on a recruitment drive from here on out," Dave countered. "We keep this up, we're going to lose turf to other clubs. We're going to fucking *disappear* at this rate."

"Is it better if we keep recruiting assholes like Pete Lundy and Dwight what's-his-nuts?" Drill pointed out.

"We make do with what we've got," Catfish said, sounding like he was saying it through gritted teeth. "Hell, you were just a sixteen-year-old farm boy when we picked *your* ass up, remember? I brought you in myself."

"You might be older," Drill said, "but you'd only patched in a few years before."

"You were both useless," Dirty Dave added, with a laugh. "But look at you now. Arguing over how to run the club."

Drill shook his head. "Nah. I'm not running anything," he said, with a low sigh. "That's all Catfish."

Frankly, he didn't want to run the club. He'd been a valued member of it for a long time. It had been his family, his safe place. It had given him purpose and a place to belong. That was why he'd done so much for the club — why he'd fought so hard, and why he'd spent the past six months wrestling with assholes to make sure that Catfish took over. At least he knew Catfish had some principles. Not many, but a few. And Catfish had signed him up and mentored him. He felt loyalty there, and there was precious little in this world that he felt he owed loyalty to.

Catfish rubbed a hand over his face. "We gotta get numbers up," he said. "Dave, start hitting up those high schoolers. If they're old enough to ride, they're old enough to join."

Drill winced a little at the thought. Yeah, he'd been sixteen. But he'd had a damned good reason to want to get out of the house. He needed a place to escape, and the club had provided it.

Maybe there will be kids out there who need an escape, too.

He tried comforting himself with that thought, and was so engrossed that he missed what Catfish had said. He looked up. "Sorry, what?"

"I said, where were you last night?"

Drill froze. He'd left the Dragon after his talk with Pete, and after he'd had a talk about loan collections with Catfish. Catfish had then disappeared into a room with one of the dancers, probably to get a quick blowie or something. That's when Drill had gone back to the farmhouse. He hadn't been followed, he knew that — it would've been easy to tell on those old back roads. Still, ever since becoming president, Catfish was developing a fine sense of paranoia.

"I went home," Drill lied easily.

"At nine-thirty?" Dave looked skeptical. "What are you, eighty? Need to take out your dentures and go nighty-night?"

Catfish's eyes narrowed. "Pete was shooting his mouth off about your sister."

"Don't have a sister," Drill said. "Remember? The Wraiths are my family."

"Oh, I remember fine," Catfish drawled, his brown eyes glaring at Drill with intent. "Just wanted to make sure *you* remember."

"There was bad blood between you and your Daddy, as I recall," Dirty Dave said. "Surprised you didn't go over to piss on his grave."

Drill recoiled. He had hated his father, that was true. But it had been years. And the thought of disrespecting the grave — the one that was right next to his mother's, one he hadn't seen in years — made his stomach roil.

Catfish looked down at the papers again, then tilted his head. "Rumor has it Old Man Blount grew weed. Any truth to that?"

"No," Drill said. "He'd sooner stab himself than break the law, and besides, he thought weed was immoral. He had greenhouses, and I know he was growing specialty plants for fancy nurseries on the side of hay farming or cattle ranching. But weed?" Drill shook his head. "Not even if it was legal."

"Damn it." Catfish sighed. "Well, at least we've got the loans coming up, and the gambling is doing okay. Gonna need you to get some stragglers pretty soon."

"Got it," Drill said.

"Remember: we need more cash, and more recruits," Catfish told both of them, standing up and giving an obvious gesture of dismissal. "Dave, get me some more goddamn money."

"Doin' my best, boss." Dave's laugh was guttural, and he headed out the door.

Catfish put a hand on Drill's arm, stopping him from following. He shut the door. "You sure there's no weed at your Daddy's place?" he asked.

"I'm positive. I don't know how that rumor even got started."

Catfish sighed. "Probably because of you," he said. "Must've thought that the apple didn't fall far from the tree. That, and your Daddy had a talent for pissing people off."

"That he did," Drill admitted. His father had been an Old Testament man, with little patience for idiots. He counted his son, the thug, as one of those idiots. He'd disowned Drill, kicking him out of the house when he found out that he'd signed up as a prospect for the Wraiths. Literally kicking the shit out of him and sending him down the dirt road, until he'd made his way to the clubhouse. He'd spent the night on a dirty mattress. He hadn't gone back to the farmhouse until he'd seen Maddy last night. And he hadn't spoken a word to his father since.

I seriously doubt the old man left me anything.

Still, he promised Maddy he'd at least try to go to the will reading, if for no other reason than to see Maddy again.

And maybe that sexy little friend of hers. Thuy.

He took a breath. "Listen, I, um, got this thing tomorrow."

Catfish's eyes narrowed. "What thing?"

"Will reading," he said. "Um, my dad's lawyer contacted me. I need to be there."

"Your sister gonna be there?"

Drill hesitated, then nodded. He knew that Catfish could — and probably would — double-check his story.

Catfish looked lost in thought for a moment, then nodded. "Yeah, okay," he said. "You should go to that. Who knows, maybe you'll get something valuable."

"I still know who my real family is," Drill emphasized.

Catfish smiled, but it was a tired smile. "Damned straight," he said. "But even Darrell Winston knew when to use blood family. When it comes to money or getting shit, am I right?"

Drill thought about Maddy. He didn't want to use her. He just wanted to make sure she was all right.

"Right," he agreed weakly. And wondered, absently, when his "true family" had started to feel so damned exhausting.

CHAPTER SEVEN

"Damned GPS," Thuy muttered, as she found a place to pull a U-turn and catch the turn she'd missed. "I think reception's a little spotty."

Thuy was driving their rental car, headed to the lawyer, with Maddy strapped in the passenger seat. Maddy probably could've driven herself, but since the news of her father's death, she'd been sleeping like crap. She had dark circles under her eyes, and kept yawning. Thuy decided to make herself useful and act as chauffeur. Considering Maddy's size at only seven months, odds were good she'd probably need to stop driving herself during the later months, so Thuy figured she'd better get used to it.

"Aren't the trees beautiful?" Maddy asked, not caring that they might be late. She was staring at the multicolor foliage with a small smile on her face. "I always loved autumn. It's my favorite season. And there's nothing quite like fall in the Smoky Mountains."

"It is pretty," Thuy agreed, although she paid more attention to the roads than the trees. She was a decent driver, but she was more used to Oakland's bustle and even the chaos of San Francisco's one-way streets than she was these poorly marked country roads. Not to mention she usually took the BART train to work and was a big fan of public transit.

The forty-acre farm was hardly public-transit friendly. She wondered absently if Green Valley even had Uber or Lyft.

"My mom used to make apple pies around now, with apple pie filling she'd put up from our little orchard," Maddy enthused, sounding wistful. "I'd come home from school and the house would smell incredible."

Thuy felt a tiny pang of envy. When she got home from school, it was… well, radically different. Although sometimes she'd stay at her aunt and uncle's house, before they moved away, and sometimes they'd make pho broth overnight. She'd wake up, and the house always smelled delicious, rich with oxtail and cinnamon and star anise.

"I don't suppose there's a pho restaurant out here," she said offhandedly, smiling at the memory. "I could totally go for a bowl for dinner tonight. And maybe apple pie afterward." Her mouth watered at the thought.

"I don't think so," Maddy said. "This is more of a barbecue and steak sort of town. Oh! Speaking of barbecue… someone at the memorial told me about the Green Valley Community Center. They have jam sessions on Friday nights, and they have barbecue and a bunch of different kinds of salads — potato and macaroni, not just green — and coleslaw and things."

"Jam sessions? What kind of music?"

"Lots of different kinds," Maddy said. "Bluegrass, and blues. And country. And, um, folk, I think."

"Any EDM?" Thuy teased, then mimicked the electronic dance sounds. *"Umm-tss! Umm-tss! Umm-tss! Umm-umm-UMM-tss!"*

Maddy shook her head, laughing. "Yeah. There's a wicked club scene in room five. Total rave."

Thuy laughed with her. "Sorry. It's just… it's so different than anywhere I've ever lived."

"You've only lived in Oakland and Berkeley," Maddy pointed out.

"Well, it's different than there, that's for damned sure." Thuy sighed. "You can drive for miles and not see *anybody*. There isn't a rush hour. No buskers, no homeless people panhandling. No graffiti. You know the names of everyone on the police force around here. Which is, what, four guys or something?"

"Not exactly," Maddy said indulgently.

"There are literally, *literally*, white picket fences around houses." Thuy's mind boggled.

"It's not perfect," Maddy said. "It's just a town. There are plenty just like it all around Tennessee. But I have to admit, it's a pretty great place."

"I never touched a cow before I came to your dad's house." Thuy shuddered. "I think I saw one in a petting zoo, but the damned thing seemed really big."

Maddy burst out in a peal of laughter. "They're just cows. They're not even carnivores."

"Hippos aren't carnivores either, but they kill more people every year than lions," Thuy said, then ignored Maddy's increased hilarity. "Hey. I saw that on the Discovery Channel."

"Afraid of cows," Maddy said, shaking her head. "When I was a kid, we used to take care of fifty head. I fed 'em myself."

"Berkeley must've been a real shock for you," Thuy said, just now realizing how much of a culture shift Maddy had gone through. "I mean, it was a big change for me, but for you, it must've been like going to a whole different world."

Maddy's smile was tired. "It was," she admitted. "If it weren't for being so busy with softball, and you being my roommate, I might've tucked tail and headed home. It was all so overwhelming. So many people I didn't know, and the sheer crowds of people, just headed to class and back. Nothing in Green Valley could've prepared me for it."

"Well, you're a pro at big city living now," Thuy reassured her.

"Now, I can also see some of the benefits of living here that I couldn't see before," Maddy said. "Someday, I'm going to own a farm."

Thuy knew that this had been a dream of Maddy's for years. She'd talked about it a little after they'd graduated, even though her degree was in Sociology rather than anything agricultural. When

Thuy had gotten her advanced degree in library science, Maddy had gotten a job with the farmer's markets in Oakland. That was how Maddy had met, and fallen in love with, her ex David. David had been working on an organic farm, saving up to get his own, one the two of them had planned on buying and running together when the time was right. He had a one-year research trip to Australia planned, to learn new farming methods, and then when he got back, they'd start looking at locations for their agricultural utopia.

Of course, having an accidental baby had thrown a wrench in that plan. David hadn't been ready, freaking right out. And Maddy had cut him loose rather than have him just propose to her because they'd had a birth control malfunction.

Thuy gripped the steering wheel a little tighter. She wondered if Maddy's sleeplessness and melancholy were because she was thinking of David. Thuy knew Maddy wasn't over him, even though she'd done her best to talk about David in cool, logical terms. Personally, Thuy wanted to kick his ass. Even though she knew that Maddy had all but shoved the guy on a plane, if you love someone, you do whatever you have to, to be with them.

The fact that he got on that plane and left made him an asshole as far as she was concerned.

"You'll have a farm someday," Thuy finally said to Maddy, trying to sound comforting. "In the meantime, you've got a great job, and you're going to have a baby that loves you to pieces. And you'll have me, Auntie Thuy, ready to help out."

"You are a godsend, Thuy," Maddy said, wiping at her lashes with her fingertips.

"Whoa, whoa! It's nothing," Thuy said. "Come on, now. It's okay, it's fine."

The GPS voice came on. "Your destination is on the right."

Thuy looked over. There was a Victorian-styled house, not very big, with a wooden sign out front. *Walter Graham, attorney at law.*

"Looks like we're here." Thuy pulled into the drive.

Before she'd even turned the engine off, she heard the rumbling growl of a motorcycle engine. She looked in the mirror to see Drill pulling up behind them.

"Teddy!" Maddy hopped — well, as best she could — out of the car. "You made it!" she called out.

Drill shut down the bike and stepped off, peeling off his helmet and putting it on the bike. He had Maddy's eyes, Thuy realized — that same startling blue. But everything else on him was the complete opposite. Where Maddy was rounded and soft and gentle, everything about him seemed to be rippling muscles and hard, corded flesh. He was wearing his beat-up leather jacket with DRILL emblazoned on it, as well as his club insignia.

That should have turned her off. God knows, she'd seen enough club patches in her day. But she had to admit, the way he filled that pair of black jeans, as well as the Doc Martens he was rocking…

The guy was a total yum. She hated to acknowledge it, but it was true. He looked better than apple pie, and had a helluva lot more kick.

Thuy watched as he gave Maddy a careful hug with a small, almost sheepish smile.

"I'm so glad," Maddy said, rubbing at her eyes again. He looked taken aback.

"Told you I'd be here," he said. "Jeez. Why are you crying?"

"Hormones," Maddy replied. "I'm a soda bottle full of 'em, and it's like I keep getting shaken up."

"You get used to it," Thuy said.

He released his sister and smiled at Thuy, this time wider and much, much hotter. "Miss Thuy," he said, his words a slow, honey-drizzled drawl. "Just like you said. I hoped I'd see you again."

What the hell was it about accents? The guy was hot enough without that slow, dreamy cadence in his low rumble of a voice. Thuy felt her pulse pick up and dance a little bit. She cleared her throat.

"Maddy's been a little tired. I figured it's better if I drive."

He immediately looked at his sister with concern. "You need to take care of yourself," he said, with just an edge of sternness, mixed liberally with a sort of gentle warmth that made Thuy's heart melt a little. "Especially with the baby and all."

"Yes, big brother," Maddy said, rolling her eyes.

The three of them trooped into the house/office. There was an elderly woman sitting at a small desk in a large foyer that acted as a lobby. "I'll let Mr. Graham know you're here," she said, after giving Drill a baleful glare. Drill looked supremely unmoved by her scrutiny.

"I'm guessing she doesn't get men like you in here very often," Thuy murmured. The place was so quiet, she felt like she might as well have been yelling.

Drill's grin was wicked. "Maybe because there aren't many men like me." He gave her a wink.

She couldn't help it. She grinned back. "I meant bikers," she clarified.

"Did you, though?"

Maddy looked at Drill with some surprise. "Stop hitting on my friend. Trust me, she's not your type."

"All women are my type, Mads."

"And *that's* appealing," Thuy said, shaking her head.

"All right. *You're* not *her* type," Maddy said.

Drill looked at her, and it was like his blue eyes were boring into her soul. Thuy felt her mouth go dry.

"You sure about that?" He was answering Maddy, but the question felt directed at her.

Thuy swallowed as best she could over the Sahara that was her throat.

Mr. Graham emerged from the back, flanked by the disapproving receptionist. "You must be Edward's children," he said, offering his thin hand first to Maddy, then to Drill. He was wearing a suit complete with a tie and a vest. Thuy thought he might have one of those pocket watches on a chain. He reminded her of Ichabod Crane. "Come with me."

"I'll wait out here," Thuy said, her voice cracking slightly. She gestured to one of the seats in the lobby.

Maddy gave her a grateful look, then Drill ushered her into the office. Mr. Graham shut the door behind them.

Thuy sighed. She hadn't brought a book, and she wanted to save her phone battery in case the GPS on the ride home was as squirrely as it had been on the way there. She took a deep breath.

"I don't suppose you have anything to read?" she asked the receptionist.

The receptionist gave her a withering look.

"Didn't think so," Thuy mumbled, then settled down in the chair, hoping that the meeting didn't take too long... and that Drill left soon afterward. She wasn't sure what was going on there, but the more time she spent with him, the less she liked her reactions to him. The sooner they left this town, the better.

CHAPTER EIGHT

Drill felt out of place. The lawyer, Walter Graham, had an office that was as fussy as the rest of the house: dark paneling, shelves with nautical knick-knacks and thick leather-bound books. Diplomas with fancy cursive writing hung on the walls. The guy gestured to the leather seats.

Drill sat down. He saw that Maddy had gotten at least a little dressed up, wearing a flowing green dress thing that encompassed her enormous belly. She'd done her make-up, which only accentuated the rim of redness in her eyes. He, on the other hand, was wearing his scuffed and dirty black shit-kicking boots, black jeans, a Dragon Bar T-shirt and his leather jacket, complete with fraying patches. He looked like he'd just stepped out of jail. At least he'd taken the time to shower and shave his head.

Walter Graham looked just as finicky as the surroundings. He was a thin man with graying mouse-brown hair that was going high on his forehead. He had wire-rimmed glasses and cleared his throat a lot. Drill could probably snap him like a twig without breaking a sweat. That said, Walter the lawyer did not seem intimidated by him at all. If anything, he seemed to be looking with more concern towards Maddy. Probably because she looked like she was ready to pop.

"I'm so sorry to see you during this difficult time," Walter started, sitting at his desk and adjusting his glasses. "Your father wanted everything cut and dried, so at least this shouldn't take too long."

Drill heaved out a breath. No, it probably wouldn't take long at all. It's not like his father had a lot of stuff: no stocks and bonds, no fortune. All he had was that damned farm. And it wasn't like he'd left anything for Drill, either. It was probably stupid to have shown up, only to be slapped in the face with that stark reminder.

Just suck it up. Maybe he could have coffee with Maddy afterward — back at the farmhouse. Not anywhere that Catfish's spies might see. He sank a little lower in the chair, hating that he had to sneak around to see his own damned sister.

"All of the possessions — furniture, memorabilia, and whatnot — inside the house goes to his daughter, Madison Abigail Blount."

Maddy made a sniffling sound. Drill felt like hugging her. He knew that she'd had her differences with the old man, even if they weren't as extreme as his. But he also knew that she had a tender heart and was way, *way* more forgiving than he was. This was obviously hitting her hard.

"Are you okay with that?" Maddy asked him.

He shrugged. "I'm good. What the fu... er, the hell am I gonna do with a bunch of old chairs and a couch?"

She sent him a watery smile. "If I see anything like photos, I'll make you copies, okay?"

He nodded, then looked back at the lawyer, who had paused during their exchange. Walter cleared his throat again nervously.

"He also had two vehicles: the Chevy Silverado 1500, and a Lincoln Continental. The truck was his farm truck," Walter explained. "He said that you two could pick which one of each you wanted."

Drill startled. "He said I could have one?"

"Insisted on it, actually." Walter sent him a small smile. "He figured you'd go for the Lincoln."

Drill looked at Maddy, who was now smiling more broadly. "I'm okay with that," she said. "I like trucks. They're more useful."

"Yeah, but you've got another passenger to consider," he said, nodding at her stomach.

She let out a little peal of laughter. "I think we can figure it out. Kid's going to have to get used to riding in trucks, I think."

He frowned, wondering what she meant by that, but Walter continued. "The farm itself is completely paid off."

Both siblings stared at him. "Completely?" Drill repeated.

"How is that possible?"

"Your father was supplying seed and specialized plants to a number of nurseries," Walter explained. "He was also haying, and he winters cattle. Which is something you're going to need to deal with, by the way. At any rate, between that and living very frugally, he managed to pay off the mortgage. The house and farm are free and clear. If the farm is sold, then the proceeds are to be split evenly between the two of you."

Drill felt his jaw drop. It was as if someone had shoved him into a frozen pond. "Both of us?"

You mean, even me?

This was much, much bigger than leaving him a car. It was mind-boggling.

Walter's expression turned compassionate. "I know that you didn't see eye to eye with your father," he said, his voice lowering a little. "I know that things between you were… strained. I don't think it's betraying a confidence to let you know that earlier drafts of the will left you out for several years."

Drill's stomach churned.

"But as he got older, he told me that he felt he may have been partially responsible for the path you've taken," Walter added gently. "He felt like, had he not been quite so harsh on you in your formative years, perhaps you would've made different choices. He was of the belief that once your mother died, he had to be extra vigilant, and he was… well, this is my opinion, but I think he was frightened that he would make mistakes with you and your sister, and ruin your lives."

Drill blinked at this bit of insight. He couldn't imagine his father afraid of anything. And yet, his father's descent — and the punishments — had started in earnest after his mother's death. It was something to think about.

Walter cleared his throat. "I think that the money from the farm might have been his way of helping you have the leeway to have other options. If nothing else, it might be an apology, of sorts."

"My father never apologized." Drill's voice came out harsher than he intended. And it was true. In his entire life, he'd only ever heard his father apologize to one person: his mother. Once she died, it was as if his father forgot how to say "I'm sorry."

There had to be a catch here. There had to be. Yet Drill still felt a wild fluttering of hope in his chest, like a bird flapping futilely against a cage.

"You said 'if the farm is sold,'" Maddy pointed out, bringing Drill back to the present. "What does that mean?"

"There is a further stipulation," Walter said, pushing his glasses back up on his high, thin nose.

And here it comes. Drill braced himself.

"If one of you wants to keep working the farm, then ownership will go to him or her," Walter said. "Or both of you can split it evenly. I understand there are two residences?"

"The farmhouse, and the guest cabin," Maddy clarified. "The guest cabin's awfully small, though. I guess you could build some extensions, there's space around it, but..."

Drill shook his head. "It doesn't matter, someone's bound to like it," he said. "It'll look good on the real estate brochure. Because we're going to sell it. I mean, I've got the club, and I can't be a farmer. And you've got..." He motioned to Maddy's stomach. "... all that going on. So obviously you're not going to..."

He stopped abruptly. Maddy's expression was thoughtful.

"Maddy?"

She bit her lip, her complexion reddening.

"Oh, Jesus, no. Tell me you're not honestly thinking about this."

"I want to raise my baby in Green Valley," she said. He could hear the stubborn lilt in her voice. This was the sound of Maddy digging in.

God damn it.

"You can raise your baby somewhere else in Green Valley," he said, his own voice going harsh.

"I wanted to raise him on a farm," she argued. "I always wanted that. Do you know how long it would take me to afford a place like the homestead? Even with a nest egg of half of the proceeds?"

"You can't even take care of a farm!" His voice was raising, and he forced himself to keep it down. It wouldn't do to yell at a pregnant woman, even if said woman was his sister and driving him nuts. "You're in no state to run a farm, and you know it, Mads."

"I'll get help. And I've got Thuy," she said.

"Has Thuy ever worked a farm?"

"Well... no." Maddy looked thrown off, but then she rallied, her expression turning mulish. "But she's tough."

He shook his head. Then he looked at Walter for help.

Walter looked at Maddy, and shrugged. "If you agree, we've got some paperwork to fill out, to transfer the business. And you'll want the books and things. I can put you in touch with Edward's accountant."

"Maddy, you need to think about this," Drill said. Almost pleading.

She sighed. "You could come help," she said tentatively. "We could run the farm together."

He growled. "You *know* I can't."

She looked impossibly sad for a moment. Then her face set stubbornly.

"Then I guess you're still making bad choices," she said. "And that's not my fault. I want this farm, for *my* family, and I'm willing to work for it."

"So, you're screwing me over, then?" Drill couldn't believe it. Couldn't believe his sister was capable of it.

"You said you didn't expect Dad to leave you anything anyway," she said, sounding only a little sorry. "I will do everything I can to make sure some money comes your way. But I want to keep the farm in the family, and I want to raise my child there. I want you to be a part of that, not part of some damned criminal biker gang."

Her words bit into him, and he winced.

"So no, I'm not selling. You do what you want."

He glared at both Maddy and Walter. Then, without another word, he stormed out the door, past a startled Thuy, and off to his bike.

CHAPTER NINE

Thuy watched Drill's retreating figure as he got on his bike, put his helmet on with jerky motions, and roared off. She looked back at the door to the lawyer's office. Maddy was shaking hands with the spindly looking man, who patted her on the back kindly. Maddy looked a little upset.

"What happened?" Thuy asked. "Are you all right? Did Drill upset you?"

"Not as much as I upset him," Maddy muttered, then shook her head. "Come on, I'm starving. I feel like cake."

"Cake?" Maddy was a prime comfort-eater, and cake signaled definite upset. "Um, okay. Grocery store?"

"Let's go to Donner Bakery. They have the best cakes, I hear," Maddy said instead.

They headed out to the rental car. "What happened?" Thuy tried again.

"I don't want to talk about it."

Thuy suppressed a sigh. Maddy was her best friend, but she knew the woman could and would be stubborn. She wasn't going to spill the beans until she was damned good and ready. Which was probably when she'd gotten some cake in her system.

After only getting lost twice with the GPS before finally resorting to Maddy's hazy sense of direction, they finally made it to Donner Lodge and Bakery. It was a pretty place. With its fresh awning and French-styled wrought iron tables and chairs, it could fit in as a café anywhere in Berkeley, and the college's café game was fierce. She was impressed. It reminded her a bit of Artis Coffee or Espresso Roma, only with a ton more pastries.

Seriously. The glass cases were filled with glossy, decadent creations, from cupcakes to eclairs to petit fours. And the smells coming out of the kitchen were like God's own bakery.

She considered going for something chocolate (because, hello, chocolate) but finally went with their special, a hummingbird cake. "It's like a spice cake with banana and pineapple," Maddy explained, ordering two of her own slices.

It was around one in the afternoon by now, but the place was still doing brisk business. They grabbed a small open table by the window and settled down with their cake and some coffee, decaf for Maddy, fully leaded for Thuy.

"Ready to tell me?" Thuy asked, taking a sip of the coffee. Ahhhh. Caffeine.

Maddy held her hands around the winter-white mug, staring down at the cake. "Well. Things started out pretty good. My Dad left each of us his car and truck. However, we wanted to split them."

Thuy waited. That wasn't what had pissed Drill off, or had left Maddy looking so shaken but determined when she left the lawyer's office.

Maddy sighed. "The farm. The house. He left it to both of us… if we sold. We'd split the proceeds from the sale, I mean."

Thuy stared at her for a second, but Maddy picked up her fork and started eating. "And…?" Thuy prompted.

Maddy kept on eating methodically, not meeting her gaze.

"Is it because you have to split it with Drill?" Thuy asked, puzzled. Maddy had spoken about her brother with such fondness, she had a hard time believing that her problem with Drill was going to be money. And besides, if Drill was getting half the sales price, why was he so pissed?

She took a bite of the cake, and momentarily, her brain went on the fritz. "Holy shit, that's good."

Maddy smiled. "I know, right? Lives up to its reputation. This is Southern cooking, right here." She paused. "I've missed it. I didn't realize how much. There's a lot of good cooking in the South."

"So you've pointed out," Thuy said. "We'll have to hit as much of it as we can while we're here. Are you feeling overwhelmed? Is it about finding a realtor, or emptying the house? Because you know I'll do whatever I can to help you out. I've got your back."

Maddy went silent. Then, to Thuy's shock, she put her fork down.

Maddy adored cake. Even when she suffered morning sickness, cake was the thing that brought her out of her funks in the afternoon. For her to stop eating — especially cake this monumentally delicious — meant something really serious.

Thuy felt a ball of ice form in her stomach. Maddy was finally looking at her. And her look was sad, but no less determined than it was when she'd left the lawyer's office.

"Ah, crap," Thuy breathed.

"I'm staying," Maddy said, her voice shaking slightly. "I'm keeping the farm, and running it."

Thuy blinked for a few seconds. "You're *running the farm?"*

"Whoever runs the farm gets to keep it," Maddy said. Then she looked at Thuy imploringly. "You know I always talked about wanting to raise my kid in a place like Green Valley. And that I always wanted to have my own farm."

"Well, yeah," Thuy spluttered. "But that was, you know... back when you were with David-the-farmer, before he went to Australia."

Maddy looked more pained, and Thuy wished she'd bitten her tongue. "It was," Maddy said, with dignity. "But we both wanted to have a place we could set up a small-scale organic market farm. I wanted to grow vegetables and plants for sale, either at a farmer's market or to private nurseries. And of course, I wanted it to be a working farm."

Thuy put her own fork down, which was a crying shame. "How big's your Dad's farm, again?"

"Forty acres." Maddy swallowed. "It's a lot, I know…"

You're just one woman! One pregnant *woman!*

Thuy took a deep breath, then another, letting the wonderful scent of the bakery act as a sort of aromatherapy tranquilizer. "It is a lot," Thuy agreed quietly.

Maddy's mouth turned down at the corners. Then she straightened her back. "This isn't what you signed on for," she said quietly.

Thuy blinked. "Hey, now. I didn't say that."

"You've got a job, and a life, back in Berkeley," Maddy said, her voice gaining resolve as the words tumbled out. "I can't ask you to give all that up, just to move with me here in Tennessee. I'm *not* going to ask that of you."

Thuy felt cold lashes of panic strike her, but outwardly forced calm. "You can't handle a farm all by yourself," she pointed out. "It'll be hard enough handling a baby all by yourself. The two together… Maddy, are you sure?"

Maddy was silent for a long, torturous moment. Then she nodded firmly.

"I'm doing this." Her blue eyes blazed. "I want to raise my child like I was raised."

"But your childhood sucked!" Thuy blurted out, surprised.

Maddy's eyes widened, then she laughed softly, shaking her head. "Not… I mean, not later. When my Mom was alive, the farm was the greatest place on earth. I want that for my child. Not living in the city, or the suburbs. I want my kid to get to know where his food's coming from. I want him to be able to wander in the woods. I want him to get to know the Smoky Mountains, and see the trees changing color, and love nature as much as I do."

Thuy watched as her friend's expression grew dreamy. She was truly home here, Thuy realized.

Thuy bit her lip.

Maddy would walk across fire for her, she knew that. And quite frankly, Maddy had given Thuy her future. If it weren't for Maddy, she wouldn't have any of her degrees. She'd still be…

Thuy shuddered. God. It didn't bear thinking where she might be, if Maddy hadn't stepped in and helped her out.

Thuy nodded. "All right, then. So… I guess we're farmers now."

Maddy looked resolute. "I mean it, Thuy. I can't…"

"Oh, shush and eat your cake," Thuy said, rolling her eyes. "We're in this together, remember? You're probably my favorite person on earth, and I am *not* letting you struggle with this baby and a farm all by yourself. Besides, what am I getting rid of?"

"Your job, for one," Maddy pointed out.

That would suck, a little. She'd been at the biosciences library at Cal for a few years now. "It's time I branched out," Thuy said, then wiggled her eyebrows. "Get it? Library? Branch?"

Maddy rolled her eyes. "Oh, lord."

"And if you move here, I'm losing a roomie, and you know finding a new one would be nightmare," Thuy said. "You're my best friend. Where you go, I go. So, I'll move here with you, and we'll make it work. Okay?"

Maddy smiled, and her eyes watered. She reached out, and Thuy took her hand.

"I owe you so big time," Maddy said, as tears started to roll down her cheeks. "But it's just temporary, okay? I don't expect or want you to give up your job and your whole *life*, just to help me. I felt bad enough that you moved in to help with the pregnancy, but…"

"Are you kidding? You are my bestest best friend in the whole world," Thuy pointed out, squeezing Maddy's fingers. "I liked the library, but I could work anywhere. I can't just find a best friend anywhere."

Maddy's smile was watery, but grateful.

Thuy nodded decisively. "I've got this. *We've* got this. How hard can farming be, right?"

Even as she said it, her stomach clenched.

She looked over, only to see several people staring at their joined hands. She sighed.

"It appears we're still giving them stuff to talk about," Thuy said dryly. "Honestly, are we that shocking?"

Maddy laughed, releasing her. "You mean out-of-wedlock preggo homosexual life partners?"

"Don't forget that I'm Asian," Thuy added. "Bringing the Asian contingent of this place to probably, what, one percent?"

"Don't worry. They're a good group of people, mostly," Maddy said. "You're going to fit in before you know it. And even if they're curious, they're also kind. They'll help out."

Thuy smiled. "Well, that's..."

"I just hope Drill gets over it." Maddy's eyes clouded, and she poked at her cake. "He was really, really mad at me. I think he thinks I cheated him out of his inheritance."

Thuy stared at her. She could see how he'd feel that way.

"Maybe I'm being selfish," Maddy said, her voice contemplative. "Maybe I should offer to buy him out."

"With what?" Thuy asked. "You don't have that much in savings." Honestly, with the baby on the way, Thuy knew that Maddy had very little in savings and she'd need every penny she could get.

"I don't know," Maddy admitted. "Maybe I can promise him part of the profits of the farm."

Thuy felt a little sick. That was assuming the farm made a profit — and that could be a while. She wished that she knew more about farming. She couldn't even keep houseplants alive.

That did not bode well for her future as a farmer, she realized.

"Well, it won't be planting time until spring," Maddy said. "I've got a month or two to plan and get stuff laid out. And I don't know when Drill's going to talk to me again."

Thuy frowned. She knew how unpleasant family could turn, especially when something like money was involved.

You can try to leave, girl, but you will always *be a part of this.*

Her father had been furious when she'd moved out, and for a brief, fiery moment, she wondered if his words were literal: if he'd hunt her down, drag her back — do God knows what to her. She'd often wondered if she would have made it out alive if it hadn't been for her brother's tempering influence.

She had deliberately shut down those thoughts, those memories. She wasn't going to dredge them up today. She had too much to do. She had to quit her job. And move their stuff, and break their lease. And then she had to help her hugely pregnant best friend run a farm, with like cows and plants and things.

Thuy took another bite of the cake, only this time it felt like sawdust in her mouth.

Oh my God. How am I going to do this?

CHAPTER TEN

Drill rested his head against his knuckles. He was on his fourth whiskey, and the burning sensation and subsequent numbness still hadn't put a dent in his anger. He felt like a volcano, seething and bubbling.

Maybe it wasn't fair. After all, he was surprised his old man had considered leaving him anything in the first place. When he'd been kicked out at sixteen, his father had pulled out all the stops. He'd trotted out the "you're not my son" line. And if they'd ever crossed paths in the street — and even for a town as small as Green Valley, that hadn't happened often — his father had stared through him like he was plate fucking glass. As far as he knew, his father had died hating him, even if he felt a little bit sorry for his actions.

So maybe he should be grateful that his father had left half the farm to him.

But then Maddy snatched it away.

That was what hurt the most, he thought, motioning to the bartender to give him another double. He was getting good and plowed tonight, and crashing in one of the back rooms. God willing, the haze of alcohol would help curb the feeling of ripping someone's head off.

The thing was, if he'd simply been left out of the will, he'd have been depressed, *but he wouldn't have been surprised.* It would have conformed to his admittedly pessimistic world view. His father hated him, he was cut out, end of story.

But he had a chance... *only* if he stayed on the farm. Or if his sister had decided to sell it.

He shook his head, downing the liquid in front of him with no shudder. That was what he couldn't believe. Maddy had deliberately chosen to stay on the farm and screw him out of it. She knew, she fucking *knew* that he couldn't and wouldn't leave the Wraiths. Why toy with him? Why ask if he'd share the farm — and all its responsibilities — with her? What did she honestly think he was going to do in response to that?

He felt his blood pressure throb in his temples. She'd screwed him, plain and simple. His father had taunted him from beyond the grave, and his own sister had totally hosed him.

He'd made the mistake of looking up prices for farms in their area. It wasn't a huge fortune, but it still would've been a nice bundle for forty acres of prime farmland and several outbuildings. Not that he was hurting for money, either. He got his cut from the club's profits for the work he did, even if that cut had gotten leaner since they'd lost Darrell and Razor and the place had gone haywire. He didn't spend much. He didn't have a woman to blow money on, like other bikers often did, either buying gifts for their old ladies or tossing bills at strippers or hookers. He certainly didn't waste money on drugs, especially after seeing the wake of destruction that occurred after several of his biker brothers had partaken of their own product. He might spend some money on his bike, but he was handy and did all his repairs himself, usually with their stolen parts. He had a shithole apartment and shabby furnishings, since the place was just somewhere to crash when he needed to sleep. He had a pocket of savings that he didn't touch. He considered it escape money, if and when he ever really needed it. So technically, it's not like he *needed* the money from the sale of the farm.

But it was mine.

At the very least, he'd had a moment where his father had left him something, had given a damn. Before his sister, conforming to their father's last wish, took it from him.

He growled softly to himself before realizing it.

"What crawled up your ass and died?"

Drill closed his eyes. Of all the people to run into, the last thing he needed right now was Peter Goddamn Lundy.

Pete plunked himself on the barstool next to him, ordering a beer from the bartender. "Is it the holidays? Can't stand the holidays, myself," Pete said.

Drill shook his head. He hadn't celebrated Thanksgiving or Christmas in longer than he could remember. It's not like they had a big get-together in the Wraiths, for God's sake. He looked over at Pete scathingly, mentally wishing the man would disappear.

"So, what's the problem?"

"Nothing." Drill hoped that the short answer would shut the man up, but he realized that it wouldn't… that the guy would needle at him, like a small biting fish, until he gave up more information. "I was just thinking about people who screw other people over."

Pete made a sympathetic sound. "Can't trust anybody these days."

"Damn straight." Drill drank his other shot. His head was swimming a little, which was better.

"Listen… I've got something to ask you." Pete looked around, as if to see if anyone was listening to their conversation. Then the weasel-looking guy had an expression of almost fear. "Is it true? About Razor?"

"What about Razor?" Because if it were psychotic, it was probably true.

"That he had bikers killed, when he was laundering that money." Pete definitely looked scared now. "Like twenty of them or something?"

"Well, yeah," Drill said slowly. "I heard that, too." Most of them weren't Wraiths — but one member was, along with his family. When the news had come out, about Razor's scheme, it had been a bit of a scandal. Also, because people found out that Razor was keeping more of the money than the club realized.

"But he killed other club members, too, didn't he?" Pete's voice dropped low. "I mean, not a lot. But like… what's-his-name. Lube? This would've been a while ago, but…"

Drill tensed. Nobody talked about Lube. It had been years — and yeah, it was common knowledge that Razor had the guy killed. That's why nobody talked about it.

"And nobody's seen Christine St. Claire in a while," Pete said meaningfully, looking at Drill for confirmation.

Drill stared back at him. "That was after Razor went to jail."

"Yeah. That was when Catfish was taking over," Pete pointed out nervously.

Drill grimaced. "Is this all just occurring to you now, or what?" he asked, in a normal voice.

Pete looked pained, his eyes quickly darting around the room. "I'm just saying, what kind of loyalty is that? Killing other guys, I get, but our own? I've been considering signing up with the Wraiths and getting patched in and all, because I think it'll really help move my product. But there are other clubs, more powerful clubs, ones that might be a little more reliable, you know? And I'm considering — *gack!*"

Drill barely had time to register what happened. Catfish moved quicker than a snake when he wanted to. He'd quickly grabbed Pete, yanking him off the stool like a fish on a reel and spilling him out on the dirty, sticky floor.

"Get up," Catfish said, his voice sharp as a blade. "*Get. Up.*"

Pete scrambled, staring at Catfish in terror.

"You're going to question *our* loyalty? You're acting like signing up with our club is like signing up with the local fucking Elks Lodge, or some kind of business networking, and you're questioning how loyal we are to each other?" Catfish's eyes blazed with fury. "In our house. In *my fucking house.*"

Pete's already pale skin went paper white.

Catfish aimed a kick that caught him right in the ribs. Pete let out a squeal, then a whimper.

"Let me make it easier for you. You're not a member of the Wraiths. You're not *ever* gonna be a member of the Wraiths." He looked at a few of the club members, who surrounded him. "More than that, I'd get the hell out of Green Valley if I were you, because you're on our turf as long as you're here. You take your shitty-ass skunkweed to Knoxville, or Nashville, or goddamn Timbuktu. I'm giving the order that if any member of the Wraiths sees you anywhere in Green Valley, he's allowed — no, he's *required* — to drop you wherever the fuck he finds you."

He looked at the other members. "Take this garbage out, kick the shit out of him, and drop him off on his daddy's doorstep. Keep his bike."

Pete made weeping noises as they carried him out. Drill didn't particularly like the guy, but he felt sort of sorry for him. Still, he knew that Pete had earned his own beating. Or rather, Pete's own stupidity had earned it.

Drill had been the recipient of a few stupid-beatings, first from his father, then from the Club. He shrugged. You got used to it. If you didn't, you were in the wrong world.

Catfish motioned for Drill to follow him, and he did, feeling the numbness from the whiskey slowly setting in. The pounding music of the bar retreated as they went into the back office. Catfish sank down at the desk. "Fucking Pete," Catfish said, shaking his head slowly.

"Thought we needed new recruits," Drill said. "Not that Pete was any great candidate, but..."

"He was stirring up more trouble than he was worth." For the first time, Drill realized that Catfish looked exhausted. "We're hanging on by our teeth, man. If I'm going to get the Wraiths back to where it was, I can't have some punk questioning loyalty and talking up other clubs."

Drill nodded, seeing his point.

"How'd the will thing, go, anyway?"

Drill grimaced, the pain rushing back to the fore. "Shitty," he admitted. “Coulda gotten half the farm, but my sister decided to stay rather than sell. So she gets to keep the whole thing.”

Catfish’s eyes narrowed. “You’re telling me that if the farm sold, you would’ve gotten half?”

“Yeah.” Drill sighed, then let out a low, mirthless chuckle. “Ain’t that a bitch, huh?”

“Good sized farm, huh?”

“Forty acres.” Drill felt a little dizzy. The shots were finally kicking in.

Catfish looked contemplative. “You need to talk to your sister.”

“What’s the point? She’s made up her mind.”

“I don’t think she’s thought it through,” Catfish said. “Maybe you talk to her, show her why it’s a lot better that she sells.”

Drill stared at his old friend. “Why?”

“Because we could use the cash, man.”

Drill blinked. “Wait. What?”

“We need money,” Catfish repeated. “The Wraiths. We’re bleeding out financially. You know that. And as one of the most trusted lieutenants in our club, I’m asking you — no. I’m ordering you: talk to your sister. We could really use the money.”

Drill felt blindsided. Catfish wanted him to talk to his sister, and then give all the money from the farm to the Wraiths?

They were there for you when you needed them...

Drill swallowed.

“I... okay. I’ll talk to her tomorrow.”

Catfish’s grin was wide. “Great. Now, let’s finish getting you wasted.” He put his arm around Drill and led him back to the bar.

CHAPTER ELEVEN

The next day, after starting to write lists of things that she'd need to get done, Thuy realized that she was woefully unprepared for... well, farming.

This looks like a job for Google, she thought in her best superhero voice, pulling her tablet out of her messenger bag. She had only opened it to read since they'd gotten there. She'd been checking emails on her phone when they were in town or when she could get reception, which was in odd places of the house, like the downstairs bathroom by the tiny window, or out on the front porch if she leaned just right. Now, she wanted a slightly larger screen to do some internet searching. If push came to shove, she'd break out her laptop.

Maddy had been on the phone most of the morning, handling her father's affairs, and submitting her resignation to her job at the Oakland Farmers Market, where she worked as a marketing associate. "Hey, Maddy?" Thuy said, when Maddy hung up on her latest conversation.

"Yup?" Maddy crossed something off of the to-do list she'd written on a yellow legal pad.

"What's the Wi-Fi password here?"

Maddy stopped, looking up, blinking. "Um... there isn't one."

"Sorry?"

Maddy laughed. "Yeah. There isn't Wi-Fi here."

For a second, Thuy went blank. "What do you mean?"

"Just that. There isn't Wi-Fi."

"So… there's a hard line?"

Maddy sighed. "I'm sorry, sweetie. I forgot to tell you. The farm is way too far out of town for them to run cable out here. We don't get cable, so… no hard line, either."

Thuy goggled. "What did your father do for internet?"

"I don't think he did anything," Maddy mused. "We only talked on the phone, and that was only in the last year. I think he may have still had a flip phone, actually, and the old landline. And he never sent emails. I don't think he had an email address."

"Huh." *What do you mean, he didn't have an email? Who doesn't have email or a smartphone in this day and age?* Thuy tamped down on that line of thinking. These were first world problems, she scolded herself. So they didn't have internet. So what?

But how the hell am I supposed to figure stuff out? Being disconnected made her skin itch.

"You might try using your phone as a hotspot," Maddy offered apologetically. "And we can look into something like satellite internet, but if I remember right, it's really expensive."

"Oh-kay," Thuy said. "No problem. I'll, um, use my phone."

She retreated to the porch, not wanting to turn the bathroom into her office just for an internet search. It was brisk, but the sun was shining, at least. She bundled herself in her thick coat and pulled her phone out.

"How… to run… a profitable… family… farm…" she typed, muttering to herself.

The phone whirred for a second.

Wi-Fi not available.

"I *know* Wi-Fi isn't available," Thuy said sharply, switching the setting. She entered the search term again.

The phone whirred obediently. Then another message popped up.

Phone is offline. Return search when online?

"YES," Thuy grumbled, twisting and contorting, struggling to get a signal.

After two hours and a game of signal Twister, Thuy came back into the house feeling demoralized and cold. The articles she'd managed to scavenge were very general. It gave her just enough information to realize how much she needed to learn. There was probably something Socratic and profound in knowing she knew nothing, but that wasn't going to help her run this damned farm with Maddy, and if there was one thing she hated, it was feeling incompetent.

"You doing okay?" Maddy asked, looking concerned.

"Yeah," Thuy said. She didn't want to stress Maddy out. Since Maddy had decided to keep the farm, she'd been sleeping better, humming to herself as she moved throughout the farmhouse. She seemed really happy, and Thuy didn't want to take that away from Maddy by revealing her own anxieties. "I'll, um, figure something out with the internet."

"Yeah. I forgot how bad tech can be in rural areas," Maddy said. "You get so used to high speed at your fingertips, you know?"

"I'm going to go into Netflix withdrawal," Thuy said ruefully, and Maddy giggled.

"You're going to be a farm girl," Maddy pointed out. "That means early rising, and early to bed. You'll be tired."

"So, what exactly are you planning on doing with the farm?" Thuy asked. "And, you know, how can I help?"

Maddy looked down at the multitude of scribbled notes she had jotted on the legal pad. "I've worked with farmers markets enough to know which farmers make the most, and a lot of their practices," Maddy said carefully. "My father was an amazing gardener. He's got the greenhouses filled with plants, even now. The electricity bill's going to be kind of high from heating them, but I think I can keep a lot of his customers. And when spring hits, I think I can plant produce for sale. Sort of an artisanal organic farm. Maybe not with the certification, because that costs an arm and a leg, but one that runs without pesticides."

Thuy stared at her friend, watching her face light up with passion at the project.

"What about the cows?" Thuy asked.

"From what I can see, we're wintering some cows for a neighbor, Jake McMasters," Maddy said. "We're giving his lands time to recover. We're sort of renting our land and taking care of his stock for him. So that'll be extra income. It does mean we need to feed the cows, though, and look after them."

"But what can *I* do?" Thuy asked.

Maddy bit the corner of her lip. "I'm still figuring that out," she admitted. "At the least, you can check fences. Maybe help with feeding? I did that when I was a tween."

Well, if Maddy did it before she was thirteen, then a grown-ass woman ought to be able to do it, Thuy reasoned. "That doesn't sound too bad." She paused. "I don't know much about gardening, though, organic or otherwise. And I know absolutely nothing about livestock."

"You'll pick it up. You're smart, and you're the best researcher I know," Maddy said confidently. "Besides, the best way to learn is practice. I'll walk you through it."

Thuy sighed. She wished she felt as confident as Maddy sounded. "Okay," she said. "Anything I can do for you now?"

"You could grab the mail," Maddy suggested. "I want to make sure I'm staying on top of Dad's bills. Oh, that reminds me... I need to contact his banks." She hurriedly turned back to her lists.

Thuy headed out, then realized that the mailbox was down at the end of the driveway — about half a mile, maybe more, away. She considered walking, then reached for the car keys hanging on a hook by the door.

"You can take the side-by-side, if you want," Maddy said absently.

"The what, now?"

"The side-by-side. That golf cart looking thing," Maddy clarified. "It's by the barn."

"Um... okay."

Maddy looked indulgent. "It's just like driving a car, basically. Only smaller."

"Gotcha." Thuy struggled to keep the trepidation out of her voice.

"It's what you'll probably use to get hay to the cattle," Maddy added. "I don't think you'll use the farm truck, it's too big. Again, I've driven side-by-sides since I was twelve or so."

"Right." Thuy nodded, leaving the rental car keys where they were. She swallowed hard.

"Key's in the ignition," Maddy called out after her.

Thuy headed out towards the barn. It was a faded reddish-brown, with a metal roof. The side-by-side was painted in camouflage colors, its black seats patched with duct tape. She climbed in, carefully buckling the seat belt.

"Just like driving a car," she muttered. Except it wasn't, not exactly. There were buttons for lifting and lowering things, from the looks of it. And there was... what the hell was a "diff lock?" Did she need it?

Cars were *so* not her jam.

She bit her lip, then turned the engine. It growled to a surprisingly noisy start.

"Shit," Thuy muttered. She looked for a clutch. Not finding one, she struggled with the gear shift, putting the thing in drive and tapping the gas pedal.

It jerked forward.

She grimaced, then pushed the gas pedal forward, gripping the steering wheel for dear life. For a little thing, it went pretty fast. Of course, she couldn't have been going more than twenty or thirty miles an hour, but the wind rushing over the half-windshield and the roar of the engine made it seem like it was going a lot faster. She bounced down the dirt road, heading for the mailboxes.

She slowed down carefully, braking as she got to the box and then putting it in neutral since there didn't appear to be a "park" setting. Getting out, she grabbed the mail. There were a few bills, a mailer, a local newspaper. She stuffed them in the little glove compartment.

As she got back into the small vehicle, she abruptly realized that the driveway was narrow — like, one-lane narrow. It was flanked on one side by a ditch and on the other side by several large trees.

She had two options: turn around, or drive in reverse all the way back. Driving in reverse seemed stupid, and honestly, she wasn't all that confident in her backward driving anyway.

She looked at the main road. She could try turning around there, she reasoned. A simple three-point-turn. It didn't look like there was a lot of traffic on this road.

She moved the gear shift. Only this time, the thing decided it didn't want to leave neutral.

"Oh, come on," she muttered, cursing under her breath. "Come on, baby. Work with me, here."

She got it in drive, the lowest gear. It lurched forward, then stalled out.

"God *damn* it." She turned the key off, then put it in neutral, starting it back up again. It made a sick sound, like a nauseous cow, but slowly warmed up.

She felt a wave of relief, and put her hand on the gearshift.

It shifted, all right. Only this time, it went into reverse — and her foot slipped from the brake to the gas.

"*Fuck!*" she yelped, as the thing jerked back. And next thing she knew, she'd rolled into the ditch.

CHAPTER TWELVE

Viciously hungover, Drill rode his bike to his father's farm, grimacing to himself. He hoped that Maddy's decision to keep the farm was hormonal, just something she thought of out of nostalgia and maybe a misguided sense of family. It would make it that much easier to convince her to sell the thing, so they could split the profits.

And then he could... give the proceeds to the Wraiths.

He frowned, pouring a little more speed into his bike, feeling the rattle of the machine beneath him as he tore across the pavement.

It had made sense, when Catfish had told him last night. The Wraiths were in trouble. They needed cash. He could get his hands on cash. He needed to hand it over to the club.

Of course, when he'd agreed, he'd been pretty damned drunk, he realized.

When he was sixteen, he would've handed it over without blinking. They were his family, his soul. They were his brothers. If they told him to rip out his own liver and cook it over an open flame, he'd have done it without a second thought.

That was sixteen years ago. Half his life.

A lot of shit had happened since then.

Unbidden, he remembered Pete's remarks at the bar last night.

Bikers killed... like twenty of them? He killed club members too, didn't he?

Drill gritted his teeth. That had been Razor, though. Razor had been a psychopath. That said, he'd also been one of the most effective leaders the Wraiths had ever had. With Razor and Darrell Winston at the helm, the Wraiths had brought in more money, run more rackets, and had absolutely zero attrition. Once you were a recruit, you didn't fucking leave the Wraiths, period. Not unless it was in a box.

That Razor might've put you in.

Since Razor was in jail and Darrell had gone state's evidence, it had taken nearly a year for Catfish to take the reins and get the club in some semblance of order. Drill had beaten a few pretenders to the throne to make sure that Catfish stayed on top. He'd kept assholes like Timothy King down when they started getting too big for their britches, thinking they were running the place. He'd taken over the bulk of the loan collection, and he'd provided muscle when their car parts racket was being threatened.

But I've never killed anyone.

He felt tired, and it had nothing to do with the hangover.

Maybe he was being selfish. Maybe he was overthinking things. But he felt taken aback that the club wanted his half of the farm. It'd be a good deal of money, tens of thousands of dollars. Maybe even a hundred thousand, if he was lucky.

But it'd all go to the club.

It's like an investment, he seemed to remember Catfish saying. And he'd half-heartedly agreed. But the thing was, the Wraiths didn't really pay out like an investment. What was yours was theirs. They gave him enough of a cut to keep him afloat, and comfortable. But he knew that Darrell and especially Razor and Dirty Dave, kept the lion's share for themselves. Management fees, Dave used to joke.

Drill felt a little hesitant about handing over the lion's share of his family farm to fucking Dirty Dave.

It's not to him. It's for the Wraiths.

He was still muttering that to himself when he pulled up to the farm's driveway. He stopped immediately at the sight of a side-by-side that had somehow slid ass first into the drainage ditch alongside the drive.

He turned off his bike, getting off and quickly going to the vehicle. Thuy was in the driver's seat, her head on the steering wheel.

"You okay?" he asked, feeling concern. He rushed into the ditch to her side.

"Yeah," she said quickly, rubbing at tears that were in her eyes. "Well, I mean, no, obviously. I'm in a fucking ditch. But other than that, I'm peachy."

He barked out a surprised laugh. "That you are, baby. So how'd this happen?"

"I was — don't laugh — getting the mail," she said. "I wanted to get used to driving this thing, since I'm probably going to need to. You know, to help out with stuff around the farm. Anyway, it slipped out of gear, and then I guess I hit it funny when I was pressing the gas, and next thing I knew..." She gestured at the ditch.

He nodded, not trusting himself not to chuckle. When he finally got it together, he cleared his throat. "I see," he said solemnly.

"I tried driving back up and out, but it's too steep," she said. "I was afraid I'd burn out the motor if I kept pushing it. So I was trying to figure out a way to get out when you came along."

He nodded again. She looked miserable, and frustrated. He looked around, seeing a solid oak tree behind the mailboxes. "Tell you what. I'll get you out of there."

"With what? Your motorcycle?" She looked skeptical.

"No, darlin'. With the winch."

She looked at him blankly.

"Here. Why don't you hop out a sec, and we'll get this fixed right quick."

She did as he requested, clambering out with little grace. She was such a tiny thing. Perfectly proportioned, but short and slight. She was wearing a pair of jeans and a thick jacket, her cheeks pink from the cold.

He ran the winch line out, getting enough of it to drag to the nearby oak and loop around. Fastening it, he walked back to the side-by-side. "All right. See this button here? That operates the winch," he instructed.

Thuy watched, looking fascinated and a little wary.

He pushed the button. The winch heaved, struggling for a moment as the metal line tightened. Then slowly, inexorably, the cart inched up the incline and settled on the driveway.

He turned it off, then turned back to her, smiling. "See? Not so bad, was it?"

She nodded. "Thank you," she said, with feeling. "I had no idea what I was going to do. I hate feeling helpless."

"No big deal."

She put a hand on his arm, stopping him. Her dark eyes were solemn. "I'm serious. Thanks."

He puffed up, feeling his chest warm. He couldn't remember the last time someone had thanked him for something. For that matter, it had been a long time since he'd done something to help someone. He felt an odd sensation seep through him, like a shot of whiskey on a cold night. It was nothing like the numbness and disquiet he'd been feeling with the club.

He immediately smacked the thought away, feeling traitorous and uneasy.

Quickly, he undid the winch line and retracted it. "No problem," he said to Thuy. "Can you get it turned the right way from here?"

"I think so."

"Let me help you get it into gear," he said.

She climbed in, buckled up, and he leaned over her, putting his hand over the key. He tilted his head to look at her.

She was inches away from him, looking at his hand. Then she turned her attention to him. Their gazes locked, and he felt a blast of heat that had nothing to do with the sharp November sunshine.

She was cute as hell. He'd thought so earlier. Now, he realized, she was even prettier than he remembered. That full lower lip, that rosebud mouth. Her eyes, that dark rich brown of polished walnut. Her determined little chin, currently tilted up at him.

"Um... the engine?" she asked slowly, sounding out of breath.

He could lean forward and kiss her. She'd probably smack the shit out of him. He thought about it anyway, just for a second.

"Drill?" she asked, her voice a mere breath.

He wanted her, he realized, and it was like a punch in the gut. And it wasn't in the casual way he normally hit on women, which was more for entertainment than anything, a way to fend off the numbness. It wasn't because it'd be casual, a simple way to pass the time.

It was strong, almost scalding, in its intensity. He wanted this woman.

She was Maddy's friend, and he couldn't just have a quick roll in the hay with her. Maddy would kill him. Hell, he got the feeling *Thuy* would kill him.

But what if she didn't? He could see her pulse, pounding in her throat. The way her breathing went shallow, and her pupils went big.

Maybe she would be up for something. The barest of images, of the two of them wrapped around each other, flashed across his brain. Before he could pursue the train of thought, another question popped into his mind.

Would one time be enough, anyway?

The concern was shocking, one he couldn't remember having about anyone. He shook his head, trying to clear it.

Lock this shit down, idiot. Get yourself together.

"Maddy's home, right?" he asked, his voice coming out hoarse.

Thuy nodded slowly.

"C'mon then," he said, and with some effort moved away from her. "Let's go see my sister."

CHAPTER THIRTEEN

Thuy followed Drill back up the driveway to the house, parking it in the spot by the barn. She felt shaken, and not just from the fall into the ditch.

What the hell was *that?*

The last thing she needed was an attraction to a frickin' biker. She'd known criminals most of her life, and she found nothing sexy about the lifestyle. So, what was it about Drill that had her hormones twerking every damned time she saw him, for God's sake?

She climbed out of the side-by-side, watching as he got off the bike and put his helmet down. He was ripped, no question, and did nice things for a pair of jeans. She realized he was a hell of a lot more solid than the guys she usually dated. She tended to lean towards thin, diminutive guys. Guys who knew their way around a bistro menu, who knew the latest memes, who could tell you the latest Bethesda game release and why it was better (or worse) than the last one.

You tend to date guys who don't threaten you.

She frowned at the realization. *Threatened* might not be the right word. *Challenged.* Because it wasn't that Drill threatened her, per se. If anything, she felt a strange safeness in his presence.

It doesn't matter. You're not going to date the guy. End of story.

She followed Drill into the house, wondering if he'd want privacy to talk with Maddy. The way his strong jaw was set, he looked like a soldier on a mission. She wondered absently what that mission was, and why it made him look so grim. She'd seen how pissed he was when he left the lawyer's office.

It suddenly clicked, why he was there. She felt her heart fall into her stomach.

He held open the door for her, and she walked in, feeling him fall in line behind her and shut it. She went to the kitchen.

"Thuy? I was starting to think you got lost," Maddy said, with a laugh, sitting at the kitchen table. The surface was absolutely strewn with notes, open farming books, and her laptop. "I… Teddy?"

Drill sighed.

"Sorry, *Drill,*" Maddy corrected. She started to cantilever herself out of the chair, but Drill put a hand on her shoulder, nudging her down.

"Don't get up on my account," he said, his voice low. "I'm here to talk, Maddy."

She looked at him earnestly. "I'm glad," Maddy said. "I hate the way we ended things yesterday."

Thuy saw Drill's Adam's apple bob, and his eyes looked melancholy. "I… it took me by surprise," he admitted.

Maddy looked sad in response. "I know," she said. "I've been trying to think of ways to make it up to you, and I think I've got a couple…"

"I think you should sell the farm."

Maddy sighed. "I know. But I'm not going to. I hope you can understand that."

Thuy felt a little out of place. "Maybe I should let you guys discuss this in private," she hedged.

"No. You're staying. This affects you, too," Maddy said. Thuy knew that while Maddy was including her because this was her future, too, she also looked like she needed some moral support. Thuy nodded, taking a seat next to Maddy.

Drill turned a chair backward, straddling it, so they all sat at the table, like it was a business meeting. Which, Thuy supposed, it was, even if it was filled by a hugely pregnant woman, a menacing bald biker, and a dirt-smudged Asian woman.

"I don't think it's fair that you get to make this decision without my say-so," Drill said, his voice sharp.

"I didn't set up the will, Dad did," Maddy countered. "He wanted it to stay in the family. He wanted someone to work it. So whoever was willing to work it got to keep it. I'm willing to stay, you aren't. So, it's going to be mine."

Drill sighed. "Here's the thing, though. You *can't* work it."

Maddy bristled. "And why not?"

Drill looked at her like she was insane. Then he glanced down at her stomach.

"Being pregnant doesn't make me useless," Maddy said, her blue eyes sparking. "Lots of mothers before me worked the land, believe me."

"Yeah. *With their husbands*," Drill said. "They had help. It wasn't just a pregnant woman plowing the back forty."

"I'll have help," Maddy protested.

"Besides that," Drill said, in a reasonable tone that had Thuy's teeth on edge, "it's not like it used to be. Family farms are harder and harder to stay afloat, you know that. Most farmers I know have a day job, too, just to make ends meet."

Thuy saw Maddy's expression falter a bit. "Well, if I need to..."

Thuy felt a rumbling of unease.

"You're going to, what? Have a day job, *and* do all the work that a farm needs? All while you've got a baby to take care of?" Drill's voice gentled. "And who's supposed to take care of the baby while you're working, huh? I don't know a lot about it, but sounds like daycare costs a whole wad of cash."

Thuy sank a little lower in her chair. She hated to admit it, but he was making sense.

"I'll keep working with the nurseries," Maddy said. "Dad has a good business set up there. I can work with farmer's markets once I get produce set up. I can have the baby with me while I'm working in the greenhouse. And besides, Thuy is going to help me."

Thuy immediately felt Drill's scrutiny as his sharp blue gaze turned to her.

"Ever worked on a farm before?" he asked, even though she was sure he'd guessed that she damned well hadn't.

"No." She straightened, lifting her chin pugnaciously. "But I can learn."

"You got the side-by-side stuck in a ditch," he said. "*Getting the mail.*"

She looked over at Maddy, whose eyes widened almost comically.

"Are you all right?" Maddy asked quickly.

Thuy felt her cheeks heat with embarrassment. "Yes, I'm fine," she reassured her friend. She then glared at Drill. "It was my first time driving it."

"Do you know how easy it is to get hurt? A cow steps on your foot. You get a piece of clothing caught in some machinery. You flip the tractor over on you." He stared at her, as if by sheer intensity he could burn the words into her brain. "And even if you don't have anything go wrong, there's the sheer *work* of being on a farm. You need to move hay bales, and feed cattle. Maintaining farm equipment. Taking care of the million little things that need taking care of. It's not some day job you can call in sick to, or leave at the office."

Thuy felt a little sick to her stomach. She'd been a city kid, admittedly, all her life. What the hell did she know about any of this?

She looked over at Maddy for help, and saw her best friend's expression, pleading with her.

"Thuy is stronger than you think," Maddy said to her brother, but her eyes never left Thuy's face.

Suddenly, Thuy remembered their sophomore year at Berkeley. The year everything had changed. She'd lost all hope. But Maddy had been there, believing in her.

You're stronger than you think, Maddy had said stubbornly.

Thuy had never had someone believe in her like that. Someone who had supported her, and convinced her that her wild dreams of getting a college education and making something more of her life were more than just dreams.

Maddy needed her help now. And she'd be *damned* if she let her friend down.

Thuy turned to Drill, feeling purpose and determination well up in her like a geyser. "I will do whatever it takes to help your sister keep the farm," she said, in a low-voiced oath. "I know it'll be hard. But I've done hard things in the past, and trust me, I can do this."

Drill stared at her for a long minute.

"I'll bet you have," he said, his voice tinged with a grudging admiration.

Maddy sighed. "I have been thinking about how to make this more equitable," she said. "I was thinking some profit-sharing, until I can buy you out…"

Drill waved his hand. "That's making the assumption that there will actually be profits," he said, pissing Thuy off. Even if she'd initially had similar thoughts.

Maddy's mouth pulled into a tight line.

Drill stood up. "Listen. I know this is what you want now, but I want you to think about it. It's going to be winter here… we've got the holidays coming up, and nobody's going to want to buy farmland until early spring," he said, his voice imminently and infuriatingly reasonable. "And you haven't even had the baby yet. You still might change your mind."

"I'm not," Maddy said, her voice flat.

He looked at Thuy. Thuy glared back at him.

He sighed heavily. "I'll be in touch," he said, heading for the door.

"If it's about me selling," Maddy called after him, "don't bother."

He shook his head, then left.

"Oh my *God*," Maddy said. "Could he be more condescending? I know how hard running a farm can be! It's like he forgot I *grew up here*, just like he did!"

Thuy reached over, patting her on the shoulder. "We'll just have to prove him wrong, then," Thuy said.

But even as she said it, her stomach knotted. Her burst of confidence slowly wilted, as Maddy continued to rant.

Can I do this? Thuy thought, feeling suddenly shaky. Because the last thing she wanted was to let her friend down.

CHAPTER FOURTEEN

To Drill's surprise, Catfish was waiting for him at the Dragon Bar, perched on a barstool and watching the door. "We need to talk," he said without preamble, motioning Drill to follow him.

Ah, shit, what now? After his disappointing and frustrating talk with Maddy, the last thing he wanted was to hear more bad news. Catfish was wearing his serious expression — pretty much the only expression he wore, for the past six months — and his edgy impatience and hawk-like pounce meant that whatever it was, Catfish wanted it dealt with. Immediately.

They were in the office, and Dirty Dave was waiting there, throwing a knife at a dartboard. He looked over, taking a swig from a beer bottle. "So? You take care of things?"

Drill blinked at him. "What are you talking about?"

Dave scowled at him. Catfish's expression grew more irritated. "The farm, Drill. When's it going up for sale?"

Drill scowled back at both Dave and Catfish. What the fuck was Catfish doing, talking to Dave about this, anyway? "It's not," he said. "At least not right now. My sis... *Maddy* dug her heels in. She's being stubborn, hasn't thought it through. She keeps saying she wants to keep it."

"Women." Dave spat the word out like a curse. "Always fucking things up."

Catfish's face went carefully blank. "That's not what I wanted to hear."

"I know. Trust me, it wasn't what I wanted to hear, either." Not because of the club, either, or at least not only because of it. He was genuinely worried about Maddy and Thuy, and their chances on the farm without any help. It was going to be a brutal undertaking, one he wasn't sure either woman fully understood or was prepared for. He thought of Thuy, stuck in the ditch.

Jesus wept. They were in for a rough road.

"You say she hasn't thought it through," Catfish said, drawing out his words. "So, you're thinking she might come to her senses?"

"God, I hope so," Drill muttered. Then he cleared his throat. "I mean, she's pregnant and she only has her city friend to help her..."

"Her *girlfriend,* you mean?" Dave wiggled his eyebrows suggestively. "Heard about her in town. Can't believe your sister's a lez!"

Immediately, Drill pictured plunging his fist right in Dave's dirty face. He suppressed the urge. "It's her friend," he corrected. "But who gives a shit?"

"She's not his sister anymore. And I don't care what she is," Catfish said, and Dave shut up with a small smirk. "Gay, straight, doesn't fucking matter. She's getting in the way of business, Drill."

Drill felt his muscles lock in surprise. Catfish's brain was working — he could see that. What worried him was Catfish's announcement.

She's getting in the way of business.

"How likely is she to stay stubborn?" Catfish asked, his brown eyes probing.

Drill squirmed. He didn't want to give Catfish false hope, but he didn't like where this was going. "I don't know," he finally answered. "She can be very stubborn. But I figure by the time spring hits and the baby gets here, she's going to realize just how tough it really is, and give up. Besides, that'll probably be a better time to put the farm up for sale."

"No," Catfish said, and his tone was patient, like he was

schooling a kid. "You want to sell the thing before spring, so whoever buys it has time to plan and… I don't know, plant and shit. Besides, it takes a while to sell land. If it goes up for sale in early spring, might not get the money until, what, late spring? Maybe early summer?"

Drill shrugged. "How the hell should I know? I don't know real estate."

Dave nodded. "There's stuff like closing, that can take like forty-five days," he said, sounding surprisingly intelligent. "And there's inspections. And financing stuff can fall through. You want to give plenty of time — the first buyer's not gonna work out, more likely than not."

There was a reason Dirty Dave was their money guy, Drill realized.

Catfish was frowning, thoughtful. "The sooner it goes on the market, the better," he summarized.

Drill *really* didn't like where this was going.

"She needs to see the light, then," Catfish drawled. "Like, right fucking now."

"I can keep talking to her," Drill said immediately. "She might not like it, but she'll see it makes sense. She's just got all these hormones and stuff, and she's still overwhelmed by my dad's death. She just needs a little time."

"We don't have time." Catfish's voice was a low growl.

Now it was Drill's turn to frown. "What the hell is going on?"

Catfish looked at Dave, who shrugged, then walked over, pulling his knife from where it was embedded in the dartboard. "You know we've been taking hits. Losing members. Losing some of our biggest money makers," Catfish said. "Somebody took money, too. Cleaned out some of our hidden reserves."

Drill couldn't help it. He shot a look over at Dave.

Dave held up his hands, which would've looked more convincing if he didn't have a switchblade in one of them. "Hey, if I was stupid enough to grab the money, I wouldn't still be here," he said, with a chuckle.

Drill thought he might be smart with money, but he might be *just* that stupid. Still, he turned back to Catfish.

"We'll make it," Catfish continued. "But I won't lie, that farm of yours would mean the difference between scrabbling on the streets like damned losers trying not to get patched over, and being back on top, on our turf. Just like we used to be. We could finance more ops, get more rackets going, attract more than just the dregs. Get some of our own back."

Drill sighed. He knew, he *knew* he ought to be more interested in what Catfish was saying. He ought to be on board with Catfish's plan. But he just felt exhaustion hit him like a wave.

What difference does it make? So what if the Wraiths got taken over by a bigger club? It'd be the same shit, different day.

And I'm getting really tired of it.

"I'll talk to her," Drill said again. "I'll do everything I can to get her to see reason. I can't promise more than that."

Catfish tilted his head, then chuckled softly. The sound raised the hairs on Drill's arms. He'd only heard his friend chuckle like that before they did some seriously questionable shit.

"I think," Catfish said slowly, "that we can convince the little lady pretty damned quick."

Dave cackled. Drill's blood went ice cold.

"Catfish," he said, his voice holding a note of warning. "I said, I'll talk to her."

Catfish's eyes narrowed. "She's not your sister. She's not your family. *We are.*" He slammed a hand on the desk, emphasizing his point.

"Is this what it means to be in the club now? Terrorizing pregnant women?" Drill put every ounce of disgust he could into his voice.

"If it means saving the Wraiths, *hell yes,*" Catfish countered. "Are you getting squeamish on me now?"

"There's worse we could do," Dave added, with a crooked smile. He threw the knife, which landed with a thunk inside the outer ring of the dartboard.

Drill couldn't help it. He took a menacing step toward the older man, whose eyes widened in surprise. Dave took a step back. Catfish moved between them, shoving Drill a step back.

"Listen. We came up at around the same time. We're brothers," Catfish said. "I know how you feel about Maddy. You always looked out for her, even when you didn't think anybody noticed. Yeah, I knew," he said, when Drill made a reflexive sound of protest. "Because I need you on board with this, I'll give you until December to change her mind. That's because you've put in sixteen years in this club, and I know you'll do the right thing."

Drill grunted.

"But if you don't change her mind," Catfish said pointedly, "then we're going to. Got it?"

Drill gritted his teeth. Then he nodded, once, a sharp motion.

"Good." Catfish sat down. "Now. We've got some collections I'm gonna need you to handle. It's small change — just a couple of G's — but it's what you're built for."

He means beating guys up. Drill frowned. Gamblers who were late, stupid assholes who decided to take their chances on a quick loan. Drill had done that enough in the past. Darrell and Razor had figured that his farm-boy physique, built from carting hay bales and doing the hard labor of bringing in harvests and taking care of animals, was better used kicking the shit out of people.

"Yeah, okay," Drill said, taking a seat, glad at least that they weren't talking about his sister, even as he felt a little… uneasy. "Just tell me who, and when."

CHAPTER FIFTEEN

After the great ditch disaster and Drill's anti-pep talk, as well as her inability to access the internet, Thuy spent the weekend going through Maddy's notes, grocery shopping, and taking back the rental car. Now it was Monday afternoon, and she was driving the big Chevy truck that Maddy's dad had left behind. She'd made it into town, and was going to the one place she knew would not only make her feel better, it would better prepare her for the challenges ahead.

The library.

She found it more easily than the lawyer's place, at least, she consoled herself as she pulled into an empty parking spot. She was still getting used to the sheer size of the truck, which was a behemoth next to the old Honda Civic she was accustomed to driving. She scrambled out, reaching down with her toes to touch the ground. With a huff, she slammed the door shut, then headed toward the building. The front windows were decorated for fall, with leaves cut out of multi-color paper and gourds of some sort. It had just been Halloween; they'd be moving on to Thanksgiving soon, then shooting the holiday gauntlet from Christmas to New Year's. She headed for the front door eagerly.

There was a smell to libraries and bookstores that Thuy always found comforting. She took a deep breath, soaking in the ambiance. Cliché as it probably was, it felt like coming home.

It was a small building — nothing like the cathedral-like libraries at Berkeley, like Doe or the sprawling expanses of Moffitt or Main. Still, there were books, neatly shelved, and plenty of them. There was a bulletin board with flyers advertising local events and services. There was a teen's night advertised, as well as a local poetry gathering, which she found encouraging. There was a children's section where she could see lower shelves and a number of colored bean bags. The circulation desk had a woman with curly hair who was helping a patron, discussing something about a mystery author.

Thuy's gaze stopped when she saw an odd but familiar piece of furniture.

Tell me that's not a card catalog.

She walked straight to the set of wooden drawers. Holy shit. It really *was*. She hadn't seen one of these in years. She pulled out one of the drawers, and sure enough, the little index cards were lined up there like soldiers. For giggles, she picked one at random.

"Zelazny, Roger. 1937-1995. Nine Princes in Amber, [1st ed]," the card stated. Then, in red caps over to the left, it said SCIFI, ZEL.

It was like stepping into a Wayback Machine, Thuy thought, shaking her head as she pushed the drawer back in place. She glanced around, looking for a computer, hoping that the system here was automated and the card catalog was just for show. Not that she needed to look up titles on the computer — she was familiar with enough library cataloging systems, both Dewey Decimal and Library of Congress, that she knew the area she'd need to search — but the thought of being in a library that used only the cards suggested they might not have automated check-out, and *that* was kind of daunting.

To her relief, there were three computers, over by one of the walls, next to a few tables. One of the computers had a paper taped to the screen, obviously out of order. The second had a middle-aged man scowling at it. The third was crowded by a number of teenagers who were obviously playing video games, much to the consternation of the man next to them. There was a printed sign on the wall above all the computers:

The internet is still a net. Don't get caught up in it.

She shook her head. While she appreciated the sentiment, and imagined whoever had put it up wanted people reading rather than falling down the latest Youtube rabbit holes, the fact was that the internet *was* a huge part of people's lives. When she'd gotten her Masters of Library and Information Science, they'd emphasized that helping people navigate the internet, and getting information in different ways, was crucial to the job.

She went over to the 630s: *Agriculture and Animal Husbandry.* She ran her finger along the spines, looking at the titles. Many of the books were old, she noticed — from the forties and fifties. There weren't any books on permaculture farming, one of Maddy's favorite topics, but it was a little avant-garde (and a bit hippie-esque) so Thuy wasn't terribly surprised. She grabbed a book on running a homestead, and another on expenses of the small farmer. There was a book on cattle ranching that looked detailed, so she grabbed that, too. She wished desperately that there was a For Dummies book on the subject, but she guessed in this town, if you were dumb enough to need one of the books, you were probably too dumb to have your own farm.

Thuy sighed. Then she grabbed another few books, and headed toward the circulation desk.

As she headed over there, she saw the man at the second computer shove his chair away. "This goddamned machine!" he hissed. The librarian looked over with concern, but was still talking with the other patron. The teens next to him snickered.

Thuy had worked in libraries too long to simply leave a patron frustrated and cussing. "Anything I can help you with?" she said easily, her voice dropping into the hushed tones she was so used to.

He looked surprised. He ran a hand through his hair. "This damned thing," he said in a low voice, gesturing to the screen. "I'm just... well, I'm trying to apply for a truck driving job, and I can't get the screen to work."

She looked over the website. It was set up poorly, she realized, but he was also making things more difficult than they needed to be by minimizing the screen. She clicked the box at the right, expanding it to take up the whole monitor, and increased the font size. "Better?" she asked.

He nodded.

"Okay. Why don't you tell me what you're having trouble with?"

It took about twenty minutes, but with her quicker typing and his renewed enthusiasm, they got his resumé entered and submitted. He looked drained and relieved when they finally closed out the site.

"Thank you, miss," he said.

"No problem. Really," Thuy said, smiling. And it wasn't. That was part of why she liked being a librarian: helping people. That, and of course, the books.

"'Bout time," one of the teens said, in a low, surly voice.

The man glared at them. "You watch it," he warned. "Playing video games. What the hell's wrong with y'all?"

They rolled their eyes. Thuy shook her head. Teens, she thought.

The man walked away, a teen springing into his place. He quickly called up the Epic website, logging into the same video game as the other screen.

Thuy recognized it immediately. "Fortnite, huh?"

They all stared at her for a second. "Yeah. What, you play?"

"Not for a while. RPGs are more my bag," she admitted. "Just finished *Zelda* for the Switch. Good times."

They looked at her with a new sense of respect. She shot them a small smile.

"So, you guys come here for video games, huh?"

"We can only play an hour," one of the teens, a boy with wheat-colored hair that flopped in his eyes, said woefully. "Then they kick us off. Even if nobody else is using it!"

"What about on teen night?"

The kids, two boys and a girl, looked at each other, then rolled their eyes, laughing. "Teen night?" the girl said. She looked like a young proto-Goth, with dyed-dark hair and burgundy lipstick, and heavily kohled eyes. "More like *baby night.*"

"They're mostly middle graders," the wheat-haired boy clarified. "They do arts and crafts, crap like that, and read little kid books."

"What do you guys read?"

They stared at her, then looked at each other, like no one had ever asked them that. "Uh... I don't know," the second boy, a freckle-faced redhead, said with a grimace. "Not really interested in anything."

Thuy's heart broke a little.

"And it's not like there's a huge selection," the Goth girl said derisively.

"Where's the YA section?"

They all laughed. "There *is* no YA section," she said.

Now Thuy's heart broke even more. There was a ton of YA literature out there, truly quality diverse reads... adventure and sci-fi/fantasy, issue books, even great manga and graphic novels. "That's a shame," she said, and meant it.

They shrugged. "They were going to shut the library down until a few weeks ago," Wheat Hair said.

"Which would have *sucked,*" Redhead said. "I live outside of town, and my internet sucks."

"I know those feels, bro," Thuy muttered. "Well, I'll let you get to your gaming."

They nodded, friendly now, and went back to teaming up and parachuting down into the battle royale. She smirked, then went up to the circulation desk.

"I was wondering if I could check these out," she said, pulling out her wallet. "I don't have a utility bill or anything, but I'm planning on moving to the area very soon, and I was wondering if I could give you my driver's license or a credit card number to..."

"You're staying with Madison Blount, aren't you?" the curly-haired woman asked, looking her over.

Thuy took a little step back, surprised. "Um, yeah."

"I'm Naomi Winters." She held out her hand, and Thuy shook it. "Old Man Blount didn't use the library very much, but he did have a card. And we all know Maddy, or at least we did until she moved away ten years ago."

Naomi's smile was wide and genuine. Thuy felt some of the tension she hadn't realized she was holding relax.

"I'll just put these on my card," Naomi said. "They'll be due in two weeks, but if you need them for longer, we can always renew them. That okay?"

"That's fantastic," Thuy said. "Thank you."

"Thank *you*," Naomi said. "Jim Thompson's been struggling with that computer for the better part of an hour, and you helped him when you didn't have to. And not a lot of people have patience with the kids who come in to play video games," she admitted. "You'd be a good librarian."

Thuy grinned. "I am a librarian, strangely enough."

"Well, that explains it!" Naomi said, with a laugh.

Thuy walked out with an armful of books and a spring in her step. She'd definitely be back, probably within the next week. She wanted to check out the fiction selection.

As she headed to the parking lot, she saw someone was leaning against the door of her truck. As she got closer, she recognized the black leather jacket, the form-fitting jeans, the boots.

Drill.

Her heart gave a little traitorous trill, and she grimaced. The guy had all but called Maddy incompetent and declared the two of them unable to hold onto the farm, and yet her pulse still danced the mambo when she saw him. *Stupid good-looking biker. Stupid hormones.* She walked over to the truck.

"What are you doing here?" she asked, without preamble.

He looked at the books she carried, and smirked. "Some things you can't learn from books."

"You know, I have yet to find one thing I couldn't learn more about," she said. "That all you're here for? To make fun of me for researching? Because I've got stuff to do."

"I saw my Dad's truck, and figured that Maddy wasn't driving it," he said. "Too tall, given her condition. So that left you."

"You were looking for me?" She sounded a tiny bit breathless at that, and frowned at herself. "What do you want?"

"You," he said.

Her heart beat like a trip-hammer. "Oh?" she squeaked, then winced.

"C'mon. We need to talk," he said. "I'll buy you a doughnut."

CHAPTER SIXTEEN

It had taken about ten minutes of back-and-forth to convince Thuy to follow him to Daisy's Nut House.

"If you're trying to push me about the farm, it's not going to work," she'd said pointedly.

"I don't want to upset my sister," he replied, which was true. That, and he'd figured out that Thuy was the lynchpin to this whole scenario. If Maddy didn't have Thuy's help, then Maddy couldn't keep the farm, and the sale was a done deal.

Therefore, he just had to persuade Thuy that selling was the right thing to do.

You could just tell her that the Wraiths are moving in.

He frowned as he parked his bike outside the Nut House. That would definitely be one approach, he thought ruefully. Maddy might take the threat seriously — or she might just tell him to shove it. Thuy was an unknown quantity: she seemed fearless, not to the point of stupidity, but definitely to the point of recklessness. If she thought she was protecting Maddy…

His jaw clenched. He didn't want to put them in that position. And as much as he couldn't believe it, he didn't want to see his sister's face when he said that his biker gang insisted that she sell the property so they could fund their criminal activities. Or that he'd let her come to harm if she didn't go along with his demands. He'd just have to find another way to persuade them.

Thuy pulled in, deliberately parking further away. She trotted over, looking over the restaurant. "So, they sell doughnuts here? I wondered."

"The best doughnuts," he said, ushering her inside. "They're famous around the state."

They sat down at a table. She got a raised chocolate glazed, and he got a slice of pecan pie. They both ordered coffee. He watched as she put a bunch of cream and sugar in hers.

"Want some coffee with your sugar?" he asked indulgently.

She rolled her eyes. "You should see Vietnamese pour-over coffee. You just get a little cup of it, but you could float your spoon in it, it's that thick. And it's served with condensed milk. So good." She took a sip, testing out the flavor. "This is okay, too."

He leaped for his advantage. "Aren't you going to miss where you come from? California, I mean?" he pressed. "I'm sure you weren't expecting to move to a tiny town in Tennessee. Is that what you even wanted?"

The waitress, Rebecca, brought over their doughnut and pie, and Drill nodded. Rebecca looked at him suspiciously, glancing between the two of them, then turned and walked away.

"Just jumping right into it, are we?" Thuy smiled tightly. "I don't know that I had a clear idea of what I wanted. I was cruising along, but my life wasn't exactly exciting. When your sister told me she was pregnant and that she'd kicked her boyfriend off to Australia, it was a no-brainer. Of course I was going to help her. She's my best friend. My *family*." She took a deep breath. "So that's what I'm doing. Helping her out, however I can."

He frowned. She sounded loyal. He valued loyalty: it was why he'd joined the Wraiths.

"There's more to farming than she realizes," he said. "Stuff I don't think she's thought of. The costs alone. There's feed, there's a lot of electricity, there's fuel. Vet bills." He sighed. "And then there's maintenance. Do either of you know how to fix the side-by-side, if it breaks down? That transmission can be touchy. Do you know how to change the oil on the tractor? How to sharpen the mower? How about tune up the Chevy?"

She looked miffed, but she also looked thoughtful — and a little nervous.

Good. He wanted her nervous.

She took a bite out of the doughnut, avoiding answering his question. Then her whole expression lit up, and her eyes went low lidded.

"Oh. My. *God.*" She chewed, then let out a soft sigh. "This is maybe the best doughnut I've ever had *in my life.*"

He jolted. She sounded and looked like she was talking about sex. There was a little smile playing along her lips, and her tongue reached out slightly as she put the fried dough on her tongue.

He found himself swallowing hard, imagining what else she could do with that tongue.

Stay focused. He had a job here. He cleared his throat.

"Well, ah, it's a lot of hard work," he continued, but got the feeling she wasn't even paying attention to what he was saying. Finally, he stopped, staring at her. "Really enjoying that doughnut, huh?"

"Mmmm." She looked like she was in heaven.

"Don't they have 'em where you come from?"

"They have doughnuts in Berkeley," she said, looking amused. "But not this good. Not by a long shot." She paused. "Guess that's just another benefit to staying here."

"Tell you what. I can mail you a box once a month if you can convince Maddy to sell."

She sighed, her dark eyes zeroing in on his. "I don't blame you for being pissed. Maddy doesn't, either. But it'd be really hard for her to afford a farm, even a small one, right now. Even with half the sale of your dad's property," she pointed out. "She's always wanted this — like, *always*. She's smart, and she's thought this through. If she thinks we can pull it off, then I believe her."

He sighed. The damned thing was, she was probably right. Maddy had grown up on the farm, same as he had, and they'd both helped their father with farm chores. While Maddy might not be as mechanically minded as he was, she was a whiz when it came to growing plants, just like their father had been. If anybody could make a go of specialty plants and such, it'd be Maddy.

"Why are you pushing so hard, anyway?" she asked. "Is it because you need the money? Or because you think Maddy's screwing you over?"

He stiffened, surprised by the casual way she asked the question. She surveyed him, finishing her doughnut, then sipping coffee like it was the most natural thing in the world for them to be talking like this.

"I… okay. I was angry," he admitted. "Pissed, like you said."

"Because you weren't getting your fair share of the farm."

He grimaced, trying to figure out a way to explain. "You know how in those comic strips, Lucy holds the football for Charlie Brown, and his dumb ass keeps trying to kick it, and she yanks it away at the last second?"

Thuy's expression was compassionate. She nodded.

"I felt like I couldn't believe my father had left me something — and then Maddy, my little Maddy, had yanked it away at the last second." He pushed his half-eaten pie away. "I love my sister. You don't have to believe me, but I do."

"Then let her have the farm," Thuy said softly. "It means so much to her. It'll be hard, I understand that. No, I do," she said, when he snorted in disbelief. "But she needs this. It's her lifelong dream. I don't know when or how she'd get another chance at it."

"What's *your* dream, Thuy?" he asked. "Doesn't that count for something?"

She blinked. Then she bit her full lower lip, looking thoughtful.

He wanted to bite that lip for her, he realized. There was just something about her that turned his engine over. He wasn't sure if it were her full lips, those high cheek-bones, or the way her dark eyes snapped. Her expressiveness. Or her fierce loyalty. Maybe it was the whole package. But he was attracted to her in a way that he'd never been to any woman, ever.

"I want to be part of something meaningful," Thuy said. "I like helping people. And Maddy has helped me more than I can possibly repay. My dream is helping her the way she's helped me. I'm right where I want to be, Drill. I hope you can understand and accept that... and stop trying to convince me otherwise."

He stared at her. The problem was, as it stood, he couldn't accept that. He *needed* them — both of them, he now realized — to be safe.

But damn, if he didn't admire her tenacity and drive.

"See me again," he heard himself say, his voice gravelly and low. "Not about this. Just go somewhere with me."

She tilted her head, looking at him like a surprised bird. "That's a bad idea," she said, with a gentle chuckle.

"Nobody has to know." Meaning Maddy. Although he certainly wouldn't tell the Wraiths, either. "Don't tell me you're not curious about how it'd be between us."

"Ego much?" She grinned.

He leaned forward, his voice dropping to a rough whisper. "You really gonna sit there and tell me you aren't interested?"

He heard the tiny gasp in her breathing, saw the way her pulse pounded quickly in the column of her neck. Her pupils dilated, and she wet her mouth reflexively with the pointed tip of her tongue, as she stared at him. His body went taut with desire, starting to harden. He wanted to devour her. But he sat there, waiting.

"Do you... read?"

He paused, sure he hadn't heard correctly. "Do I what?"

"Read. You know. Books. Novels, especially."

"What does *that* have to do with anything?" he asked, pulling away. Did she think he was some kind of idiot or something? Did she think he was illiterate?

"There's a great quote by John Waters. He said we need to make books cool again. So if you go home with somebody, and they don't have books, don't fuck them."

He barked out a surprised laugh. Of all the ways he thought she might turn him down, this was one he hadn't expected.

She smiled. "Librarian's gotta have her standards, even for one-night stands, Drill. Sorry."

He hadn't read a book since he was required to, back in high school. And he hadn't finished high school. He thought about lying, but knew she'd see right through it. "I'll pick up some books right away," he drawled. "Read right through 'em. And then maybe we can revisit the situation."

She blushed. It was adorable.

"Yeah, well," she muttered. "Until then… I'm going back to the farm."

He paid for their food, then accompanied her to the truck. He'd hoped that he could sway Thuy, but now he saw she was immovable. Where his sister went, she went.

He wished, for a second, that they could stay. He wanted to get to know her better. A *lot* better.

But that was stupid, wishful thinking. And if he kept it up, it might get them all hurt. Or worse.

CHAPTER SEVENTEEN

The next night, Thuy and Maddy decided to go out for dinner at the town's famous steak restaurant, The Front Porch. They probably should be more careful with their money, since Maddy had been worrying over ledgers and crunching numbers all day. But she also knew that today was Maddy's anniversary with David, so Maddy had been by turns melancholy and then hyper, trying to distract herself. Thuy decided that a night out might do them both good.

For her part, she couldn't stop thinking about what Drill said at Daisy's Nut House... not about the logistics of running the farm, but his invitation at the end.

You really gonna sit there and tell me you aren't interested?

The damned thing was, she *was* interested. Very interested. More interested than was healthy.

And now she was staying put — in the same town he was in.

Worst of all, she couldn't talk to Maddy about it. It was Maddy's brother, and that just felt weird. There were enough problems between the siblings. Thuy didn't want to add more oddity to the mix.

Maddy sighed, cutting into her prime rib. "I have something to admit to you."

"Yeah?" Thuy tried her steak. It was decent, just as Maddy had promised. The sides of cheesy broccoli and a loaded baked potato were tasty, as well. She tucked in. "What'd you do?" she asked around a mouthful of spuds.

"I, erm, emailed David."

Thuy's forked stopped mid-air, halting her next bite. "Oh, come on, Mads."

"I know, I know," Maddy groaned, covering her face with one hand. "I didn't mean to."

"Did you need something from him?" Thuy asked carefully.

Maddy shook her head.

Thuy sighed. "Did you find something he needed to have?"

"No."

Thuy paused. "Did you tell him he's an unmitigated dickhead and that you hope he dies by one of the multitudes of venomous animals Down Under?"

"No!" As she'd hoped, Maddy laughed, shaking her head. "You know it was amicable, mostly. He wasn't ready, and I wasn't interested in somebody who couldn't commit."

"So why'd you email him?"

Maddy turned red. "I said I… um, missed him."

"Oh, *Maddy*." Thuy shook her head. "He was the one who left. You might've told him to go, but he still made the choice."

"I know, I know!" Maddy peeked through her fingers. "It was a bad idea. But I was feeling nostalgic, with the anniversary and all. And I still love him."

Thuy didn't quite get that. She'd been in relationships, but she'd never been so in love that she wouldn't have kicked the guy's ass for deciding that going to another frickin' *continent* was a viable option when his girlfriend was pregnant.

Hell, she hadn't been in love enough to overlook a guy who chewed his cereal too loud.

Of course, that probably said more about her than it did about Maddy, she realized with a frown.

"I told him about the farm, at least. That the baby was fine. And how I was going to make it without him," Maddy said, with a teary little smile.

"That's good. You are. *We* are," Thuy corrected.

Maddy's expression fell a little. "I am a little concerned, though."

Thuy gripped her fork tighter. "What's up?"

"Looking over the numbers… Drill was right about one thing," she said. "Well, he was probably right about several things. It's going to be hard. And even owning the farm outright, we're going to have a lot of expenses. The electricity for the greenhouses is astronomical. And I hadn't taken into account health insurance, especially with the baby coming and all."

Thuy felt anxiety twist in her chest. "We need to stay positive," she said, keeping her expression schooled so Maddy didn't feel more concerned than she currently was. "Drill said that a lot of family farmers had a day job in addition to running the farm, right?"

"Yeah." Maddy nodded, looking glum. "But that's another place where he's right. I can't hold down a job, care for a baby, *and* run a farm."

"So I'll get the day job," Thuy said.

Maddy reddened. "Thuy, I can't ask you…"

"You're not asking me. I'm volunteering," Thuy said decisively. "You can take care of the baby. I'll handle the day job, and then we'll figure out how to take care of the farm stuff. I'll feed the animals or whatever, and you can tackle the plants in the greenhouses, and we'll… I don't know. We'll hire out for getting stuff seeded…"

"Sown." Maddy looked amused.

"Okay, *sown*, in the spring. If we have, um, a bigger crop in mind for some of those fields."

"It looks like my dad grew hay," Maddy said. "I can still see us growing some, even if I want to expand our vegetables and such for market."

"Right." Thuy nodded. "See? It'll work out."

Maddy looked hesitant. "I really am never going to be able to thank you enough."

"Remember all the times I slept on your floor? The times you hid me from the R.A.?" Thuy shook her head. "That time when my parents came looking for me, and you lied to their faces when I was hiding in your closet?"

Maddy paled, even though she chuckled weakly. "Yeah. That was scary as shit."

"You still don't even know the half of what they'd done, or what they're capable of," Thuy remarked. "Trust me. You don't owe me a damned thing."

"Well, we've come a long way from eating ramen in the dorms," Maddy said quietly.

Thuy raised her glass of water, and Maddy did the same. "To being farmers," she said.

"To new beginnings," Maddy added. They clinked glasses.

After they finished their meal and paid, Maddy spoke with the hostess —they'd gone to school together, back in the day. Thuy wandered outside, taking in the cold November air. It'd be Thanksgiving that Thursday, she realized. She wondered if she and Maddy ought to get a little turkey to celebrate. She also wondered if they should invite Drill.

Because you want to see him again.

She frowned at herself. At least once they showed they weren't going anywhere, he'd probably steer clear of them, per his motorcycle club's orders. She knew what it was like. The criminal family was your family: you owed them supreme loyalty. And they enforced that "loyalty" if you did something they disliked.

Sex with a biker like Drill was the last thing she needed to get mixed up in.

She thought about that wicked smile of his, as he looked at her over the rim of his mug of coffee. The heat of his gaze, as he surveyed her like she was something on the menu that he'd like to eat — slowly, and with great enjoyment.

Her body stirred. It had been a long time since she'd had sex, at least nine months, and even then, it hadn't been anything to write home about.

She got the feeling riding a biker like Drill would be plenty noteworthy.

She waved a hand in front of her face. Apparently, the cold November night had nothing on thoughts of Drill. *Stop it, you ninny,* she chastised herself. Whatever it was about him, she needed to let it go, right now.

Maddy waddled out, and they headed for the Continental. She helped Maddy climb carefully into the passenger seat, then she clambered into the driver's side.

"I will be glad when I'm not so damned large," Maddy complained, as she carefully buckled herself in. "It's like being one of those hippo ballerinas from Disney's *Fantasia*."

"At least you're graceful," Thuy joked, causing Maddy to laugh.

"I don't feel graceful. I feel like a lump."

Thuy was still getting used to the town, so she relied on the GPS. It led them through the main street of town. She stopped at a stoplight, taking the moment to look at the quaint shops around them. It really was a pretty town.

Suddenly, there was a loud snarl of engines. She looked in the rearview mirror to see lights — not of a car, but from a number of motorcycles. A large number.

"Thuy…" Maddy said, with a note of uneasiness. A biker had pulled up along either side of the large car.

Thuy watched as one pulled in front of the car. Even though the light had now turned green, he turned the bike lengthwise. There was no way to go around; there was no way to pull forward. They were surrounded.

What fresh hell is this? Thuy thought frantically. She considered gunning the engine, signaling that she'd run the guy in front over, but she didn't want to make matters worse. Odds were good they were armed. She needed to think this through.

There was a tap on her window. She looked down at the man who flanked the door.

"You two are the new girls, huh?" He was a vaguely handsome man, with an ugly sneer. He stared at her, then gestured for her to exit the vehicle. "Huh. Well, be friendly. Come out and say hello."

CHAPTER EIGHTEEN

Drill knew there was no question: Timothy King was an asshole. Right now, though, he was an asshole that was up to something.

Ordinarily, Drill didn't give a shit what Tim did, as long as he kept his side of the street clean and didn't cause too many problems for the Wraiths. He didn't like how Tim was with women, probably because Tim didn't have a sister or a mother himself. The guy was grabby, and Drill had to push him to stay in line, especially when they were in town. He also didn't like how Tim thought he was bigger and tougher than he actually was. He had delusions of grandeur, which had led him to campaign heavily to become the next leader of the Wraiths. When Catfish had beaten him — both figuratively and literally — he'd nursed a grudge.

It was the grudge thing that had Drill keeping an eye on Tim. He still had some followers, people who had backed his play when he'd attempted to become captain. They were idiots, too, honestly, but right now the Wraiths couldn't afford to be choosy. So, when the pack of them decided to leave the bar on a Tuesday night, after Tim got a phone call, Drill knew that he'd better follow and make sure the idiot and his posse didn't do something stupid.

He'd been hanging back, and they hadn't even noticed him — another mark of how clueless they were — when they arrived in town, gunning their engines and generally making a scene. They used to do this all the time, until Catfish told them to knock it off. They were never going to be taken seriously as a motorcycle club if they kept showing off like dumbasses.

As he drove up, he noticed that they were blocking the intersection, and had a car surrounded. His eyes narrowed. It was a black Lincoln Continental — his dad's car.

He clenched his jaw so tight, it was a wonder his molars didn't disintegrate.

He pulled up as Tim knocked on the window. He could make out Thuy in the driver's seat, looking supremely bored.

"I just wanna talk to you. Get to know you. Show you around town," Tim said. "Both of y'all. Surely two pretty women don't want to spend the night all by their lonesome, do they?"

One of the other bikers, a bearded lunk named Grizz, laughed like a braying donkey. He was on the passenger side. "C'mon, sweetie," he crooned.

That's when Drill noticed his sister was on the other side, in the passenger seat.

He watched as Maddy rolled down the window a little. "Got no interest in a needle-dick like yourself," she said sharply.

Grizz grinned. "It's a lot bigger than a needle," he said, reaching for his crotch. "Wanna see?"

Jesus wept. Drill shut off his bike and got off, storming towards them.

"If you don't move," he heard Thuy say from the cracked window, "I am going to run your goddamned bike over. Got it?"

"Now, that's not very friendly," Tim said, his eyes bright with malice. He tried the door, which was thankfully locked. "Come on out. Or do I have to—"

"Leave them alone," Drill ground out, grabbing Tim by the scruff of his neck and whirling him away from the truck. Tim staggered, then righted himself, his eyes narrowing.

"Dammit, Drill. You never let me have *any* fun," he said. "I was just greeting your sister and her little friend here, welcoming them to town."

Drill felt anger like lava in his stomach, churning and bubbling, ready to explode.

"But wait — she's not your sister, is she? Once you're in the Wraiths, *you don't have family.* So what difference does it make to you, if I get friendly with some women here in town?" His shit-eating grin was wide and smug.

So that had been the phone call. Someone had sighted Maddy and Thuy, and told Tim about it. Which meant Tim was looking to stir up trouble… and probably to get a little payback on Drill by bugging his sister, knowing that he couldn't acknowledge her. Not without Catfish going batshit.

But then again, Tim had never been that bright.

"You're fucking terrorizing women in the middle of the street, you idiot," Drill said. "Now move your bike, and let them through, before the cops get here."

"I'm just saying hello," Tim said.

"At a stoplight? With your bike stopped in front of them?"

"Stalled." Tim's smirk was arrogant. "Maybe they'll give me a ride, help me out."

"The *only* way a woman would give you a *ride* is if she took pity on you!" Drill heard Maddy call from the truck cab.

Please, stop helping. His sister, once she got going, had a mouth on her.

Tim turned an ugly shade of red, and started heading back towards the truck. Drill grabbed him again.

"Grab your bike, get it out of the way, and let the girls go," Drill said, lowering his voice. "Christ, Tim. Catfish is *not* gonna be happy when I tell him that you're stirring up trouble here in town."

"Fucking tattle tale." Tim spat on the ground. "And what do I care, whether Catfish is happy or unhappy? We're gonna be patched over anyway. Get taken over by one of the bigger clubs. One of the *serious* clubs. I hear some of 'em have links to bigger outfits, like the Bandidos or Hell's Angels, or even the mob." Tim sounded excited by the prospect.

"Like they're going to be excited to take *you*," Drill said with exasperation. He looked over at the other bikers. "Move the damned bike."

They looked at each other, hesitant, unsure of who to listen to.

"Unless you want me to fucking pound every single one of you," Drill said, in a serious tone, "I'd get moving. *Now*."

Quickly, one of them hopped off his own bike and moved Tim's ride out of the way.

Drill's gaze met Thuy's in the side mirror. He nodded to her. "Go on home," he called.

Thuy hit the accelerator, and the car sped away into the night.

Drill was about to deal with Tim, who looked ready to fight, when the *whoop-whoop* of a police siren interrupted them. It was Jackson James, sheriff's deputy and general pain in the ass.

Just what I needed. Why hadn't the guy been here five minutes ago?

"I got a call that there was a disturbance," Jackson said sternly, surveying the group. Drill noticed that his hand didn't stray far from his gun. "Something about a bunch of bikers circling a car with two women in it. Anything I should know about?"

"No car here now," Grizz said, his smile revealing a lost eyetooth.

"So why are y'all here, blocking up the intersection?" Jackson pressed.

"Um... Tim's bike, uh, stalled," the guy who moved it answered, giving Tim a nervous glance.

Tim looked like he'd eaten worms. "Yeah," he finally said. "My bike stalled."

"Well, move it to the side of the road then," Jackson said, with the *dumbass* silent but heavily implied. He looked over at Drill. "You corroborate his story?"

He could say that Tim had been scaring Thuy and Maddy, but it wouldn't do anything but make him a narc in his own club, and that was something he wouldn't do. He'd been too loyal for too long.

"His bike *stalled* before I got here," Drill said. "Guys, do as the sheriff says and move the thing, will you?"

Going along with it, they rolled it off to the curb. Tim looked irritated.

"Figured that's how you'd play it," Jackson said, shaking his head. He stepped closer to Drill, lowering his voice. "I got the call from Maddy, you know."

Drill froze, struggling to keep his face completely expressionless.

"She said that the guys were catcalling them. That they'd stopped the car and were trying to get in."

Drill shrugged, even though it felt like shit to do so.

Jackson sighed. "Lucky nothing happened then," he said, in a voice ripe with frustration.

"I wouldn't have let anything happen," Drill hissed back, then caught himself. "If anything like that had occurred, I mean."

Jackson rolled his eyes. "Whatever. Just keep your dogs in line."

"Will do," Drill drawled. He watched as Jackson got back in his cruiser and drove away.

"Fucking cops," Tim said. "Should've known those bitches would…"

Drill turned around and punched Tim square on the jaw. Tim's eyes rolled, and he went down to the ground like a dropped bag of flour.

"When he comes to, bring him to me at the bar," Drill said. "Apparently, he needs a lesson in manners… and who's in charge."

The rest of the bikers scurried to follow his orders. Drill spared one last look down the darkened road. The car was nowhere in sight.

He wanted to call Maddy, make sure she and Thuy were all right. But maybe it was for the best. If they were scared, maybe they'd rethink staying in Green Valley. It sucked, but it was what Catfish wanted anyway.

And he knew, with ugly certainty, that Catfish would do a lot worse to get the money.

CHAPTER NINETEEN

Thuy drove back to the library. It was the Wednesday before Thanksgiving, so she knew that the library would probably be empty as most people prepared for the holiday. She was starting the job hunt, just as a way to feel like she was doing *something*. Between the two of them, she and Maddy had a bit of savings. Maddy had suggested they hire a teen to help with the animals, so Thuy had also brought a flyer they'd printed up for the bulletin board. She'd pin one up at the Piggly Wiggly and Daisy's Nut House, as well, to see if there were any takers.

But the main reason she was there was to see if the library was hiring. It would be the perfect match for her, a good use of her skills, and it would allow her to spend her days in one of her favorite environments on earth. Win-win.

Just need to see if they were hiring.

If they weren't, she'd looked online (as best she could, with her phone) at other options. So far, the only thing in the nearby area was a night stocking clerk at the Piggly Wiggly. She could do it if she had to, but she hadn't worked in grocery, or retail, and she hadn't worked a night shift. With the baby coming, she wasn't sure if that was going to be the best use of her time.

She walked into the library, squaring her shoulders. She walked to the desk. The woman she'd met earlier, Naomi, was there, and smiled at her.

"You're back already," she said. "How were the books? Did you find them helpful? Need some more?"

"Yes. That is, they were helpful, although it's going to take me a while to process all of them," Thuy admitted. They had read like Ikea instructions, unfortunately. She'd gone over soil composition and fertilization and pH balances until her eyes had glazed over. She got the feeling that farming wasn't going to be a natural fit for her. "I came back for something else, though."

"Oh?"

"Yes. By any chance, are you guys hiring?"

Naomi looked surprised, then thoughtful. "It's funny you should mention," she said. "We just got word that we received a donation, that will keep the library open. It allows for the hiring of a few more people. We hadn't really planned on hiring anybody soon, but it might be good to allow a little more flexibility in hours… hmm." She tapped her bottom lip. "You know, the person you should talk to is our head librarian, Julianne MacIntyre. Let me go get her. I'll be right back."

Just like that, Naomi disappeared into the back offices. Thuy swallowed hard, and surreptitiously straightened out her clothes. She'd brought her resume, just in case, in the same folder as the flyers. She was glad she was wearing a nice pair of slacks and a sweater, rather than her usual sweatshirt and jeans.

Naomi came back out, this time with an older woman in tow. The lady had to be in her sixties. She looked… well, strict, was the best way Thuy could describe her. She had gray hair that was cut in a bob, more utilitarian than stylish, and she wore glasses. She was also wearing a blouse and skirt with some low heels. She glanced at Thuy.

"You're looking for a job at the library?" she asked without preamble.

Thuy nodded. "If you're hiring." *Please, please be hiring.*

The woman harrumphed a little. "Come back to my office."

Surprised, Thuy walked behind the circulation desk and followed her. The back room was the usual chaos of books piled in waiting bins, ready to be sorted on carts and finally shelved. She wove around the piles and followed Mrs. MacIntyre into the head librarian's office. This was neat as a surgery tray, everything in its place. Mrs. MacIntyre gestured to the seat across from her desk, and Thuy sat down.

"We will be getting funds to hire someone full time, although that's not going to take effect until first quarter next year," she said. Her voice was unfussy, very cut-and-dried. "It's not a huge salary, but it's good for this area."

Thuy had researched what the average librarian's wage was in the area, so she knew what to expect.

"Of course, not everyone is a good fit for libraries in general, or ours in particular," she said firmly. "I'm assuming you have experience?"

"I do. I've been a librarian for five years," Thuy said, reaching for her resume.

The woman shook her head. "Library *professional*, actually. Technically, you're not a librarian unless you have a degree in library science." She said this primly. "That's not to say I don't admire and respect library professionals, but I do believe in being specific and correct."

Thuy suppressed a grin as she pulled out her résumé and handed it over. "I received my MLIS from San Jose State University five years ago," she said quietly. "I have been working at the University of California Berkeley Biosciences and Natural Resources Library for the past three years, and the East Asian Library for two before that."

"I see." Thuy had obviously caught the woman off guard. She watched as Mrs. MacIntyre scanned the document. "These are stunning credentials."

"Thank you," Thuy said, feeling pride warm her chest. She'd worked hard and overcome a lot to get them.

"In fact," Mrs. MacIntyre said, a little sadly, "you seem woefully *overqualified* for our job."

"I'm okay with that," Thuy assured her quickly. "I'm permanently relocating to Green Valley, and I'm happy working at a smaller library. My focus of study was public librarianship, rather than academic or corporate. It'll be nice to use that skill set again."

Mrs. MacIntyre's lips pursed. "We aren't a big city library," she said slowly. "This is a small town. We embrace tradition. I've been working in this library for longer than you've been alive, and I know most of the people who patronize us, and have since they were children."

Thuy nodded, not sure where this was going.

"I don't want a lot of changes," Mrs. MacIntyre said, her expression suddenly stern. "I don't need someone who's thinking they're going to revolutionize anything, or who thinks they know better than we do what's best for our town."

Ah. So that was what was wrong. She was probably the reason that there were still card catalogs, rather than extra computer terminals. She'd hung the internet sign.

Oh, joy.

Thuy liked to think of herself as a progressive librarian. She didn't look down on rural towns, or at least, she hoped she didn't, even if she'd never lived in one. She'd studied the effects of lack of resources on libraries in inner cities. She knew that rural towns had just as many problems as far as getting enough books, enough funding, helping enough patrons. And it wasn't just a matter of books. It was helping people like Jim Thompson use the internet to get a job, or giving teens a safe place to hang out, or even helping idiots like herself find out more about stuff like farming. That meant more computers, printers... even 3D printers. More eBooks and audiobooks for people who were sight impaired or had trouble physically getting to the library. More accommodations for special needs patrons. Interlibrary lending.

The more she thought about it, the more she thought she could help this little library.

If they let her.

She swallowed hard, biting down on the suggestions that wanted to trip off her tongue.

"I could work within those parameters," Thuy said carefully. "I don't want to upset your traditions, or do anything that would make you, or the town, uncomfortable."

Mrs. MacIntyre looked at her suspiciously. *And rightfully so.* Thuy felt like, after she'd been there a while, maybe she could make some suggestions. But she needed to get a foot in the door.

And honestly, it beat the hell out of stocking grocery shelves, especially when you were short.

"I could start in a part-time capacity," Thuy suggested. "Until you were sure I was a good fit."

"Confident," Mrs. MacIntyre mused. "That's a good suggestion. Let's say a month long, part-time trial period."

Thuy felt a wave of relief.

"If I feel you're not working out," she added, "then you'll be released, of course."

"Of course," Thuy said through gritted teeth.

"Fine. You start Monday afternoon, then. One o'clock to nine o'clock." Mrs. MacIntyre stood up, holding out her hand.

Thuy shook, wondering abruptly if she knew what she'd just let herself in for.

CHAPTER TWENTY

Drill had been looking for Frank Helms all day. Frank had been dodging Catfish's guys for the past three weeks, defaulting on a ten-point loan that he'd taken out. After the first week of radio silence, Catfish had been patient. By the second week, he was irritated. Three weeks earned you a visit from the club's muscle — namely, Drill.

He'd been put in the position fairly early on, mostly because of his size and his fighting abilities. It wasn't something he enjoyed, necessarily. It was something he understood. If you sold your soul to the devil, sooner or later, the tab came due.

He was the one who collected on that tab.

Now, he was in the parking lot of Genie's bar. It was the night before Thanksgiving, before a holiday weekend, so it was crowded for a Wednesday. He knew that Frank had a fondness for drinking when he was stressed, and he thought that maybe the man would wander out of whatever hole he was hiding in to drown his sorrows.

He was right. He spotted Frank's beat-up Ford F150 in the lot.

He thought about waiting by it, but it was cold, and with his luck, Frank would be in there till closing time. So instead, he walked in, scanning the crowd. Sure enough, Frank was holding up one end of the bar, looking like a basset hound with his long expression. Drill watched as Frank dropped a shot in a mug of beer and then drank it steadily.

Drill stepped up behind him. "Boilermakers, huh, Frank?" he asked quietly, taking a seat next to him.

Frank went pale as a ghost. "Shit," he breathed.

"You knew we were looking for you." Drill's voice could've been mistaken for gentle, but there was an underlying steel there. He was not fucking around, and he needed Frank to know that, even if he didn't want to cause a scene. "So why don't you finish that drink there, and we'll step out to your truck?"

"You're... you're letting me finish my drink?" Frank asked.

"Let's just say you'll want all the anesthesia you can get," Drill said in a low voice.

Frank's eyes widened. "Shit," he repeated. "Shit, shit, *shit*."

He drank the rest of his boilermaker steadily. Then Drill stood, gesturing to the door. Frank walked in front of him. Nobody looked their way, thankfully.

Drill wasn't planning on beating the man too badly. Usually, a few good strikes were enough to get the point across, in his experience. For all the talk of broken kneecaps and busted arms, it was counterproductive. He was trying to get money back for the club. What could a farmer with a broken kneecap do to earn back the cash?

No, he'd probably just give Frank a black eye, knock the wind out of him, bruise him up good. Give him something that Catfish would be satisfied with, something that expressed the severity of their concern. But nothing too harsh.

Frank was shaking like a leaf by the time they reached the truck. "I swear, I'm trying to get the money back," he all but gibbered.

"Do you know how many times I hear that?" Drill asked tiredly. "You owe six thousand, six hundred and fifty-five dollars."

Frank's eyes widened. "But... but I only borrowed five thousand!"

"That was three weeks ago. It's a ten-point loan."

Frank goggled.

Drill sighed. And now he was giving an impromptu math lesson. "A point's a percent, right?"

"O-okay," Frank agreed.

"So it's ten percent interest weekly."

"All right." He blinked. "But... wait. Shouldn't that be, like, sixty-five hundred?"

"Compound interest," Drill said, sighing. "It's ten percent of the amount of the loan at the end of the week, not an additional ten percent of the principal."

"Jeez Louise. You sound like a banker."

That was a new one. He'd been called many things, but "banker" was never one of them. Drill smiled humorlessly. "Really, you're lucky it's not more than that." He cracked his knuckles, and Frank winced. "You were supposed to pay off two weeks ago. You said that you just needed a week. You didn't lie to us, now, did you Frank?"

Frank let out a low moan. "I... my farm. I'm behind on the bills, on the mortgage. I just needed a little to get the bank off my back," he said.

Drill felt a pang of guilt, and gritted his teeth. He'd heard sob stories before, as well. Most of the time they were lies. But then again, he was usually dealing with gamblers, people who would sell their own mothers to get into another round of poker. He knew Frank had a farm, and knew that the guy had a bad harvest this year. He probably wasn't lying.

"I've been trying to sell stuff to make up the difference. I've got about three grand," he said. "But I knew you guys wouldn't accept partial payment, or whatever, and I just... I screwed up, okay? I swear, I'll get the money by the end of the week. I'm selling my goats, and I'll... I don't know. I'll sell my furniture if I have to. I'll get you the money, I swear." Drill could see his throat work as he swallowed hard. "Just... just don't hurt me, okay?"

Drill let out a long exhalation. This was the part of the job he hated. Maybe he was getting too old for this shit.

A car pulled into the parking lot, and he shielded Frank, not wanting prying eyes to pay attention. They were in a darkened portion of the lot, and the beating ought to be quick, but still. It wouldn't do to have somebody intervene.

He narrowed his eyes, watching as the truck that pulled in shut off its lights.

Ah, son of a bitch.

Chevy Silverado. He watched as Thuy opened the driver's side door, gingerly lowering herself to the ground.

He couldn't do this. Thuy already thought he was a thug. He wasn't going to underline that assumption by beating the shit out of someone while she was fifty feet away.

"You are one lucky asshole," Drill said, shaking his head.

Frank stared at him, looking like a frightened rabbit. "Pardon?"

"I'm letting you off the hook," Drill said. "Ordinarily, I'd have bloodied you up and sent you on your way. But today, you're getting a warning. It's the only warning you're gonna get," he emphasized. "You need to get the cash in by Monday, got it? All of it. Do whatever you have to do, but get the cash, and *do not run*. It'll only make things worse on yourself."

"Okay. Okay. I promise." Frank was stammering now, sweat pouring from his forehead despite the autumn chill. "Thanks, man."

"Don't mention it. Seriously — not to anyone," Drill said. "And if I have to come collect again, I'm going to make up for being nice this time. Don't make me regret it, okay?"

Frank nodded. Then he quickly climbed into his truck.

Drill watched as he pulled out, leaving in a trail of dust and screech of tires. He felt suddenly, overwhelmingly tired.

I am so sick of this shit.

He turned to the bar. Thuy was standing there, staring at him, he noticed immediately. He straightened, walking over to her.

"We've got to stop meeting like this," he said. "In parking lots, I mean. Although I've got to admit, I didn't expect to see you at a bar."

She shrugged. "It's been a long day. Maddy's home sleeping, and I just needed to get out where it was noisy," she said, with a shrug. "Blow off some steam. I thought I'd check out the nightlife here in town. Maddy suggested Genie's."

He nodded. It was pretty much the only place in town for drinks and dancing, if you didn't count the Friday jam sessions. "Can I buy you a drink?"

She tilted her head, a small smile playing at the corners of her full lips. "That's probably a bad idea," she said.

"You can talk to me about books," he said, wiggling his eyebrows.

She chuckled. Then her eyes grew serious.

"What were you talking to that man about?"

He winced. "Private business," he said, more sharply than he intended.

Her lips pursed as she surveyed him suspiciously.

"But you'll notice, he walked away unhurt," Drill pointed out. "So it wasn't that big a deal."

She seemed to process that for a second. Then she turned, heading toward the bar.

"So, can I buy you a drink?" he repeated.

She sighed. "I can buy my own drinks," she said. "But... you can sit next to me. And we can talk about books. If you want."

He smiled. It was probably stupid, to let Frank walk away, all because he didn't want to disappoint some woman he barely knew. But she was letting him drink with her, and opening up just a little. He'd take it.

CHAPTER TWENTY-ONE

Thuy stepped into Genie's, feeling Drill's presence behind her like a heat lamp even before he put a hand on her lower back and guided her inside. She wasn't sure if this was a good idea, but back at the farmhouse, she'd been climbing the walls. Maddy's pregnancy had her sleeping more and more, and Thuy knew she was perfectly safe — and could call her at a moment's notice if she felt unwell. For Thuy, there was no cable, no internet, nothing to distract her from the oppressive silence of the farm, punctuated only by the hoots of owls or faint scratching that she assumed was mice or something skittering across the porch. She'd tried reading her book, but she felt the need to get *out*, amongst people. Not that she was an extrovert — far from it. But sometimes, it was nice to get in the energy of a crowd.

Ordinarily, she'd go to a coffee house. She thought that Daisy's Nut House might be open, but after her exchange with Julianne MacIntyre, the head librarian, and going through some numbers and farm stuff with Maddy, Thuy thought the top of her head would blow off. She decided she needed something stronger than a decaf.

"I see some people leaving a booth," he said, his height an obvious advantage in this situation. "C'mon."

She wasn't sure why, but she let him lead her to the small corner booth. She slid in, and he squeezed himself next to her. She scooted so his powerful thigh didn't rub up against her wool slacks.

The waitress came up, surveying them with surprise. "Hey, Drill," she said, sounding tentative. "Usual?"

"Just a beer, yeah," Drill said, with a nod. Then he looked at Thuy.

"Amaretto and orange juice," she said. "Light, please."

The waitress stared at her for a second. "New in town? Or just passing through?"

"Um, yeah." Welcome to small-town living, she thought with a grimace. "I'm Maddy's friend. Maddy Blount?"

"*Oh.*" The waitress nodded, obviously having heard something since the funeral. She then looked between Thuy and Drill again. "I'll get your drinks."

Which left Thuy and Drill sitting there, looking at each other. He grinned, revealing a dimple. His blue eyes twinkled.

"How's Maddy?" he asked.

"She's fine. Sleeping when I left," Thuy said. "We're going to need to find a doctor for her here." Something else to add to the list.

"And how are you?" he asked, his voice lowering a little. She had to lean closer to hear him over the loud country music that was playing.

"I'm okay."

"If you were okay," he said conversationally, "then why did you decide to come out for a drink all by your lonesome?"

She sighed. He caught her there. "Maybe I'm here to pick up a guy, ever think of that?" she teased.

He blinked, then his grin grew wider. "I volunteer as tribute?"

She burst out laughing, and he chuckled with her. "I thought you didn't read," she said.

"I don't really, but I saw the movie," he said. "Caught it on cable. Pretty good."

"The book was even better, but it almost always is," she said. "Wait, you have cable? God. I envy you."

"I forgot. Dad wouldn't have gotten cable, even if they ran it out that far," he said, with a rueful shake of his head. "Dad didn't believe in luxuries."

Which made Thuy wonder, again, at what sort of life Drill and Maddy lived while they stayed under "Old Man Blount's" roof. Maddy had said it was unpleasant living with such a strict father — that he'd never hurt her, but that he'd rarely shown affection, and that he'd been very harsh when it came to getting his opinion across. She got the feeling there was a lot of verbal and emotional abuse.

She also got the feeling that Drill had received more than just that. Why else would he leave to join the club at, what, sixteen?

She was still mulling that over when the waitress showed up with their drinks. Thuy thanked her, taking a sip. It was perfect, not too strong. She was lucky to have a high tolerance, but she was still going to be driving, and she didn't want to overdo. She just wanted one drink to take the edge off.

Of course, with Drill sitting there, she had a whole new edge to her system.

"I got a job," she found herself saying, then frowned. It wasn't like he'd asked.

"You did? Already?"

She nodded. "Part-time at the library," she expanded, "with a chance at full time after the new year. So that'll help with bills on the farm. Oh, and I put up flyers to get some teenager or something to help us out with the animals." She was going to try her hand at feeding the cattle next, and after her little jaunt with the side-by-side in the ditch, it was a little daunting. Still, she didn't want Drill to know that, especially since he was still on his crusade to sell the farm.

"You guys move quickly," he said. Was there a trace of admiration in his voice? His gaze was warm, but that could just be attraction.

Jeez, did they have attraction.

"We're serious about making this work," Thuy said instead, hoping that her voice was stern enough to get the point across.

"I know," he said, with a sigh. He took a sip of beer, then reached out, stroking the back of her hand for just a second with his fingertip.

She felt it like an electric wave running up her arm, and it was all she could do not to jolt away. "I also know it's going to only get harder."

She frowned. Why? Why couldn't he be the least bit supportive?

"Let's not talk about the farm," he said, surprising her. He looked mischievous. "Tell me: what kind of books do the men you sleep with read?"

She blinked. Not what she expected him to say. She felt herself smile, slowly. "It's not like I have a required reading list," she said, then paused. "Although now that you mention it, that's not a bad idea."

He chuckled. "Probably classics, or 'literature', or whatever smart people read," he said, and there was a note of self-deprecation that somehow broke Thuy's heart. She quickly shook her head.

"I don't read a lot of lit fic — nothing too snobby," she said. "I mean, I don't just read literature or classics, although I appreciate them. I read lots of genre fiction, too. Romance, sci-fi, fantasy, mystery, thrillers. I think it's important to read outside of your comfort zone: different authors, different experiences. I have comfort reads, too, but I... well, if you hadn't guessed, I read all the time," she finally said, as she realized she was rambling.

He was staring at her like she was something brand new, something he'd never experienced before. She felt embarrassed, and quickly finished her drink.

"You know," he said, his voice tinged with amused surprise, "I don't think I'm as passionate about anything as you are about books."

She let out a half-laugh. "They are my favorite thing ever. They gave me a place to go when my life was shitty, and they have continually given me a reason to get out of bed in the morning. I read every single day. They're my lifeline."

"Now I envy you," he said, and she got the feeling he wasn't just bullshitting her — he sounded like he meant it. "What do you think a guy like me should read?"

She felt warmth, and it had nothing to do with the amaretto she'd consumed. This was the sort of challenge she loved. She scooted a little closer, so they could talk over the music without yelling. "What kind of movies do you like? What kind of stories?"

By the end of their talk, nearly two hours had gone by. She found out he liked adventure stories, and that he liked stories with justice and questionable heroes and things that had puzzles. She could think of several books, across several genres, and started to list them all.

"Whoa, whoa," he said, holding up a hand. "I'm not going to be able to remember all of them. Which one of those is your favorite?"

She paused, thinking about it. "For a true book junkie," she said slowly, "that's like asking 'which one is your favorite child?' or 'what appendage would you like to keep?'"

He laughed, and she smiled back at him.

"But, based on what you've told me," she said, "I'd say *The Name of the Wind*, by Patrick Rothfuss."

"Okay." He nodded. "I'll read it."

She must've looked skeptical, because he chuckled.

"I mean it. I'll give it a try."

"It's like seven hundred pages long," she warned him.

His eyes widened, then he shrugged. "Okay, it may take a little while. But hell, I'm game."

"Why?"

He was silent for a long moment, staring into her eyes. She squirmed as the heat from his gaze seemed to seep into her very bones.

"Do you really not know?" he asked, so matter-of-factly that she felt like an idiot.

He's volunteering to read a book for you.

She felt heat suffuse her cheeks. That might be the single sexiest thing a guy had ever offered to do for her, she realized.

"I... I ought to get going," she said, hitting the table in her haste to get out of the booth.

He got up, too, and put down enough money for both drinks, waving her hand away when she reached for her purse. "I'll see you out."

It was gentlemanly. Downright chivalrous. She noticed that several people were staring at the two of them as they walked out the door together. She was parked under a light, and he escorted her right up to the door of the truck.

"Thanks," she said. "I had a good time tonight. Talking with you, I mean. It's what I needed."

"So, I'm not as bad a guy as you think," he said.

"I don't think you're a bad guy," she protested, then winced.

He stepped closer. "You don't, huh?"

She let out a breath. The thing was, she'd known truly bad people all her life. He was involved in criminal stuff, no question, and that didn't make him a "good" guy, per se. But he loved his sister, and she got the feeling he wasn't as "bad" as others might make him out to be.

He tilted her chin up with his fingertips, and she couldn't help it. She sighed, almost moaning with longing. He leaned towards her, giving her plenty of time to pull away. "Tell me no," he said, in a low voice.

She should have. It was the smart response. Honestly, it was the best response.

But it wasn't the response she wanted to give. Instead, she stood on her tiptoes, brushing her mouth against his.

He groaned, leaning down, scooping her up, making her squeak in surprise before his lips laid claim to hers. He pressed her against the truck, his arms holding her tight as his mouth slanted against hers. She wrapped her arms around his neck, her hands reaching up to cradle his head against hers. She felt his tongue reach out, skimming across the seam of her closed lips, which she quickly opened.

The kiss ran rampant from there.

Her tongue tangled with his, his mouth demanding, hers equally so. She pressed her body against his, her hips rolling slightly as she felt the burgeoning hardness in his jeans. She trembled, actually *trembled,* with an overwhelming need. She bit at his lower lip, and he growled in approval, his big hands stroking down her sides, then holding her flush against him. Her eyes almost rolled back in her head as he continued his sensual onslaught, his head tilting one way, then the other, advancing and retreating, pressing hot kisses against her throat, her chin, then her mouth again. She was almost blind with desire, drowning in it.

She didn't know how long they were there, but they broke apart when someone honked. There was laughter. "Woo-hoo!" someone called.

Drill broke off to glare at whoever it was, and Thuy felt sanity return in a sudden, embarrassing rush. She'd all but had sex with this guy, in public. Against a truck.

This man was dangerous to her sanity. To say nothing of her panties, which she knew were a damp mess. Her heart was still beating out of control, and given another moment, she might've just ... *Oh, ugh.*

She had to get out of here, and fast.

"I... I don't know why I did that," she said, nudging at his shoulders. It was like nudging at granite.

He looked like he didn't want to let her go, but reluctantly, he did. "I'm gonna see you," he promised. "Real soon. Okay?"

"O-okay," she said. He lowered her to her feet, and she opened the truck door clumsily. She could feel his eyes on her as she started the engine, turned on the lights. She nodded to him, and then drove away, her heart pounding frantically.

That, she thought, *was epically stupid.*

And yet, she knew some part of her couldn't wait for it to happen again.

CHAPTER TWENTY-TWO

Drill was still thinking about that kiss from Saturday night. He still needed to somehow convince Maddy to sell the farm, so canoodling with her best friend was probably dumb. But damn, it had felt *good.* It had felt *right*.

And it had only been a kiss. He could only imagine what sex with her would be like. And he'd imagined it, frequently and well, since their hot embrace against the truck.

He'd been giving the Dragon a pass the past few days, using the argument that it was Thanksgiving, even if he'd spent the day by himself, scrolling through TV channels mindlessly. He'd spent Friday cleaning his apartment, of all things, until he realized he was doing it *in case he had company*.

Which meant a woman.

Which meant Thuy.

Which was, he already realized, a poor idea.

What he *ought* to be doing was figuring out some way to drive the women back to California, without actually hurting them or threatening them. He loved his sister too much to scare her with something overt, but she wasn't listening to reason, and Catfish was going to be breathing down his neck.

He glanced over to see Catfish emerging from the back rooms. *Speak of the devil.* He took another pull of beer.

"Drill," Catfish said, his voice full of quiet command, and he gestured to the back. Drill nodded, grabbing his beer bottle and following. He was growing to hate these back-office visits. It was like going to the principal's, back in the day, when he'd been sent there for not paying attention. Or, as his father had said, "for being stupid." Which had promptly been followed by stupid-beatings.

He shuffled over, down the hallway, then into the office, closing the door behind him. At least Dirty Dave wasn't there. It was just him and Catfish. Catfish looked — well, not precisely pissed, but not happy, either.

"What the hell, man?" Catfish said, without preamble.

Drill blinked. "What the hell, what?" he asked. "What'd I do?"

Catfish sighed, rubbing at his temples. "You fucked up this week, is what you did."

"What?" Drill growled. "How'd I fuck up?"

"You didn't collect on Frank Helms."

Drill winced. Okay, that was true. "I warned him," he said, knowing that was an excuse at best. "And I told him he'd better have it by Monday. He's still got time."

"When I didn't see the money, I found out that you'd talked to him on Wednesday night — and then you'd let him walk off, not a scratch on him." Catfish's deep voice was gravelly with frustration. "Do you know how it looks, when we let somebody walk away like that? What kind of message it sends?"

Drill was silent, knowing that Catfish would no doubt educate him.

"It makes us look fucking *weak*," Catfish finished, his voice rising. The office was sound-proofed, for a number of reasons, so it wasn't like anybody else was going to hear Drill's dressing down. But still, it stung. "And right now, the last thing we can afford to do is look weak! Do I need to draw a fucking picture for you to get that?"

He knew Catfish had a point. Still, Drill crossed his arms. "A few days — over a fucking holiday, no less — wasn't going to make that much of a difference. I still think it was a decent call."

"Yeah, well, I made my own call." Catfish huffed out a breath. "I sent in somebody to clean up your mess."

Drill's eyebrows went up. "You *what?*"

Catfish might've been unhappy with some of his decisions in the past, but he'd never outright countered them, at least not without talking about it first. He knew that Catfish was the new president of the club, but *what the hell?*

"I sent Timothy King out to talk to him and collect the debt." Catfish's face screwed up in distaste. "Needless to say, he fucked it up even more. I sent him to clean up your mess, and he made an even *bigger* mess."

Drill had a bad feeling in the pit of his stomach. "What'd he do?" he asked slowly.

Catfish raised his hands. "Now, this wouldn't be a problem if you'd just done your job from the beginning..."

"*What did he do?*" Drill repeated.

Catfish glared at him. "Watch your tone there, Drill."

Drill forced himself to take a few deep breaths. He put his beer down on the desk. "What did Timothy do?" he finally asked, in a reasonable voice. Or at least, the closest he could get to one.

"Timothy had a little too much fun, went overboard." He shook his head. "Kid's got a taste for light torture. He broke the guy's arm, went at him with a blowtorch a little bit, then went old school and busted his kneecap."

Drill winced. "Jesus wept," he breathed.

"I know." Catfish looked disgusted.

"How did Timothy think the guy was going to be able to get the money to pay us *now?*" Drill asked, his voice incredulous. "He's not going to be able to work the farm, he's not going to be able to sell anything... he's going to have medical bills..."

"The bills aren't our problem," Catfish said sharply. "Getting our money back is. He knew what he was getting into when he came to us for cash. But you're right, it was short-sighted, and it's not gonna help us if he doesn't have a way to pay us back. That's why you're the muscle in this operation. You know where to draw the line."

It was a dubious honor, Drill realized with distaste. That he was strong enough to beat the shit out of a guy, but smart enough not to kill the cash cow.

Christ, Tim was an idiot.

"Speaking of cash," Catfish said, with a sly grin, "heard you were at Genie's with Maddy's girl."

Drill didn't respond. He hadn't seen any Wraiths in the crowd, but he hadn't looked really hard. And in Green Valley, gossip was faster than the damned internet.

"So? Was it true?" Catfish goaded. "Heard you guys got *plenty* close."

Drill sighed.

"Man. So she's banging *both* Blount kids?"

Drill struggled to restrain himself from reaching over the desk and wrapping his hands around his old friend's throat. "She's not banging Maddy," he said, then added, "or me. She's Maddy's best friend from school. They're like sisters." He wasn't sure why he was justifying this, or why it was any of Catfish's goddamned business. But he didn't like the implications, that Thuy might somehow be... God, he didn't know. A slut? Someone who was working the Blount family?

Catfish's eyes narrowed as he picked up on Drill's discontent. "You going soft on me, Drill?" he asked, in a voice that was both quiet and dangerous.

"No," Drill said quickly. Maybe too quickly. Catfish did not look convinced.

"She the reason you didn't rough up Frank Helms?"

Maybe. "No," Drill said. *Probably.*

Catfish's neck muscles tensed, and he twisted his head, right to left, as if trying to relieve that tension. "I can't have you losing track of what's important here," he said. "Especially not for a piece of ass. Got it?"

Drill bristled. *She's not just a piece of ass!*

But that would only prove Catfish's point. The last thing he needed was Catfish digging deeper, taking more of a personal interest in Thuy and Maddy. Or, even worse, trying to put Timothy King on the case.

Drill nodded curtly.

"Get the cash from Frank," Catfish reiterated. "Get the girls to sell. If you think fucking your sister's friend is gonna get it done, then go ahead, but don't get sidetracked. Goddammit, we've got to get the Wraiths back in line, and I can't do that if we don't have money — and if people see my top lieutenant acting like a pussy."

Drill nodded, clenching his teeth. "Got it," he finally said, when it looked like Catfish wanted a response.

Drill walked out of the office, feeling Catfish's stare on him. Some of the other bikers were looking at him curiously, as well. He stalked past them, heading out the doors to his bike. He strapped on his helmet, then straddled the motorcycle, gunning the engine.

He wanted to shout. Break something. Or beat the shit out of someone. Timothy King would be a good start.

But right now, he was just going to head home, and try to figure out how to keep Catfish away from Maddy and Thuy, until he could get them out of the state for good.

CHAPTER TWENTY-THREE

It was Thuy's first day on the job. She wasn't nervous, necessarily, but she did want to make a good impression. Which meant she was wearing a blouse and a skirt, similar to what Julianne had worn on their first meeting. Her black hair was pulled back in a ponytail. She was wearing high heels only because she hadn't thought to pack low ones. Next month, when she went back to pack up the apartment and get everything ready for the move, she'd bring the rest of her clothes. Fortunately, she and Maddy had friends from the library and the farmer's market who were willing to help them pack up one of those rented shipping pods and get it ready to go.

It's real, she marveled. She was really moving to a farm, of all things. And working at the local small-town library. And she was about to be an aunt.

It was a lot.

Julianne emerged from the back room, tapping her watch. "It's been an hour," she said, her tone low but sharp. "You need to tell those teens to get off the computers now."

Thuy nodded, even though she felt a little discomfited. There wasn't anybody waiting for the computers that she could see, which was a bit surprising. And every library she'd been to had software that allowed users to put in their library card number, and it would automatically cut them off at an hour. That allowed the library to track usage and user data, which would be helpful in future funding discussions.

She walked up to the trio, the same ones who were there the first time she'd entered the library. "Time's up," she said.

They all groaned. "Man," the kid with wheat-colored hair said, turning off his game reluctantly. "That was my highest count ever!"

The girl shut off her game, as well, while the redhead looked on.

"Sorry," Thuy said. "That's the rules. Tell you what, though; I'll see if I can get the third computer fixed, so you all can play next time. Okay?"

"That'd be *awesome*," the girl enthused. Then she cracked her gum. "I'm Ginny, by the way."

"Hi, Ginny. I'm Thuy."

Ginny looked at the boys, who nodded their greetings. "I'm Kevin," the redhead said, "and this is Jeremy."

"Nice to meet you both," Thuy said automatically.

"Hey," Kevin said, "are you the one who put up the flyer about needing help with cattle?"

"Yes. Are you interested?" *Please, be interested.*

"Depends." For a second, Kevin leaned back, looking much older than his teen years. He looked like a middle-aged horse trader. "I'd need at least five dollars more than you're offering per hour, for one thing."

Thuy frowned. She wasn't sure what the going rate was for farm labor, but she trusted that Maddy did. "That seems a little steep."

"Yeah, well, I don't have a car, so I'd be riding my bike or my horse to get to your farm," he explained.

Thuy bit her lip. That made sense. They hadn't had any takers yet, but... "I need to talk about it with Maddy. It's her farm," she explained.

Kevin nodded, then his expression turned crafty. "I will make a deal, though. I'll take the price you're offering — *if* you figure out a way to get us more computer time."

Thuy grinned. *Sneaky devil.* "That is out of my hands," Thuy said.

"You can at least talk to someone, right?" Ginny pleaded. "They won't listen to us because they think we're just kids."

Thuy sighed, knowing that Ginny was probably right; it was hard for people to listen to teens. "I'll see what I can do," she said. "But no promises."

"Okay, then." Kevin looked satisfied.

"Why don't you guys check out some books while you're here?" Thuy asked.

They looked at each other. "We told you," Jeremy said. "There aren't any books for us here."

"They could definitely have more YA books," Thuy agreed, making a mental note to look into getting some donations. "But I'm sure there are some books that you'd enjoy. What do you guys like to watch?"

"I like *Twilight Zone* marathons," Kevin said, with a grin. "They're total mindfu… uh, they mess with your mind."

Thuy smirked at the near miss.

"I like stuff that's funny, but paranormal. Like *Supernatural*," Ginny said, then made a face when the boys laughed. "Shut up."

"You just like the guys," Kevin said, rolling his eyes.

"I don't watch TV. I like video games," Jeremy said shyly. "I just watch Youtube walkthroughs and Twitch streams when I get the chance. Someday, I'd like to write my own game."

Thuy nodded slowly. "Come on."

With the three kids in tow, she brought them first to the fiction section. "For you," she said to Kevin, pulling out a large hardback, "the collected short stories of Philip K. Dick."

They snickered.

"Grow up," Thuy said with a grin. Then she moved to the end of the row. "For you, Ginny, Jim Butcher's Dresden Files. Urban Fantasy. He's got a great voice, you'll love him."

Then she walked them to the non-fiction section. "It's not the most up-to-date, but there's something on Python coding here that ought to get you started," she said to Jeremy. "I'll look into getting an interlibrary loan for something more recent. Oh, and if you've got a Steam account, you might look into getting Undertale. It's an indie game that people either love or hate. It's weird, but I think you'll like it, and it might give you ideas on how to create your own game."

The three teens looked at her with surprise. "This is really cool," Ginny said. "Thanks."

"No problem."

She watched as they trooped towards the circulation desk, where Julianne was waiting with a disapproving frown.

"Here I thought I was special," a low voice said behind her.

She spun, startled, to find Drill standing behind her in the stacks, a small grin on his face.

"I thought you were just giving me book recommendations," he said. "Now I find you're suggesting books all over town."

"What can I say? I'm a book hussy," she whispered back. His low chuckle ran over her skin like mink, and she suppressed a shiver.

That kiss.

She'd been trying not to think about the kiss since it had happened, and had largely failed. The memory, and accompanying sensations, tended to creep up on her at unwanted moments, like in the shower, or during breakfast, or when she was trying to focus on Maddy's lectures about soil health and the importance of the farmer's almanac. Now that he was in front of her, larger than life, of course, her hormones were clamoring for attention.

"What are you doing here?" she forced herself to ask.

"You said I should read a book," he said. "So, I thought I'd come to the place where the books are."

She wanted to drag him to a quiet corner and just *lick* him. She tamped down the urge. "I'm working," she said, trying to sound stern and failing miserably.

"I know. You're a librarian," he said. "Maybe you could help me… find that book you were talking about?"

He was standing too close. Her nerves were going haywire, with conflicting impulses of pushing him away and climbing him like a jungle gym. She swallowed hard.

"Let's see," she said, finally getting her feet to move. She took him to the fiction section. "Rothfuss, Rothfuss," she said under her breath, then shook her head. "Sorry. Looks like we don't have the book here."

He put a hand on either side of her, trapping her against the bookshelves. "Well. What should I do now?" he murmured, his eyes intent on her.

Out of sheer self-preservation, she ducked, heading for the circulation desk. "I'll see if it's checked out," she said quickly, heading for the computer. He followed her. Julianne was checking the teens' books out on one computer, so she went to the other, typing quickly.

"It… looks like we don't have that book," she said, feeling genuinely sorry. "Maybe we have interlibrary loans, though?"

"I really wanted to get started now." His tone made it sound like he had more than reading in mind.

"Well, you could always buy a copy," she suggested. "If you've got an ereader — or a smartphone — you can always buy the eBook copy. Then you wouldn't even have to wait for it."

"I like that." His grin was sly, and sexy as hell. "I'm into instant gratification."

Oh, I'll just bet you are.

She took a small piece of scratch paper, the type that people wrote call numbers down on, and wrote the title and author on it. "Good luck," she said.

"I'll be seeing you soon," he said. "To tell you how it went."

"Okay. Goodbye." She waited until he walked out the doors, and she let out a breath. That man, she thought.

Julianne surveyed her. "Is that going to be a problem?"

"Is what going to be a problem?" Thuy asked.

Julianne's eyebrow went up, and she looked towards the door, towards Drill's retreating figure.

"You mean him?" Thuy shook her head. "No. He's my roommate's brother, and he's, um, interested in reading new books."

She didn't know if she sold it, but Julianne let out a small "humph" and let it slide.

CHAPTER TWENTY-FOUR

Drill rode out to Knoxville late that afternoon. He hadn't planned on visiting Frank, but since Catfish had dropped the news on him on Saturday, the thought of Frank in the hospital had been preying on his mind. He'd distracted himself by stopping by the library and seeing Thuy, but that had made him feel only temporarily better. What he *ought* to be doing was talking to Maddy, getting her to see reason and sell the damned farm, not flirting up a storm with Maddy's best friend. What he *really* ought to be doing was going out and finding new recruits for the Wraiths, or maybe shaking down more gamblers and loans.

But instead, he was an hour away, pulling into the visitor's lot at the hospital, ready to see a man who still owed the Wraiths money.

Because he felt guilty.

He frowned. He didn't used to feel guilty. When he was young, he took on every challenge like it was a quest, a way to prove himself. He saw everybody he beat the shit out of as a personal enemy. Anyone who stood against the Wraiths stood against his brothers and himself. It was a matter of... well, honor, for lack of a better term.

As he got into his twenties, it became more of a business. He lost some of that youthful zeal. Some fucked-up things had happened, but he knew it all balanced out in the end. The Wraiths weren't perfect. But hell, who was, right? He certainly wasn't.

Then Lube "disappeared." And he felt a little wary. Not scared, exactly. But not exactly comforted, either. He knew better than to get on Razor's bad side, or even Razor's old lady, Christine. He was by then a trusted lieutenant. He knew where the bodies were buried. In some cases, literally.

That's when he started going numb. He did the job. He went home. He got up and started all over again.

Now, at thirty-two, he was more than jaded. Darrell had gone state's evidence, and Razor was in jail. He'd worked too damned hard to help Catfish establish himself as the new leader of the Wraiths.

But was it worth it?

He walked up to the desk, asking the nurse if he could visit Frank Helms. The nurse looked at him cautiously, and he realized that he looked like a biker and that Frank had obviously taken a beating. She finally cleared her throat and directed him to Frank's room.

He thought about getting something. He hadn't visited anybody in a hospital. The occasional Wraith had been hospitalized, but since he'd usually put them there, he thought visiting was pointless. *Maybe I should grab him a magazine?*

Finally, jamming his hands into his jacket pockets, he walked into Frank's room.

There was another patient in the room, sleeping with deep, wheezing breaths. Frank was on the other side of the curtain. Drill walked over, pulling the curtain back a little.

Frank looked like shit. His face was a mish-mash of blue, purple and green, his eyes nearly swollen shut. His right arm was in a cast, as was most of his left leg. He was hooked up to a machine that monitored his heart rate.

"Hey," Drill said, in a low voice.

Frank took a second to focus on him. Then, suddenly, his heart rate went up.

"I didn't say anything," Frank said quickly. "I swear, I didn't say anything!"

The monitor's beeping was going fast. Drill looked back at the door. "No! No. It's all right, it's fine. I'm not here because of the Wraiths."

A tear welled out of Frank's eye, tracking down his marred cheek. "You said I had until Monday," he said.

Drill sighed. "I did," he said. "This is my fault. I should've talked to Catfish sooner, cut this off. I didn't know he was going to send somebody else."

"He… he broke my knee," Frank rasped. "My arm. He *burned* me."

Drill winced.

"How the hell am I supposed to work the farm now? How am I supposed to pay you back?"

Guilt almost drove Drill to his knees. "This never should've happened," Drill said sharply.

A nurse came in, looking at Drill with both anger and trepidation. "Is everything all right, Mr. Helms?" she asked, her eyes never leaving Drill.

"Yes. Thanks," Frank said, his voice sounding thin as paper.

The nurse sent Drill another scowl, then she turned and left.

Drill took in a deep breath, inhaling the antiseptic smell of the hospital. Then he let it out slowly. "You're in for nearly seven grand, right?"

Frank nodded, then winced, making a pained sound. "Yeah. Thereabouts."

"As of now, it's taken care of."

Frank stared at him blankly. "What do you mean?"

"I mean I'm paying it off. Okay?" Drill held up a hand when Frank's mouth dropped open a little. "If I'd have given you the beating you earned, you'd be in pain, but you'd be at home, figuring out a way to pay off your debt. Not dealing with all this shit. This is wrong."

Frank let out a hoarse laugh. "You've got a weird sense of right and wrong, Drill."

"You knew it was stupid to take a loan from a biker gang, pal," Drill said dryly. "Kinda the pot calling the kettle, huh?"

Frank let out a low sigh. "This gets me out from the club's loan," he said. "But what am I gonna do about the farm?"

"I can't help you there," Drill admitted. "Sorry, man. This is gonna wipe out my savings as it is. Best I can do."

Frank nodded, a little movement. Then he looked at Drill. "Thanks, man. You don't have to do this, but I'm damned grateful you are."

"Steer clear of the Wraiths from here on."

"Don't have to tell me twice."

Drill nodded, then stood up. "Hang in there," he said, feeling helpless. He turned and left.

He'd go square things away with Dirty Dave. He had about eight grand socked away… it ate away most of it, but it would be worth it. Already, his chest felt a little lighter.

He just had to make sure that they didn't go after Frank, thinking he'd found some kind of pot of gold. It would be just like that jackass Timothy King to try and rob Frank after putting him in this position.

Drill frowned. He'd always been loyal to the club — but this wasn't the club that he'd joined, and he wasn't the recruit he once was. Just for starters, Timothy King would stab him in the back, first chance. It took Catfish's boot on his neck to keep him in line — and even then, Tim would go out and raise havoc. There were others in the Wraiths that would follow him.

So why am I feeling loyal? And why am I feeling guilty for not *feeling more loyal?*

He thought about Catfish. They'd come up together, were the same age. He knew Catfish had the same issues, the same needs, when it came to having a family in the Wraiths. But Catfish had an even stronger drive. He wanted the Wraiths to be not only his family, but the most powerful club in Tennessee. Maybe in the Southeast, if it came down to it. While Drill had admired Catfish's ambition, he was starting to wonder if, when it came down to it, Catfish would have his back if it wasn't what Catfish deemed "what was best for the club."

In short, Drill was worried that after sixteen years *in* the club, he'd somehow made a terrible mistake. And if, at age thirty-two, there was another way he could go.

He needed to talk about this. But there wasn't anybody in the Wraiths he could open up to. His closest friend was probably Catfish, but he knew that Catfish would not allow dissent to be discussed, not without some serious repercussions.

Drill headed back to Green Valley, his mind whirring.

Who could he talk to?

Maddy. He needed to talk to her, anyway. Maybe he could talk to her about this.

Feeling determined, he headed toward the farm.

CHAPTER TWENTY-FIVE

Thuy was sore and tired. She'd gotten up, and put out hay for the cattle — and that had been an adventure. At least Maddy had driven the side-by-side, even though it made Thuy anxious to see her hugely pregnant best friend do so. She supposed that Maddy was right, pregnant women had been farming for millennia, but she still worried.

Also, spreading the hay had been hard. She'd always been more of the cardio than weight training type, and it showed. She felt like a complete and utter wimp.

Then she'd spent her first full day at the library. The work there hadn't been hard at all — mostly a lot of shelving and getting things checked out or checked in. The bright spots in her day had been interacting with the teens, and... well, she had to admit, it was talking and flirting with Drill. Which she knew, she *knew*, was stupid. Nothing was going to happen there.

Is it?

She sighed at herself in exasperation. It was ten o'clock at night. Maddy had gone to bed around nine. The pregnancy knocked her out. Thuy found herself staying up later and later, still getting used to everything. The farm. Tennessee. How her whole life had changed so drastically, and so abruptly.

In the night quiet, she heard the unmistakable sound of a motorcycle engine, and her heart picked up its tempo. She figured it was Drill. Who else would it be, this time of night?

She was wearing a pair of leggings and a beat-up, paint-stained Cal sweatshirt. She finger-combed her hair, then realized what she was doing and mentally berated herself.

Nothing is going to happen with this guy. Knock it off, you lunatic.

She stepped to the front door, opening it and peering out. Drill was heading towards the porch, looking nothing like the mischievous, flirty man she'd last seen in the library that afternoon. He looked sad, she realized. And her heart strained a little, as she felt the inexplicable need to relieve that burden somehow.

She opened the door wider. "Little late for a visit," she commented.

"Not too late?" His blue eyes were concerned, but also hopeful.

"No. Although Maddy's asleep."

He grimaced. "I should've figured that."

She still gestured him in. "What's wrong?"

He looked at her in surprise as she shut the door behind him. "What makes you say that?"

"You look upset."

"I do?" He frowned. "I… huh. I've got a lot on my mind. I didn't realize it'd be that obvious."

He looked lost. His hands were stuffed in his pockets, and he shifted his weight uneasily from one foot to the other.

"Why don't you sit down, and I'll make some coffee?" Thuy offered.

"I don't know. I don't want to bother you."

"Trust me. I'd tell you if you were," Thuy said, with a small laugh that elicited a smile from the big man.

"You would, wouldn't you?"

"Yup. I don't suffer idiots if I don't have to." She wandered to the kitchen, and he followed her. She frowned. "Actually… I'm still getting used to this percolator thing. I'm more of a drip or pour-over girl, myself."

"I got it." He bustled around, quietly measuring out coffee and getting the thing going. It was funny, to see this shaved-head biker almost humming to himself as he went about such a small domestic chore. He plugged the old pot in, and it started gurgling.

She leaned against the counter, surveying him. "So. Want to talk about it? I'm a good listener."

He sent her a half-grin that still looked sad. "I like you."

"Well, I don't know you," she said, with a wink, "but I'm getting fond of you, myself."

He let out a little chuckle. "That's it though. You *don't* know me." He sighed, leaning back against the counter and crossing his arms. "I'm a one-percenter, like you said. I've done some bad shit in my time."

You should probably send him away now, Thuy told herself. She'd cut herself off from criminal elements since she was a teen. When she'd gone off to college, she'd sworn she wouldn't let that life touch her. But he was Maddy's brother. She saw how much he cared about Maddy, even when he wasn't supposed to.

In a way, he reminded her of her own brother. Although, honestly, her feelings for Drill were hardly brotherly.

Rather than dwell on what *that* could mean, she cleared her throat. "Is that what's bothering you?"

"I went to the hospital tonight."

She felt alarm jolt through her system. "What? Why? Are you all right?"

He sent her a look of surprise at her obvious concern. "Yeah, yeah, I'm fine." His tone was warmer, and his small smile was thoughtful. "I was visiting someone. Someone my club put in there."

She froze. "Oh," she said, in a small voice.

"I keep thinking, I could've stopped it." He rubbed his hand over his face, then over the back of his head. "It never should've happened. I shouldn't have *let* it happen."

"Why didn't you?"

He let out a rough exhalation. "I thought I was doing the guy a favor, giving him more time on a loan he took out. Instead, they sent someone else who didn't know what the fuck he was doing, who thought that reminding someone of a debt meant nearly killing him."

"So you would… have beaten him less?"

"Jesus. I think that *is* what I was trying to say." Drill grimaced. "Listen, I don't usually have a problem with this. I never used to. I did what I was told to do. What the fuck is *wrong* with me?"

"That it's bothering you now?" Thuy probed. "Or… that it didn't bother you before?"

He looked at her, and his expression was pained. "I don't know," he said, his voice breaking as he shook his head. "Both. Maybe. I don't know."

She took his arm, tugging a little. He let her guide him into the small living room. She nudged him until he took a seat on the old, worn sofa.

"Okay. Take a few deep breaths, and let's talk about this, okay?" She sat down next to him. "You've done some bad things in your life. Seriously shitty things, from the sounds of it."

"Yeah."

"Why?"

He took a deep breath. "Because that's what I needed to do, for the club. I know, that doesn't make it right, though. Not this 'I was just following orders' bullshit. *I* did that stuff."

She nodded. "I know people who have done bad things," she said slowly.

He snickered mirthlessly. "Yeah? Like what? Stealing library books?"

"Like murder."

His laugh stopped midway, cutting off dead. "The fuck?"

She never talked about this. *Never.* She'd cut this part of her life out, for damned good reason. Not even Maddy was aware of how bad her past was. But Drill was looking so lost, so upset, and most of all, so hopeless about how he could change.

"My family," she said, her words coming out choppy and hesitant, "was — *is* — part of a club, too."

"That's how you know about one-percenters," Drill murmured.

"Yeah. That's how I know." Thuy swallowed hard. "So yeah, I've seen it. Drug running. Gun smuggling. Gambling, prostitution, the works. But this… *particular* group is known for their violence. You don't cross this group. You don't fuck with them. Not if you want to stay alive."

Drill's eyes widened. "Which group?"

She bit her lip. "It doesn't matter. I don't like to talk about it." In fact, she'd love to change the conversation *now*. But she'd gone this far… "The point is, I'm not going to judge you for what you've done."

He straightened up.

"That doesn't mean I'm getting involved with someone who plans on continuing to do it," she said firmly. "And if you keep on staying in this mess, that's on you. It's not enough to feel bad about it. You need to *do* something about it."

He frowned, thoughtful. "It's been a part of my life for so long, I don't know any other way to be."

"Bullshit." Thuy turned to face him more fully. "You don't know, or you don't *want* to know?"

He turned, too, his gaze piercing. "This is new, okay? I didn't use to think about this shit. I did what was required!"

"And now it's bothering you, right? What's required?" she pressed. Then she realized something. "You've never killed anyone, have you?"

She saw it, just the slightest glimpse of horror crossed his face. "No," he said quickly. "But… I know of some guys. Who have."

She nodded. "What if they ask that of you?" she asked quietly. "What would you do then?"

He mulled that over for long, quiet moments.

She got up, pouring two mugs of coffee. Then she walked back to the sofa. He took it, thanked her, took a sip. He still looked pensive.

"Even if I wanted to," he said, in a low voice, "it's not like it's easy to get out. Once you're in, you're in."

Thuy sipped at her coffee, then made a face and put it down on a magazine on the coffee table. "I know," she said, and meant it.

He was quiet for a second, then put down his own cup. He propped his head up on one hand, surveying her.

"So," he said, with a quiet plea. "How did you do it? How did you get out?"

CHAPTER TWENTY-SIX

Thuy looked stricken by his question. Her dark eyes clouded, and she looked away, her knee bobbing rhythmically. She fidgeted in the seat.

He was about to change the topic, seeing how much it was upsetting her, when she finally bit her lip and blurted out, "I wasn't really *in*, exactly. I mean, I saw lots of things, and covered up things — told the police my parents weren't home, or that they *had* been home when they weren't. It was just the way things were. They'd bring home people — or, um, bodies. My older brother..."

"You have a brother?" He didn't know why that surprised him, but it did. If his father had been beating Maddy, or doing anything shady that put Maddy in danger, you bet your ass he would've gotten her out of there any way he could. So what the hell had her brother been doing?

"Yeah. Trung," she said, and her eyes rimmed with tears. "He'd be about three years older. Anyway, Trung and I were just kids that saw stuff. Trung remembered a little about our grandparents. He'd heard that my dad's parents lived in Westminster, down by Los Angeles, but when my Dad joined the club as a teen he left them behind. Or they kicked him out, cut them off. Maybe it was mutual — I don't know. I've never met them."

Drill felt both a pang of sorrow for her, and an unwelcome sense of connection with her father. "So your dad joined an MC."

"Well, he started in an MC," she said. "Then I think he specialized. Sort of 'graduated.' He was always smart, but never satisfied, you know?"

Drill didn't know. He'd been dissatisfied with the club, but he got the feeling that wasn't what Thuy was trying to say.

"My father started with drug dealers, but discovered he had a better niche: getting people to talk, or getting rid of people."

Drill felt his stomach knot. Thuy had gone very, very pale, and her voice was thready.

"I saw some things..."

"You don't have to talk about them," he said quickly. She looked nauseous.

"Anyway, when I turned thirteen, I swore I was going to get out of the house. My brother had been initiated, and I'm pretty sure he killed someone. By that point, he was eager to join the life. I knew it wasn't what I wanted. They were still letting me go to school. Honestly, they didn't care if I went or not," she admitted. "My brother had dropped out and they didn't care. But I was determined to get out of our neighborhood and our family and our lifestyle, and go to college, and live a decent, 'normal' life."

He had a bad feeling about this.

"When I turned sixteen, I had straight A's in honors courses, I was in the California Junior Scholarship Federation, and I was chosen for the National Honor Society." She had a small smile. "And that's when my family started to expect me to pull my weight."

"What did they want you to do?"

"My Mom was drinking pretty heavily by then. My dad and my brother were the ones that were really into the club. But I think... I think my dad wanted me to be closer to the organization. They would've found a place for me. As a party favor, if nothing else."

Drill's fists bunched. "Son of a *bitch*."

"You've got the girls at your MC, too, I bet," she said. "Ever think about where they came from?"

The thing was, he *knew* a lot of the girls, since they were all in school together back in the day. He knew a lot of them had no hope, no sense of ambition or drive to get out of the small town. They thought this was their ticket to a more exciting life.

It never occurred to him that he could, or should, talk them out of it. Guilt crept in on him.

"Anyway, I ran away at seventeen. My brother actually helped me," she said. "We talked it over. He told my dad that if I wanted to be some snobby smart kid, then I ought to get the hell out and stop wasting their money and food. My dad bought it, but he did do one thing before I left."

She took a deep breath. Then she got up, turning, and lifted her sweatshirt.

There, on the right side of her lower back, was a patch of skin, raised and rough. A burn mark. But in a pattern. Drill looked closer.

Then he jerked back. "Is that... a brand?"

She lowered the sweatshirt, nodded. "Recognize it?"

"Jesus Christ." His mouth went dry. "That's a rose and dagger, yeah?"

She nodded. "You know the group."

"Every club knows the Red Dagger," he said. "They're a support club for some of the bigger clubs, doing shit even one-percenters don't like doing. Wait a sec..." He goggled. "That crew that got wiped out in a mass killing in Tempe? *That was your dad?*"

She nodded. "I recognized it when I heard about it. I'd already started going to Berkeley by then."

Holy shit.

Thuy didn't just know about one-percenters. She was the daughter of one of the most vicious, lethal men that any biker was aware of. In Green Valley, the Wraiths were a pretty big deal, even after the Darrell/Razor stuff. But this? This was *national* stuff. These guys were infamous.

"Did you ever find your grandparents?" he asked, wanting to change the topic.

"No. There are a lot of Nguyens in Westminster," she said, with a rueful little laugh. "I wouldn't even know where to start, I don't know their first names. My dad refused to talk about them."

There was a little pause.

"My dad gave me the brand to show that even though I wanted out, I'd never really *be* out. I don't talk about it. I pretend it didn't happen. And I'll be damned if I let him ruin my life," she said fiercely. "He's part of my past, and I'm going to keep him there."

He nodded, even though he knew how hard it was to pretend your past wasn't there. His father hadn't been nearly so brutal or cruel, and he'd tried to cut him out. But here he was, in his father's farmhouse, thinking about his future.

"So how did you get to know my sister?" Drill asked.

This brought the first real smile of the night to Thuy's face. "We were roomies, freshman year. Both of us on scholarship, even though hers was for sports and mine was for scholastics. She probably should've been with another softball player or something, but luck of the draw put us together. It turned out we both were closet Disney freaks, so that helped. I introduced her to video games. She introduced me to baking. It worked out."

He wanted her to keep talking, to keep that smile bright. "And from there...?"

Thuy's smile dimmed a little, but her eyes were curious. "Do you want to know why I'm here? Why I owe your sister so much?"

He nodded, eager.

"I lost my grants sophomore year," she said. "I still had tuition covered, but everything else — housing, food, even books — was on me. I got a job at the library, but it wasn't going to be enough to cover. I was terrified I was going to wind up on the street. Or worse — somehow wind up back with my family. I'd been couch surfing since junior year of high school, and I was running out of options. Maddy let me crash on her floor, and share her meal card. I ate a shit-ton of ramen for the next three years, but Maddy made sure I was never on the street. She took care of me."

He felt his throat tighten. "That sounds like Maddy," he said.

"The biggest thing — she never made me feel like she was doing me a favor. She wasn't saving me. She was just giving me a hand, like it wasn't a big deal. She said that it beat finding another roomie, which would be like 'auditioning a freakshow', but I knew the truth." Thuy rubbed at her eyelashes, catching the droplets that had accumulated on them, and then laughed. "She's the best friend I've ever had. She cared about me more than my own blood did, and she's always been there for me. If she needs me, I'm there — no questions, no hesitation. I love her."

They fell silent again. He stretched his arm out along the couch, resting it lightly against Thuy's shoulders. He wanted to hug her, after her story, but felt weird about it. He was so damned *emotional*, was the problem. After the hospital, and now all Thuy's stuff...

He cleared his throat. "My dad used to beat the shit out me," he said, then stopped.

Where the hell did that *come from?*

Thuy made a sympathetic noise, curling into him a little more. He could feel her body heat, a comforting warmth. "I figured as much," she admitted. "Maddy sort of hinted at it."

"I wouldn't have left if I thought he'd hit her," Drill said quickly. "But if I stayed, I would've killed him. That wouldn't have been good for anybody, especially not Maddy. And I know my Dad was an asshole to her, but she had food and a place to stay. And she was always good in school, and she loved softball, and he let her play. That was all that mattered."

Thuy sighed. He felt her head rest against his shoulder, and he felt some of the tension drain out of his body. Tentatively, he put his arm around her, snuggling her a little closer.

"The club was my saving grace," he said. "I thought it was my family. Now, I'm starting to wonder if they give a shit about me at all anymore. I feel like my life's fucked. I don't know what I should be doing." He let out a low laugh. "And here I am, whining to you."

"Don't," Thuy said. She tilted her head up, grabbing his jaw and forcing him to meet her eyes. "Don't act like because you're a guy, you're not entitled to talk things through. You're upset. You deserve someone who'll let you vent. You don't have to be alone."

And there it was. He'd felt alone, even in the crush of the club, for too long.

He leaned down slowly, not going for her lips. Just resting his forehead against hers, his eyes closed.

"You're a damned good woman, Thuy," he said, his voice rough.

He sensed rather than saw her smile. "And you," she said softly, "are a better man than you give yourself credit for."

CHAPTER TWENTY-SEVEN

Thuy was still feeling the aftereffects of her talk with Drill the previous night. It wasn't like they'd done anything — he hadn't even stayed that late, leaving before midnight. But she'd shared with him a secret she hadn't even told Maddy. She'd trusted him with her past. All because he was wrestling with his own.

They were a fucked-up pair, she thought, as she shelved books. Families could be a special form of hell, leaving an indelible stamp on you. She'd spent enough time doing everything she could to pretend that she'd simply been born fully formed in college, to no family. But talking with Drill reminded her that she'd survived a lot.

And gotten out stronger.

She frowned, flitting through the cookbook section, putting away old, large volumes. She picked up a book on knitting patterns, and put it on the shelf behind her.

She hadn't really thought about how the crazy, horrific stuff of her childhood had made her strong enough to withstand the rigors of life. Getting her MLIS online, while working two jobs to pay for it, had been nuts — but compared to what she'd gone through, it had been a cakewalk. Even Maddy would joke that living up to the expectations of her coaches and teachers was nothing after living with her perfectionist father. Maybe Drill's time at the club was the same way.

Still, she'd had a refuge. She'd had the library. From the time she'd gone to school on, library time was her absolute favorite thing. The gorgeous picture books, even beat-up, torn and taped, were fascinating to her. She learned to read very early, and borrowed as many books as she could. When she'd gotten old enough to get out of the house by herself, she and her brother would wander to a nearby public library. Her brother tended to just play video games like Minecraft or try to watch porn on the computers. She, on the other hand, would go straight to the children's section and read like crazy.

Libraries inspired her, gave her a place to escape. That was why she'd gone into library science in the first place.

There was such a renaissance in YA literature at this point, too, she thought as she put away some biographies. It was really a pity that the Green Valley library didn't have a bigger selection. She knew that it was hard, especially when you were cash-strapped. Still, there was obviously a need.

It was only her second day on the job, and she didn't want to pressure Julianne about it too much, especially since she'd need to take some time off in the new year to pack up the apartment she'd shared with Maddy in Oakland and get it moved out to Tennessee. But she did promise Kevin she'd talk to the woman about the time limits on computer usage. Maybe she could bring up the YA books as well.

Squaring her shoulders, she pushed her now empty library cart into the back room. She passed Naomi working at the circulation desk, about to finish her shift. She glanced back to see Julianne going over some correspondence at her desk.

Thuy knocked gingerly at the doorframe. "Do you have a second?"

Julianne nodded stiffly. "Is there a problem?"

"No. Well, not exactly." Thuy cleared her throat. "I wanted to ask — is there any way to extend the computer usage time?"

Julianne's expression grew pinched, like she'd just eaten a sour kumquat. "I think an hour is more than sufficient for anyone's needs," she said primly.

"Yes, well..." Thuy bit her lip, trying to think of how to word it. "Maybe we could extend it a bit on special occasions — like teen night? You've got a few gamers here, and..."

"I don't want people using the computers for games. Especially not violent ones," Julianne said immediately, rearing back a little. "They're meant for research, or helping people who need internet access."

"I'm not saying they should only be used for gaming, by any stretch," Thuy quickly agreed. "I'm just saying — it's a nice thing for the kids who don't have internet access readily available at home. They see their friends playing on phones or hear about the ones who do have access to playing, and they feel left out." At least, that was the impression she got from Kevin. "Besides, there are worse things that kids could be doing with their time."

She thought of Drill, what he'd been doing at sixteen. Hell, what her brother had been doing, at a younger age.

There are a lot *worse things than video games.*

"It could also be a good way to reel in more teenagers to teen night," Thuy said, warming up to the idea. "I was also wondering if we could... well, I don't know what the budget is, but our YA section seems a bit slim."

Julianne had shifted from looking irritated to looking angry. "We have had a skeleton budget for years," she said.

"I can only imagine," Thuy said with feeling. "I've seen how libraries all over the country are dealing with cuts, and I know that rural communities especially have suffered the worst."

That seemed to mollify her a bit. "As a result, YA hasn't been the top of our priorities," Julianne said. "There also hasn't been a huge demand there. The teens here tend to lose interest after middle grade. A lot of them are either working on farms, pursuing sports, hanging out with their friends, or... I don't know. I suppose they move on to adult books."

Maybe that's because there's not a large enough selection! Thuy wanted to protest, but she didn't want to piss the older woman off more than she already seemed to be doing. There had to be a solution to this problem.

"We still accept outside donations, right?"

Julianne looked surprised at her seeming change of topic. "We do, yes. Although mostly we get old books, cookbooks — not a lot of recent or relevant things."

"Thanks," Thuy said, smiling as some of the tightness left her chest. "I'll get back to work."

"Fine." Julianne looked at her suspiciously, then turned back to her desk.

Thuy grinned. She'd seen a Twitter campaign that a woman in California had done, requesting books for the antiquated selection in her rural hometown's school library. She knew that the YA author community was incredibly generous. She'd see if maybe she could set up a wishlist. It made her smile, to think about introducing Kevin, Ginny, and Jeremy to some great new reads. Hell, she'd recommend a lot of it to adult readers, as well. There was some great stuff out there.

Now, she just had to get the word out — and get the donations.

CHAPTER TWENTY-EIGHT

It was early, like seven in the morning, and brisk as hell when Drill went out to meet Catfish at Hank Weller's boat. They were going after muskies, so he'd brought the proper gear, but for the first time in a long time, his heart wasn't in it. He usually enjoyed the hell out of fishing, and he and Catfish and Hank, and sometimes Beau Winston, had gone out on Hank's boat a lot over the years.

But last night, after he'd talked to Thuy, he hadn't slept a wink. He was shaken at how forthright he'd been with her. He hadn't talked with anybody like that in — he frowned, doing some calculations — *ever*. He'd never been that open, with anyone.

He'd left at midnight. He wanted to talk to her more, but he was feeling sort of raw and vulnerable. Also, holding her in his arms, just snuggling with her, had been a welcome and unexpected soft place he didn't know he needed. Or craved. He got the feeling if he'd stayed longer, he would've pushed his luck, and he didn't want to fuck up the nice moment that they'd had. *And if that doesn't sound like a chick*, he scowled at himself, *I don't know what does.*

So, he'd gone home, but he'd been too wired to sleep. He'd tried watching some TV, even jerking off, but he wound up awake and bored. Instead, he'd taken Thuy's advice, gotten a reading app for his phone, and bought the book she mentioned.

He only meant to read a few pages, to see if it would even be comfortable on the little screen. How the hell was he supposed to know he'd get hooked by the first chapter? He kept meaning to shut the damned thing off, even when it had run low on batteries and he'd plugged it in nearby, so he could continue reading. When his alarm went off, telling him it was time to get ready to meet Catfish, he felt sandy-eyed and wrung out.

He was nowhere near the end of the story, and he was dying to see how it would shake out. Which was a weird new experience for him.

Catfish was already waiting for him by the boat launch when Drill rolled up. Drill sighed, knowing he'd probably fall asleep on the boat.

"Where's Hank?" Drill asked, rubbing his hand over his face after he put the helmet on the seat of his bike.

"Hank's not coming. What happened to you?" Catfish responded, his expression amused. "You look like shit."

"Thanks," Drill drawled. He grabbed his tackle kit from a side bag. He always borrowed everything else from Hank — hard to travel on a motorcycle with a fishing rod.

"What, did you finally hook up with someone?" Catfish asked, with a hoot of laughter. "Jesus. I was starting to think you'd turned into a monk."

Drill shrugged, adding a noncommittal grunt. The less Catfish knew about Thuy, the better.

"She any good?" Catfish pressed.

"Townie. You know how it is." He definitely didn't want Catfish to dig any deeper.

"Must've been decent. You look wrung the fuck out." Catfish laughed again. "Good. It's about time we lightened up a little. I know how hard the past six months have been."

"Why isn't Hank coming?" Drill asked, wanting to change the subject.

Now Catfish's expression turned somber. "Yeah. I wanted to talk to you, just us. No Hank, no Dave."

Ah, shit. Drill made a big show of climbing onto the big boat. He'd let Catfish do the driving.

Catfish took the boat out on the lake. Drill fell asleep for a while, the monotonous sound of the engine knocking him out. He woke when Catfish shook his shoulder; they'd stopped. Without a word, the two of them gathered up their rods, put on their spinning lures, and cast out into the water. Catfish started reeling the cast back in with slow, easy motions, not really paying attention to what he was doing.

"We need more order in the Wraiths," Catfish said, without preamble.

Drill didn't even pretend he was trying to fish. He let his lure just dangle there in the water. "Okay," he said, unsure what Catfish meant.

"I've stepped up as president. I think everybody's on board with that now — and if they weren't, then we've made sure they know they're not welcome."

Drill grunted again. Since he'd personally beaten the shit out of the naysayers and made sure they were shown the door if they didn't sign on, he was well aware of this.

"But that's not enough," Catfish said, and for the first time, Drill saw not only exhaustion but uncertainty cross his friend's face. "Dave wants to be co-president. Or at least vice president."

"Okay," Drill repeated.

Catfish let out a long, irritated exhalation. "And I don't trust that sonofabitch."

Drill chuckled. "Of course not," he said. Anybody who knew Dave knew that much was obvious.

"He knows too much about our money, and he's good with it. We need him. I don't care if he's skimming as long as he keeps it within bounds," Catfish said, pulling the lure out and casting again. "We need a VP, though. Promote a few more guys to captain — without Repo, there's definitely a lack of leadership. And we'll want an enforcer, or sergeant at arms. Somebody who'll lay down the law. Somebody who everybody *knows* will lay down the law."

Drill stiffened, trying not to look at Catfish. He got the feeling he knew where this conversation was going… and what job he was being offered.

"I was thinking of making Tim King the enforcer."

"*What?*" Drill turned, shocked. "Are you kidding me? The guy who put Frank Helms in the hospital?"

"Yeah. I mean, that was stupid, but I give him points for enthusiasm," Catfish said, smirking and shaking his head. "And if somebody's breaking the rules of the club, then that's the kind of response I want, you know?"

Drill was flabbergasted. He thought that Catfish was setting him up to take over the official role of enforcer — which wouldn't be a stretch, considering it was what he'd essentially been doing for years. "Fucking Timothy King," Drill said, shaking his head.

"Did you think I was cutting you out?" Catfish stopped reeling, surveying Drill seriously. "Nah. You've been my brother through all of this. I only patched in a few years earlier than you. We basically came up together." He paused, grinning a little. "Remember when we both got drunk, back when you were seventeen?"

Drill rolled his eyes. "Shit, yes. You puked on that stripper."

"And you passed out and woke up with a dick drawn on each cheek, and one down your nose. It was *hilarious*."

Drill laughed, and for a second, it was like old times — back when he and Catfish were badasses, fresh recruits. When it looked like the coolest thing in the world, to join the Wraiths.

"I want you to be vice president."

Drill stared at Catfish.

Oh, God. That's the last thing I want.

He swallowed, trying to think of some way to say no. Bad enough he still couldn't think of how to get out of the club and still protect Maddy and Thuy. But to sign on as VP? Hell, no.

"I… I'm not cut out for, you know, leadership," Drill tried. "I'm just a thug, man. Muscle. You're the brains of the outfit."

"You're smarter than you let on," Catfish said dismissively. "Besides, it's you taking cues from me, and I've relied on you for years. It'll be fine."

"Can I think about it?"

Catfish's eyes narrowed. "What's to fucking think about?"

"I've just been a lieutenant, or a captain at best." Drill shook his head. "I don't want to be promoted higher than that."

"You know what your problem is?" Catfish scowled, shaking his head. "You lack vision. You still think you're just this small-town hick thug."

"Thanks," Drill said.

"I'm serious," Catfish snapped. "I've got big plans for the Wraiths — and they *don't* involve getting patched over by another club, losing turf, and getting swallowed up. We're not going to be small-time hustlers, throwing their weight around a town like Green Valley. I think we could build up to be one of the biggest players in Tennessee. Hell, in the South."

Catfish's eyes burned with ambition. Drill knew his friend had drive, but now Catfish was in the driver's seat. He was in a position to put those dreams into action.

Drill suddenly felt nervous about his friend.

"Fine. Be a pussy. 'Think' about it," Catfish said. "But you're gonna need to give me an answer soon. Otherwise, I'm going to think you're chickening out on me for real, and we're gonna have problems."

Drill gritted his teeth and slowly pulled his lure in. He felt like a rabbit in a snare — one that was drawing, slowly and inevitably, tighter around his neck.

CHAPTER TWENTY-NINE

Thuy got back to the farmhouse at 9:40, after ending her shift at the library at nine. She'd eaten some leftovers on her break. She hung out with Maddy for about an hour, until Maddy fell asleep on the couch as they watched an old DVD she'd checked out — *The Fifth Element,* one of her favorite cheesy sci-fi classics. When Maddy went off to bed, she found herself restless.

She *ought* to go to sleep. She'd done a lot that day. But she couldn't get herself to read, and she couldn't seem to settle down to finish the film, either.

When she heard the motorcycle, she knew *exactly* why she wasn't able to settle down.

Dammit. It wasn't a guarantee he'd come over.

But on some level, she'd been *waiting* for Drill to stop by. To talk. Or... whatever.

She closed her eyes, then walked to the front door. His smile was slow and enticing, his blue eyes looking her over. Not in a creepy way, although there was definitely an edge of hunger to his gaze. More like he was just amazingly happy to see her.

She'd never had anyone look at her like that before. It shook her.

"C'mon in," she said. "Want some coffee? You know where it is."

"Not tonight," he said. "I was up all night last night."

"Oh?" She jolted. "I'm sorry. I can drink caffeine and go straight to sleep, so it didn't occur to me…"

"No, that wasn't the problem. Although it was still your fault." His smile was warm, his eyes twinkling with mischief.

"Oh?" Dammit. Her heart started pounding a little harder. He'd kept her up last night, with some lascivious thoughts, himself. "I don't know what you're talking about," she stammered. Although a part of her really, *really* wanted to find out.

This is a bad idea.

"That book you recommended," he said instead, surprising her.

"What? *The Name of the Wind?*"

"I started reading it," he admitted gruffly as they headed into the living room. "Stayed up all damned night."

She laughed, then quickly covered her mouth with her hands, not wanting to wake Maddy up. "That is the best thing I've ever heard," she said, in a near whisper, leaning closer to him. "I love it when people get hooked on books."

"You are a book pusher," he agreed, with a grin. She chuckled softly.

"Sorry, not sorry." She sat on the sofa, and he sat next to her. Close to her, like they'd been the previous night. He rested his head against his hand.

"You know," she pointed out gently, "this is becoming a habit."

"You're easy to talk to."

She warmed, sighing softly. "You're easy to talk to, too. A good listener."

He stroked a lock of hair away from her eyes. For a second, she wanted to curve into his palm, purr like a cat.

This is a very *bad idea.*

"Come up with any ideas? About the Wraiths, I mean?"

He sighed heavily. "I don't want to think about the Wraiths tonight."

She bit her lip. That meant no. Although if he'd been up all night reading, he probably didn't have time. Still — if he was involved in a motorcycle club, and he didn't have any plans for getting out of it, what the hell was she doing?

There's no harm in talking, she tried to convince herself. Only she knew that her body wanted to do a hell of a lot more than talk.

She was too busy fighting with herself, so she didn't notice when he moved in, his face getting closer to hers, until he was right there. She could feel his breathing brush against her jawline, his mouth close to her neck, her clavicle.

"What are you doing?" she squeaked.

He paused. "Should I stop?" She could *feel* the heat of his words, the tickle of his lips against her throat.

This was it. Make or break. Sanity, or madness.

Fuck it.

"No," she said firmly. And tilted her head back, giving him better access.

With a groan, he moved in, and she felt enveloped by leather and muscles and a sheer wall of *male.* She reached up, wrapping her arms around his neck as he sucked and nibbled his way up her neck, over her jaw, before finally meeting her eager lips.

She closed her eyes with a flutter when his mouth finally claimed hers. She'd hesitantly dreamed about kissing him again, since that time in the parking lot, but the reality blew the fantasy right the hell out of the water. His mouth was mobile and gifted. With a rough sound, he parted her lips with his, his tongue sweeping in, caressing the soft inner flesh of her mouth before tangling with her tongue. She sighed heavily, sinking into him, her fingertips digging into his muscular neck and the back of his head, holding him tight. If he had any thoughts of pulling away, she wasn't going to let him go anywhere.

Their heads tilted, alternating direction, as the kiss went wild and uncontrolled. She wasn't sure when he twisted, but she found herself shifted from the old sofa to his lap, straddling him. Her kiss-soaked brain slowly registered the growing hardness between her thighs, and she shifted her hips to better accommodate the length.

Oh, yes. Oh, fuck, yes.

She pulled away, her breathing rough and choppy, and pushed his jacket off of his shoulders, leaving him in only a thin T-shirt. Her nails lightly scraped over his pecs, and he tilted his head back, eyes closed, letting out a low moan of appreciation as she swiveled her hips.

"God damn, woman," he grunted. "*God. Damn.*" His hands held her hips still, then moved forward, under her sweatshirt, cupping her slight, naked breasts. He rubbed rough thumbs over her nipples, then squeezed the weight as he drove his hips upward.

"*Drill.*" She squeezed her thighs together, suddenly wishing they were both naked.

This is crazy. You've got to get a grip.

But the time for recriminations was *way* past. She wanted him. He wanted her. It was that simple. Right now, it was all her body was allowing. Rational thought could come later.

"I want you," he growled, before sucking on her neck, just below her ear, and causing her whole body to shiver. "I have never wanted any woman as much as I want you, I swear to God."

"Then have me," she breathed.

He paused. "You'll let me... tonight?"

She nodded, pressing herself against him urgently. *Quick. Quick. Before my mind interferes.*

His breathing was ragged and heavy. "Not here," he said. "Let's go to the..."

"Hello?"

Thuy and Drill both froze. Thuy looked over Drill's shoulder, at the stairs behind the couch.

Maddy was staring at them, her eyes round as dinner plates. "Um, Drill?"

He looked over his shoulder, and his entire head went red. "Uhhhh..."

Thuy bounced off of him like a rabbit. Her skin felt hot, a combination of desire and embarrassment. Maddy looked at her with surprise, and disappointment. Thuy looked away, swallowing hard.

"What the hell are y'all doing?" Maddy said, with obvious disbelief.

"About what it looks like," Drill said, rubbing the back of his head.

"Y'all are making out?" Maddy asked. Thuy had always noticed that Maddy's accent became more pronounced when she was upset. This obviously threw her for a loop.

"I came by and talked to Thuy last night. Nothing happened," Drill quickly added. "But I'm not going to pretend I'm not interested in your friend, Maddy. And really, it's none of your business."

"If you hurt her," Maddy said sharply, "it will be."

"It's not like that," Thuy quickly protested. "We're... there's an attraction, sure. But that's all there is. I mean, it got a little out of hand, that's all."

Now Drill was the one that looked disappointed. Thuy gritted her teeth. She was just pouring gas on a fire.

"I'll be by tomorrow to talk to you, Maddy," he said. "In the meantime — I am beat. Is it okay if I stay in the cabin?"

Thuy was puzzled, until she remembered. The cabin was the little mother-in-law unit that was on the property. She'd seen it when they first got there, but hadn't been in since.

Maddy looked at the two of them, then nodded. "Suit yourself," she said. "But won't the *club* mind?" She was looking at Thuy as she emphasized the word.

She was reminding Thuy: *my brother may seem sweet, but he's still a criminal.*

Thuy nodded.

He sighed. "You're probably right. But I'll give you a call or something soon, okay? We really need to talk."

"We sure do," Maddy said, her voice ripe with promise.

"Drive careful," Thuy said, seeing the shadows under his eyes.

He smiled, and stroked her cheek. Thuy couldn't help herself. She sighed, returning the smile.

Then he walked out of the house. She watched him as he got on his bike, strapped on his helmet, and rode away. Then she shut the door.

When she turned back, Maddy was staring at her, arms crossed.

"I am too tired to talk about it now," she said, "and yeah, it's probably none of my business. But you and me are gonna have *words* about this, young lady."

And being her best friend, Thuy knew she'd let her. She wasn't looking forward to it.

CHAPTER THIRTY

Drill was sitting at the little Formica table in what served as his eating area in his shitty little apartment in Green Valley. He didn't eat there often. Usually, it just served as a place to let junk mail collect, or maybe sit and drink a beer when he felt wrung out and didn't want to drink in bed. Since it was a studio apartment, he tended to watch TV from bed, or sleep, obviously. The place didn't have pictures. His clothes hung in the closet, which had no doors — they'd fallen off their runners, and he'd yanked the damned things off. He had a water glass by the sink. He took his trash out often because he didn't like the place smelling like old take-out containers. His window was rimmed in grime, which diffused the afternoon light that was pouring in. If he bothered to try peering through it, he'd have a great view of the gas station sign.

Right now, he wasn't paying attention to any of that.

It was a Friday, two days since he'd made out with Thuy in his father's house. He hadn't seen Maddy since. He'd thought about talking to her on the phone, but given her dismay at seeing him macking on her best friend, he wasn't quite sure what to say. And he was still trying to convince her to sell. And, frankly, he was still all up in his feelings about the club, and Catfish's proposal, and what he should do.

So, he was taking a break. He was propped up on his elbows, scrolling through pages from the book Thuy had recommended on his phone. He'd ordered the book in paperback, but it hadn't come yet, so he was still slugging it out on his cell, getting lost in the world of the main character, Kvothe, and the guy's struggles to learn about magic after losing his gypsy family to some horrific bloodshed. The guy had been homeless, had had to fight on the streets, begging and stealing and doing all kinds of shit to survive. Then he'd figured out a way out of it — sort of. The guy was still broke and struggling, but he was smart and talented. And he didn't back down. He had a bad period, but he got back up.

Drill flicked through, wishing he read a little faster. It was getting interesting. He really wanted to find out what was gonna happen to Kvothe. The guy had just gotten kicked out of a library, all because of this asshole who wanted to start shit with him. Drill sincerely hoped the asshole got his ass beat soon.

Drill frowned when he heard pounding on his door. "Who is it?" he asked, shutting off his phone.

"It's Burro!" a scratchy male voice said. "Open up, man!"

Great. Just great.

Drill was taking a day off from club stuff. He told Catfish he didn't feel well. He just didn't feel like dealing with Wraith shit today — not Catfish's grand plans, and certainly not Timothy King's smug bastard face. He still didn't know what to do about them, or about Catfish's offer from the day before. So instead, he was just going to take a day and read.

Yeah. It baffled the hell out of him, too.

He got up, wandering to the door and opening it. "What do you want?" he snapped.

Burro was in his forties, a stocky, grizzled guy with a square head and short-cropped, graying hair. Rumor had it he either got his club name from being mulishly stubborn, or because he'd been a drug runner in Texas back in the day. Either way, he'd been with the

Wraiths for the past few years. He wasn't particularly driven, and he tended to drink a little too much and talk a hell of a lot more than he acted. He was mostly used to run errands and messages.

Drill wondered what errand or message Burro was here for.

"Hey, bro. Is that any way to greet a friend?" Burro let out a smoker's laugh, raspy and edged in phlegm. "You're being rude to me and Nick, here."

Drill glanced behind Burro. He'd missed the kid entirely. Nick was in his twenties. Despite being thin and wiry, he was a brawler, edgy and quick-tempered. He looked around nervously, only shaking his head slightly to get his too-long bangs out of his shifty eyes. That seemed to be his default setting, nervous.

Drill opened the door, letting the two in, hoping that they didn't plan on staying long. "I told Catfish, I don't feel so hot. I'm not going to the Dragon today."

"Oh, yeah?" Burro looked around. "So what've you been doing?"

Drill's eyes narrowed. "Spent most of the day on the toilet, if you must know."

Burro's eyes widened, then he laughed. "Shee-it! What'd you eat? Tell me it wasn't a gas station burrito," Burro joked. "I know the joint's right there, but dammit, you can always have a recruit grab you some better grub than that!"

Nick looked around, his expression more skeptical. He picked up Drill's phone from the table. Drill grabbed it back from him. "The fuck are you doing?" Drill snapped.

Nick's eyes narrowed. "Even if you were shitting yourself, you could've been answering messages," Nick said sharply. "Catfish has questions."

"Nothing that needs my answer right this goddamned second," Drill said impatiently.

"So, you haven't been calling anybody or texting anybody you shouldn't?"

Drill thought immediately of Maddy and Thuy. Thankfully, he'd just dropped by the house, but still…

"What the fuck are you saying, Nick?"

Burro stood between them, holding his hands up in a peace maker's gesture. "Now, Drill," he said patiently. "You know how it's been. Ever since Darrell went state's evidence, everybody's a little jumpy, and Catfish… well, he's not sure your heart's in it. So, you don't mind if we open your phone and look around, do you?"

"Hell, *yes*, I mind!" Drill said. "Sixteen years. *Sixteen years*, I've been with the club. And this is the kind of trust I get? *This* is how I get repaid?"

"Desperate times," Burro said, and his expression showed he wasn't the least bit sorry.

Drill crossed his arms. "I'm just curious. If I say no, were you planning on making me?" He looked over Burro's paunchy form, and Nick's wiry, twitchy one. "Either of you? *Both* of you, together?" His derision was clear: even both of them armed would have a tough time getting the drop on him.

Burro grinned. "Well, then. We go back to Catfish and tell him you've got something to hide."

That was what they really wanted. Burro was a shit-stirrer: he liked drama, and gossiped like an old woman at a quilting bee. Nick, on the other hand, was one of Timothy's lackeys. He was there to catch Drill out, earn himself some favor. Get Timothy into that vice president slot, maybe.

Damn it.

Drill typed in the passcode, then handed it over. "Here."

Burro looked surprised that Drill had gone along with it. He opened up the text messages, poked around. "What's all this?" He frowned. The reading app was still open.

"It's a book."

"You're reading a book?" Burro repeated. "On your phone?"

"Yeah."

"Why?" Burro asked, obviously baffled.

"Why not?"

Nick looked off-balance. "You've been here in your apartment, sick — and *reading*?"

"Ugh. Yes." Drill grunted, rolling his eyes. "Drill not stupid. Drill can read."

Burro burst out laughing. "Dammit, son. I just didn't expect it, that's all."

Nick still seemed suspicious, and he took the phone from Burro.

"Don't lose my place," Drill muttered.

Nick flipped through pages. "This really is a book," he said. "What the hell kinda name is Kvothe, anyway?"

"What's it about?" Burro added, with mild curiosity.

Drill squelched a sigh of irritation. "It's about this guy — well, he starts out as a kid. His whole family gets murdered, all because of a song..."

"Wait, what?"

In the next twenty minutes, Drill found himself telling the two men about Kvothe and his struggles. He didn't really think of himself as a particularly good storyteller, but the story itself was gripping. He summed up what he could. "And that's as far as I've gotten," he finally said.

"What do you mean?" Burro pressed. "What happens next?"

"I don't know," Drill said. "I need to keep reading."

"Tell us what happens when you do," Nick said. His suspicion had melted, and now he was like a kid, bouncing and eager for the rest of the story.

"Yeah, yeah." He rubbed at his stomach. "I think it's time for another, um, bathroom break," he lied.

"What? Oh, yeah, sure. Feel better, man. The shits are the worst," Burro said, chuckling. He nudged Nick. "C'mon. Let's go talk to Catfish."

Nick waved a goodbye, and both men retreated down the hallway. Drill waited until he heard their steps on the stairs before letting a breath out.

Catfish's paranoia was growing, getting more dangerous. If he told Catfish he wanted to leave, Catfish wasn't going to believe he just wanted to live his own life. He'd see it as a betrayal. He'd wonder if

Drill was going to roll over on him. After all, Drill knew where all the bodies were buried — he'd been in the club for too long.

Drill rested his forehead against the door. He had to come up with something that Catfish wanted, some way to help him get out.

The only thing he could think of was the farm, he realized. Catfish needed money — and with Drill's half, maybe it would buy Drill his freedom. Which meant telling Maddy and Thuy, and using them to help him escape the mess he'd gotten himself into.

CHAPTER THIRTY-ONE

The following Monday, Thuy sat in Maddy's father's Lincoln Continental, taking advantage of a scheduled day off from the library to drive her bestie to the OB-GYN in Knoxville. It was a bit like steering a land yacht, but she managed. It would've been easier if her friend was talking to her. Not that Maddy was giving the cold shoulder, per se. It's just that Maddy wasn't being her usual cheerful, bubbly self. Instead, her comments and answers had been short, her whole countenance withdrawn.

Thuy finally sighed. "Are you super pissed at me?"

Maddy let out a little laugh. "No, I am not super pissed at you."

"You sure?" Thuy pressed. "Because you've said hardly thirty words to me since breakfast this morning. And we haven't talked about… you know. Last Thursday night."

"You don't owe me an explanation," Maddy said quickly. "But you've got to admit — it's *weird*."

"What's weird?"

"My best friend. With my big brother. *On my dad's couch.*" Thuy glanced over to see Maddy shudder. "That's just a lot of weird to unpack, is all I'm saying."

Thuy grinned, changing lanes carefully. "That's fair."

"It was like the perfect storm of weird." Maddy added. "At least you weren't, y'know, totally having sex. That would've been even weirder."

Oh, God. That didn't even bear thinking about. Thuy felt her cheeks flame at the thought.

"Mostly, I'd say I'm... worried," Maddy said thoughtfully. "I love you, Thuy. And despite the butthead my brother has been at times, I love him too. I just don't see how this ends well, for either of you."

Thuy sighed. "It's not like we're a couple or anything," she said. "I just — we talk. Talked. He's going through some stuff with the club."

"Is he in trouble?" Maddy's voice went sharp with fear.

"No. Not... no." She didn't want to worry Maddy any more than she had to. "I think he's just questioning some of his choices."

"Really? Huh." Maddy's voice sounded contemplative. "I would've thought he'd be in that damned club till he died. Which, unfortunately, would've been sooner rather than later, the way they run."

"Anyway, he needed somebody to talk to, so I listened. And I told him some stuff about my past that I thought might, you know, help. Give him some perspective," Thuy said carefully.

"You told him about your family?" The shock was evident in Maddy's tone.

"A little," Thuy downplayed, then shrugged.

"And then..." Maddy paused. "You... jumped him?"

Thuy let out a surprised laugh. "Um, yeah? More or less?"

"That sounds like more than just some attraction," Maddy said. Thuy glanced over to find Maddy worrying at the handle of her purse, fidgeting nervously. "I mean, Teddy — Drill — wasn't exactly a ladies' man, but he was only a kid when I knew him. He's never been that serious about women. I could imagine him hitting on you, because you're beautiful —"

"And you are my best friend and you always say that," Thuy said, touched by Maddy's loyalty.

"Regardless, it'd be one thing if he just flirted with you. I saw him doing that. If you were attracted to him, too... well, okay, that'd still be weird," Maddy laughed. "But it'd be your business. As long as I didn't have to see or hear anything, I wouldn't say anything. I'd be a little grossed out, but hey, he's my brother."

Thuy snickered.

"But it looks a little more serious than that. Especially if you're telling him stuff about your past. You never talk about that."

Thuy knew Maddy was right. "He looked so lost, Mads."

"You trust him?"

Thuy thought about it, then nodded slowly. "I don't know why, but I do."

"I'm worried for both of you, then." Maddy sighed. "He might be having second thoughts, but given any opportunity — the club has been his life. He'll always choose the club. He chose it over family. I know he's still steamed at me for not selling the farm, but I know that if the club tells him to stay away from me, even if we're living in the same town — he'll pretend I don't exist. He'll do the same to you, too. Or ask you maybe to sneak around with him. And you deserve better than that."

Thuy fell silent, focusing on guiding the big behemoth of a vehicle down the freeway. "It's too early for me to be thinking relationship with him. For God's sake, I just met him a couple of weeks ago. And so much has happened — I mean, I quit my job, got the new job at the library. I'm going to be living on a *farm*. I've fed *cows*!"

Maddy snickered. "That, you have."

"I'm not looking to settle down and have fat babies and live a good long life," Thuy said. "I fooled around a bit with Drill. And talked with him a little. It's really not a big deal."

She wasn't sure if she was trying to persuade Maddy, or herself, but she kept up a brave face.

"All right," Maddy said, after a long pause. "It's a free country, and like I said, it's none of my business."

"Yeah, but when you say 'it's none of my business', isn't that totally a Southern thing?" Thuy pointed out. "Like when someone says something judgy, then sips tea and murmurs 'but that's none of my business'?"

Maddy laughed out loud. "Next thing, I'll be blessing your heart."

"Heaven forbid," Thuy said. "Not a drive-by heart-blessing."

They both laughed at that, until Maddy wiped at her eyes. "Just… be safe, okay?"

"Okay, Mom," Thuy said. "I'll make sure he wraps that rascal before I…"

"Oh, *eww,*" Maddy interrupted. "I meant, don't get your heart broken, okay?"

Thuy blinked. "I've never had my heart broken, sweetie," she said firmly. And it was true. She'd been in several relationships, and she'd ended most of them. But even the ones who had broken up with her hadn't broken her heart. Pissed her off? Yes, absolutely. But she'd never felt the need to bury her sorrows in ice cream or anything. Usually, it was Maddy talking her down from slashing somebody's tires.

"You haven't told anybody about your family, either," Maddy reminded her.

Thuy swallowed against a throat that was suddenly dry as the Mojave. Drill was different, she realized.

I'm not getting my heart broken, she told herself sternly. *I won't even mess around with him again. Things are getting too serious.*

She just needed to remind herself the next time the two of them were alone… and hope to God this time, her body actually listened.

CHAPTER THIRTY-TWO

Drill went back over to the farmhouse the next day. The truck was gone, and he knew that Thuy had gone to the library to work. He'd texted his sister that morning to ensure she'd be at home. He parked. He could hear music coming from the greenhouse, so he moved that way. The day was sunny, even if the air was crisp and cold.

Walking into the greenhouse was like walking into a sauna. It was warm and wet and smelled like soil and leafy, living things. Maddy was misting something in one hand, holding a small pair of pruning scissors in the other, trimming off deadheads. It had been a long time since he'd been in the greenhouse, but he recognized a few plants. Some of them were fruit trees that would be put up for sale in spring, or shipped off. Some of them were things like various orchids, specialty stuff his father seemed to have a deft hand with. There were dwarf plants, bonsai trees, even some vegetables that shouldn't still be growing, like tomatoes.

"Dad got really random," he said, wondering why his father hadn't specialized more.

"I'm still trying to figure out what his system was," Maddy agreed, moving placidly between the plants. She was wearing a pair of leggings and an oversized sweater with an unzipped coat over it. Dirt already smudged the side of the coat, and one knee of her leggings. He grinned at the sight.

"You really want to work with all this again?" he asked quietly, gesturing to the haphazard mess of pots and dirt and seeds. Right this second, and just for a moment, it wasn't about Catfish. This was about Maddy. "Have you really thought this through?"

She pursed her lips. "I'm trying really hard to think of this as you asking me because you care about me," she said slowly. "Not because you think I don't know what the hell I'm doing, or that I don't know my own mind. I know I can make decisions quickly, but that doesn't mean they're rash. And I already told you: this is what I want, what I've always wanted."

"You didn't want it enough to stay," he pointed out, but winced. "But yeah, I know why you wanted to leave."

"You know, you really don't," she said, putting down the misting bottle and crossing her arms. "I loved Dad, in my own way. But he was harsh."

Drill rubbed his jaw, remembering some of his "discussions" with their father. The kind that ended with him getting smacked around. "I know."

She looked immediately sympathetic. "I know I was lucky he was never as hard on me as he was on you," she said. "And I think... well, I've gone to therapy about this. And Walter touched on it a little, at the will reading. I think that once Mom died, he thought that we'd be ruined. He didn't know how to handle kids. So he was just as hard on us as he could be, out of fear of screwing up."

"And *that* worked out really well." Drill clenched a fist, then stuffed it in his jacket pocket. He hadn't had therapy. And he wasn't feeling quite so fucking forgiving. "But this isn't about the past. This is about what we're going to do moving forward."

She was quiet for a second. Then she looked at him, her gaze both piercing and pleading.

"When you left — when you got in that big fight with Dad, and you decided never to come back — it meant a lot of changes for me."

Drill huffed, his chest feeling like concrete. "Dammit, I couldn't stay. You *know* that. And if I thought he was mistreating you, hitting you, I'd have figured out some way to get you out, too!"

"I know what the teen girls who wound up with the Wraiths turned into," she said quietly. "Strippers, if they're lucky. Junkies if they're not. Somebody's old lady, or just somebody's toy. They never get the chance to become a biker and make a difference in the club. They just get used."

He stopped. "It wouldn't... I wouldn't have let anything bad happen to you," he said, but he realized he was shaky. It hadn't come to that. It wouldn't have come to that, if he'd needed to take her away from their father.

Would it?

"I thought about running away," she said, and though her voice was dispassionate, there was a lot of pain in her eyes. "I mean it. Dad felt like with you gone, I was the last chance he had to do something right. If I didn't get straight A's, he wouldn't let me leave the house. He told me I was lazy. I had to beg him to stay on the softball team, because I knew it would be my best way out. He thought I'd just go to Knoxville for school, or maybe skip it altogether and run the farm with him." She rubbed her eyes. "He was so angry when I told him I was going to Berkeley on a full scholarship, he tried to stop me. But I was eighteen by then. He couldn't. Still, he shoved me out and told me never to come back."

Drill hadn't known about this. How could he know? Guilt gnawed at him like a feral dog.

"Hey. Hey! I'm not telling you this to make you feel bad," she said quickly, moving to his side and putting a comforting hand on his wrist. "I'm telling you because I had to make choices for myself. I had to take care of myself. I love farming; I just didn't want to farm with Dad. Now that he's gone, I have the opportunity. I know that cuts you out, and that sucks, and I'm sorry. But I am making the best choice for me, one that will take care of me and my baby. It will be hard, but I know I can make it work. It'd be easier with some help from my big brother, but I know that you've got your own problems and you've got to make your own choices. I just want you to respect mine."

He sighed. "I am trying," he said quietly. "But… like you said. I've got my own problems."

"Oh?" She waited. Then her eyes widened. "Oh. Shit. You mean with the club, don't you?"

"Yeah."

"So… this isn't about me," she said quietly, rubbing her stomach in an unconscious protective gesture. "You're in some kind of trouble. And you need the money."

"Not exactly," he said. "But… yeah. The money's an issue."

"How much?"

"However much half of this farm is," he said quietly.

She blinked slowly. "What do you mean?"

"They want my half of the farm."

"And you'd just *give* it to them?" She looked appalled. "They… you'd… what the hell!"

"I'm still working that out." Drill shifted his weight, haphazardly picking at a plant until Maddy walked up and smacked his hand. "I can't even get into all the shit the club's been through, especially in the past year. They're in trouble."

"So, you feel you're responsible for bailing them out?"

That was the thing. He *didn't* feel responsible — or at least, he didn't *want* to feel responsible. And he was getting pretty damned resentful at Catfish's attitude. "I'm wrestling with it," Drill finally said, through gritted teeth.

Maddy looked paler. "I'm *really* not selling the place so you can bail those assholes out," she hissed. "I don't care what you think you owe them. I have never asked what kind of shit you've gotten into since you left the house. I love you, and frankly, it was better for my sanity to not know. But I am *sure as hell* not selling this place so you can fund their criminal activities. And don't try to bullshit me!" she shouted, half-shoving him when he started to try and talk. "Don't act like I'm stupid! I *know* what the Wraiths do… run drugs and guns and God know what else. Selling the place would be like *me* handing them cash to keep doing it, and *I am not doing it, damn it!*"

"C'mon, Maddy," he said quickly. Her color was now getting hectic, and she was rubbing her stomach, which made him nervous. "Don't get yourself all worked up. It's not good for the baby."

"Don't fucking bring up the baby," she yelled. Yes, yelled. Her eyes were wide, her hair wild. "As far as I'm concerned, if the Wraiths just disappeared, it'd do the world good! So don't you *dare* come in here and ask me again about selling the place, because it'll be a cold day in hell before I give up the farm, you hear me?"

"I think they can hear you in Nashville," Drill said, trying to joke a little. She was breathing hard. "Come on. Let's go inside. I'll make you a cup of tea."

She harrumphed at him. "I mean it, Drill. Don't bring it up again."

"I won't," he said. "I promise."

"Oh, and another thing," she said. "What the hell were you doing, making out with Thuy?"

"That question sort of answers itself, doesn't it?" He put an arm gingerly around her shoulders, leading her out of the building, back towards the farmhouse.

"I don't want you to play with her, Teddy," Maddy said, her tone reprimanding. "She's my best friend, and if you hurt her…"

"I don't want to hurt her. Why? Did she tell you something?" He found himself very interested in the answer. More invested than maybe he should have been.

She stopped, and he stopped with her. She stared at him for a second.

"You *like* her," Maddy marveled.

"What? Yeah. She's cool." He winced. He sounded like an idiot.

"No. You like-like her."

"What are we, twelve?"

Maddy shook her head. At least she wasn't looking stressed out over their talk anymore.

Unfortunately, he still was. Maybe he shouldn't have been honest with her. Or maybe he needed to be *more* honest with her. But now, he saw that she'd dug in, and he couldn't blame her. She wanted the farm, the life, for her kid.

Now, he just needed to figure out how to placate Catfish, before Catfish decided to do something more serious.

CHAPTER THIRTY-THREE

It had been a good day, if a long one. Thuy rubbed at her shoulder a little after waving to Naomi Winters, who was locking up. She'd spent some of her shift shelving, but most of it getting that third computer fixed. Fortunately, it wasn't anything major — nothing some re-booting and hardware driver replacement couldn't fix. Julianne looked surprised when she said that it was taken care of. She still hadn't agreed to let the teens use the computers for extra time, but Thuy hoped that she might wear the woman down… gradually, of course, and gently.

She'd spent her lunch break on the internet, putting out the call for YA book donations. So many of the authors she knew on social media were both delightful and generous. She had high hopes that the YA section of the library would be filled very soon.

That night had been teen night, and as usual, it was mostly middle-grade readers. She'd let Naomi handle doing a craft with them, something Christmas related, while she focused on the teens who'd attended. Her "usual" crew of Kevin, Jeremy and Ginny had shown up, along with a few friends. She'd deliberately brought a few decks of *Magic: The Gathering* and made some fantasy reading recommendations. She was lucky she'd packed a few decks for the trip to

Tennessee in case she and Maddy got bored. She'd definitely bring more from the apartment in Oakland once it was all packed up and moved.

All in all, she was feeling pretty pleased with herself. She waved another goodbye to Naomi, who drove away in her car, and headed for the truck. She hadn't thought she'd fit in as well or as quickly, but she felt like Naomi was beginning to be a friend, and she liked the kids. Now, all she wanted to do was head back to the farmhouse, have a quick dinner, and settle down.

And maybe Drill will come over again tonight.

She knew she shouldn't be thinking that way. She hadn't seen him since Maddy had walked downstairs and interrupted their ill-advised make-out session.

She shook her head, reaching into her purse for her keys. That sounded so juvenile! Like they'd been playing spin the bottle or swapping kisses in a movie theater.

The more appropriate term would be: that time when she'd climbed him like a telephone pole.

And let's face it: if you hadn't been in the damned living room of your best friend's house — with her brother, no less! — *you would've gone a hell of a lot farther than that.*

She ought to be more embarrassed by it. Not that she was embarrassed by wanting sex; she wasn't. But to be caught like that? And, again, with her best friend's brother?

She rolled her eyes. So. Not. Cool.

So, what will you do if he stops by again?

She sighed. She wasn't sure what she was going to do. Indulging in her hormones wasn't a smart idea. But they were going to be in the same town from here on out, and she'd see him again if he ever saw Maddy.

Which he might not.

Because he's in a biker gang.

She frowned. That was a lot more concerning than the best-friend's-brother problem. She'd done too much to cut that element out of her life. She'd never hooked up with a biker, and she'd done everything possible to basically forget what her family was or that she had any connection to it. Being with Drill, even in their quiet moments, brought back the memories she'd fought so hard to dismiss and destroy.

So why couldn't she seem to walk away from him?

The man stepped out of the shadows behind the tall truck. "Hello, cutie."

She froze. She'd been too deep in her own thoughts and feelings. *Stupid,* she berated herself, even as her hands clutched her keys tighter in her purse.

He stepped a little closer, and leaned against the truck's door. He was wearing jeans and a biker's leather jacket. She could see the patch for the Wraiths.

Drill's gang. The ones that were threatening her and Maddy the other night.

She clenched her jaw. "What do you want?" she said, in a low, even voice.

"That's not a friendly way to say hello," he said, with a leering smile.

He was taller than her. Of course, she was five foot nothing, so many people were. He was probably about five foot ten, with some paunch. Meaty fists and a thick neck. She would bet he wasn't that fast, but had a punch that meant he didn't have to be. She quickly looked over his jacket, his jeans. He didn't appear to be packing a gun. Didn't mean he wasn't. Just meant that there wasn't one easily accessible or obvious. She watched to see if he reached towards the back of his waistband, just in case.

"What do you want?" she repeated, her tone almost robotic. She didn't want to sound afraid. That just encouraged them. That said, she didn't want to challenge him, either. If he was a bully, he'd feel the need to prove himself. It was a knife's edge to walk.

Then again... she was used to being underestimated.

"What makes you think I want something, little girl?" the biker said, with a rough laugh.

"You're here with a message." She shrugged. "You haven't threatened me, and you haven't taken me." *Yet,* she thought, feeling her heart rate accelerate.

"Wow. You're good," the guy replied. "Yeah, I got a message. You're not welcome here. That farmhouse needs to sell. Convince your *girlfriend* to get her fat ass back to California." His grin was crooked — he was missing an eyetooth. "Next time, we won't be so polite."

She moved her fingers slowly on her keys, careful not to jingle them too loudly. She felt what she was looking for on the bottom of the purse.

And Maddy made fun of me for buying bear spray, Thuy thought, keeping her face calm.

He reached out, lifted her chin. "You're what? Chinese?"

"Vietnamese," she ground out. "Third generation."

"Huh. Always liked them Asian girls," he said, and the way he said it made her stomach churn with disgust. "Maybe I can add a little message of my own."

Her heart raced. "Leave me alone. I mean it."

"No need to rush off," he said, leaning closer. He grabbed her shoulder, pinning her against the truck. "Why don't you just…"

She pulled out the bear spray and nailed him right in the eyes.

He started screaming, and she kicked him hard in the groin. He went down like a wrecking ball, shrieking and crying.

She unlocked and opened the door, slamming it shut. Then she screeched out of the parking lot, tears of residual panic falling as she hit the main streets.

Should she try to figure out where the police station was? Adrenaline in her system made her shake. Should she…

Wait a minute.

Maddy!

If they'd decided to stalk her at the library, what would they do to Maddy, who was all alone?

One hand on the steering wheel, she clawed through her purse with the other. She dialed 911.

"What's your emergency?"

"I just got threatened outside the Green Valley Library," she said, her voice shaking. She gunned the engine, racing towards the farmhouse, knowing she shouldn't be on the phone and driving but spurred forward by fear. "By a large man, a member of a biker gang. And I'm afraid they've sent someone to my roommate, as well. I need help."

"We'll get someone to the library as soon as possible."

"No! No. I'm headed to the farmhouse," she corrected, starting to give the address. The connection broke off, and Thuy cursed. "*Fuck!*"

She floored it.

CHAPTER THIRTY-FOUR

Drill was still at the farm at 9:30 that night. He'd spent the day hanging out with his sister, helping out around the farm, and avoiding Catfish's texts. He'd walked the fence line, making sure that there weren't gaps or breaks in the barbed wire. He'd looked at the shape of the driveway, making notes of where to add gravel and try to get ahead of ruts before things got too muddy in the spring. He'd even made dinner with Maddy, something he hadn't done since he was a teenager and she was a pre-teen. It wasn't anything special, just mac and cheese with ground beef and peas. But they'd laughed, and talked.

He felt better than he had in a long time.

He knew he could've left earlier, but Maddy had mentioned that Thuy usually got back at around 9:30 or quarter to ten after her shifts at the library. And yeah, after that kiss, he wanted to see her. He didn't know if he'd kiss her again — although who was he kidding, *of course* he wanted to kiss her again. But he didn't know if she'd allow it. Or if she did, he didn't know if Maddy would be hovering around cock-blocking him. Not that he supposed he could blame her. He wasn't good for a woman like Thuy.

Didn't stop him from wanting, though.

He heard the engine of a vehicle coming up the driveway, and he grinned to himself, drying his hands and then putting away the towel he had slung over his shoulder from when he was washing dishes. Maddy was sitting on the couch, watching some DVD from the library. He decided to do what Thuy so often did: meet her on the porch. That would at least give him a second to maybe get his arms around her before they were in front of his sister.

He frowned as soon as he got outside. He knew the distinct sound of the truck; this was the sound of a motorcycle.

What the hell?

A bike drove up. It was Nick, the nervy young recruit who had stopped by his apartment, insisting on looking through his phone. The kid took his helmet off, shaking his bangs away from his face, looking surprised.

"Did Catfish send you, too?" he asked, sounding incensed. "I can handle jobs on my own, you know!"

He sounded so surly, so pouty, that it took Drill a second to process what the kid was saying.

"Exactly what 'job' are you doing here, Nick?" Drill asked, forcing himself to remain calm.

Now Nick looked a little unsure of himself, his defensive confidence sliding. "We're telling these chicks they need to get the hell out of Green Valley," he said, then cleared his throat. "Right?"

"Did he tell you why?"

"Didn't ask why," Nick said, his eyes wide. "Are you nuts?"

So, Catfish wasn't waiting until Christmas. Drill felt his blood boil. "Did you know the 'chick' you were going to talk to tonight is pregnant?"

For the first time, he saw the cocky kid look actually uncomfortable. Even if he was one of Timothy King's cronies, the kid had at least a shred of conscience. "Uh, yeah," he said. "Jesus, Drill, I wasn't gonna, you know, *hurt* her or anything. Just scare her a little. Get the point across."

Drill walked up to him, grabbing him by the shirt. The kid ought to be thankful it wasn't by the throat. Nick's eyes went wide.

"Now I'm getting *my* point across," Drill said sharply. "You aren't coming back here. You are going to leave these women alone. *Period.*"

Finally, fear registered on Nick's face. It was one thing to be a twenty-year-old brawler amongst a bunch of drunk young assholes. It was another entirely to go toe-to-toe with a man who had been the hired muscle of the crew for the better part of a decade, who was completely sober. And who was itching for you to make a wrong move so he could crush you to powder.

"Sorry, man," Nick stammered. "I'll leave her alone."

"Leave Thuy alone too," Drill added, in case he had any other orders. Catfish probably would've wanted his bases covered. At Nick's blank look, Drill rolled his eyes. "The other girl."

"Oh. That wasn't my job. Catfish sent Sledgehammer after her."

Drill's eyes widened. "He *what?*"

Before he could pursue that line of questioning, he heard the familiar thrum of the Chevy roaring quickly up the driveway. It screeched to a stop in a cloud of dust in front of the farmhouse, and he rushed to the driver's side.

"Is Maddy all right?" Thuy asked as soon as the door was open.

"Yeah." He looked her over. She had tear stains streaking her cheeks, but otherwise, she looked unharmed. "Are *you* all right?"

"Better now," she admitted, getting down from the truck. He couldn't help himself. He checked her over, then held her tight against his chest. Just for a minute.

"What happened?" he asked, stroking her hair, patting her shoulder.

"I was at the library, when this guy..." He felt her shudder. "He told me that Maddy and I had to get the hell out of Green Valley. Then he said he wanted... he grabbed me..."

Drill saw red. He held her tighter, forcing his murderous thoughts aside to continue hearing her.

"So, I maced him," she said. "Bear spray. Stuff I'd picked up for the farm, believe it or not. Then I kicked him, and got in the truck. I headed straight here to make sure they didn't do anything to Maddy."

"I've been here all day," he said, and noticed that she curved against his chest. Like she felt safe there. It warmed him, easing away some of the icy rage that had crowded his thinking as he considered what Sledgehammer had done. Or worse, what he could have done.

Another roar of a bike engine. Drill turned, automatically releasing Thuy and nudging her behind him. "Get into the house," he said. "Get the shotgun."

She didn't say anything, just turned and ran to the house, the door slamming behind her. Nick goggled at him.

"What is going on?" Nick said, more baffled than angry.

As Drill suspected, it was Sledgehammer. When the guy got off his bike, he was limping a little. A swift kick to the balls would probably do that. His eyes were red as a weasel's.

"Where is she?" Sledgehammer demanded, tossing his helmet aside and stalking toward the house. "Where is that little bitch?"

Drill didn't respond with words. Instead, he walked over and dropped Sledge with a right hook that had all his anger and power behind it.

Sledgehammer's head swung around, and his eyes rolled up a bit. *Glass jaw,* Drill thought with the clinical part of his mind.

"Jesus," Nick breathed behind him. "You knocked him out!"

"Yeah, I know." Drill shook out his knuckles.

"But.. but Catfish told us…"

"Catfish and I had an agreement," Drill said, his words tinged with frost. "He broke the agreement. I will be having words with Catfish."

"But Catfish's president." Nick was practically whining now. "And Tim said…"

"*Fuck Timothy King.*" Drill snarled it, baring his teeth. "Get out of here. *Now.* Or you're gonna be next on the ground."

Nick didn't need to be told twice. He quickly hopped on his bike and took off, leaving Sledgehammer's prone body behind.

Drill waited for Sledgehammer to wake up. He came around slowly, rubbing at his jaw and moaning. "What was that for?"

"She's mine," Drill said. "Got it?"

Sledgehammer looked wary, but also stubborn. "Catfish didn't say nothing about the girl being yours," he said. "Besides, I thought she was gay!"

"Didn't stop you from grabbing her," Drill said. "And I don't care. *She's mine.* If you touch her again, I will fucking *destroy* you. Nod if you understand."

The dude was slow, but Sledgehammer finally registered the precarious position he was in. He nodded, swallowing hard. "Got it," he said. Then reluctantly added. "Sir."

Drill nodded in response. "Get the fuck out of here."

Sledgehammer shot him a look of resentment, but did as he was told, getting on the bike and following Nick's trail of dust.

As the adrenaline left his system, Drill turned back to the house. He found Thuy on the porch, shotgun in hand, looking at him.

A wave of exhaustion hit him. "I'm sorry," he said.

"For which part?" Thuy asked, the gun shaking a little in her hands as it pointed at the ground. "For your biker gang guy coming to my work? For the threats against Maddy and me? For telling a guy I belonged to you?"

He winced. She would take offense at that. Jesus, he'd only kissed her twice, hadn't even slept with her… but the moment the words had come out of his mouth, he couldn't deny how utterly *right* they'd felt.

This woman is mine. He wanted to protect her, defend her, and hold her. And do a hell of a lot more than that.

He walked up to her, taking the gun from her hands.

"Maybe," she said slowly, "you ought to explain to me exactly what's going on."

CHAPTER THIRTY-FIVE

Thuy watched as Drill deflated, his shoulders hunching a little. He looked pissed, and sorrowful, and frustrated. She could understand those feelings. Take all of them, add a few cups of fear and adrenaline, and shake it around, and you'd have the cocktail of emotions *she* was experiencing. She crossed her arms.

"C'mon," he said. "Let me just tell Maddy everything's okay first." He stepped into the house.

"*Is* everything okay, though?" Thuy pressed.

He nodded, his expression grim. "It is. Or it will be." He walked into the living room, where Maddy was sitting on the couch. The TV was muted, and she was clutching a pillow, her eyes wide. "I'm so sorry about that, Mads."

"They're gone?" Her voice sounded higher pitched than normal. "Are they coming back?"

"I'm going to camp out in the cabin tonight, okay?" he said, rubbing her shoulder. "I seriously doubt anybody's coming back tonight, but if they do, I'll hear them. And I'll make them sorry."

Maddy's eyes welled with tears. "I hate this," she murmured. "I *hate* this."

"I know," Drill said. "I'm sorry."

"I'm going to bed," Maddy said, turning her back on him and clomping up the stairs. She paused halfway up the stairway. "The sheets are in the linen closet, if you're going to stay. I haven't been in there."

"All right. G'night, Maddy."

Thuy looked at her friend. "I'll sleep down here," Thuy said. "Don't worry."

Maddy looked sad. "If they show up, do you think sleeping on the couch will really make that much of a difference?"

"I'll have the shotgun."

Maddy shook her head. "Let *Drill* have the shotgun. If he's going to be a guard dog, he might as well be armed."

With that parting zinger, Maddy went up the rest of the stairs.

Thuy looked over at Drill. "C'mon," he said. "I'll explain it over there."

They grabbed a set of sheets and pillowcases and a spare quilt, then trooped across the driveway to the small "cabin", which was more of a mother-in-law unit. Thuy had looked at it when they first arrived. There was a queen-sized bed in a loft with a desk, as well as a small living room, and absolutely tiny kitchen and full bath. It was actually a nice little structure. "Why do you even have this place?"

"My mom's brother was kind of a drifter. She wanted to give him a place to stay, a place where he'd feel welcome. My dad built this because she asked," Drill said, turning on the lights. It was cold in the cabin, and musty smelling, the way a place that has been closed off for months would smell, like dust and staleness. He grunted. "Can you put the sheets up on the bed while I get the wood-burning stove going? Just to take the chill off."

She nodded, climbing the shallow steps that led to the loft. There was a window. It was a clear evening, and she could make out the stars from the skylight. It was a nice cabin, and a beautiful night.

Too bad it was ruined by those assholes.

She grimaced. She stripped the bed, replacing the sheets, pulling and tugging the pillows into their cases. Then she tossed the quilt over the blanket and comforter, straightening everything out. By the time she was back downstairs in the living room, he had the fire going, slowly pouring out warmth and light.

He looked at her. "You made the bed? You didn't have to do that."

She shrugged. "Are you going to tell me what's going on, or not?" she asked bluntly.

He nodded, patting the really old, sagging couch that leaned against the window. "This is my fault," he said. "I told Catfish — that's the president of our club — about the will. He wants my half of the farm for the Wraiths."

She grimaced. "So it wasn't that they were targeting Maddy and I because they thought we were a couple," she clarified.

"They might've given you a hard time — the Wraiths aren't exactly open-minded," he said, rubbing at the back of his neck like he had a knot there. "But no. This is about the money."

"And they're convinced you're going to just give them thousands of dollars?" Thuy asked, then shook her head. "Or does it really not matter what you want?"

Drill's frown was intense. "Apparently, it doesn't matter what I want. I'd made a deal with Catfish: I had until Christmas to convince you guys to move, to sell. He jumped the gun, and I want to know why."

That little tidbit had her sitting up straighter. "You wanted until Christmas? But… wait. You were that sure you could convince Maddy and me to move?"

He looked at her, and for a second, there was a lopsided smile on his face that was so filled with tenderness that it melted her defenses.

"Why would you want to stay here?" he asked quietly. "You're a smart woman — an educated woman. You're used to a big city, with… I dunno, sushi restaurants and lots of movie theaters with subtitled films and shit. Why the hell would you want to stay here, on a farm, working in a Podunk library? I get why my sister wants to stay, but she wouldn't stay without you, especially not when she's pregnant. I thought I could either show her that it was a bad idea, or show you that you weren't going to be happy here. That there isn't enough here to keep you happy."

"You didn't do a very good job," Thuy said, with a gentle smile of her own. "If anything, you provided some of your own incentive for me to stay."

His eyes glowed with warmth, and her heart trip-hammered in response.

She cleared her throat, shifting away from the emotions that were starting to flood her. "Besides. I'm liking it more than I thought here. The air's clean, the trees are breathtaking, and the town's like a postcard. It's amazingly beautiful. I like the library, too. I mean, it needs some work," she closed her eyes for a second, thinking of just how much work it needed, "but I like helping people, and there, I feel like I am. I have that chance. And I'm getting used to the farm. I don't know much about plants, but Maddy's teaching me stuff. I'm even getting used to the cattle. I'll miss them in the spring when Mr. McMasters takes them back."

Drill looked at her indulgently, and he reached out, stroking her cheek, tucking her hair behind her ear. The gesture ought to annoy her, she supposed, but she found herself tilting a little, until his hand cupped her face.

"You really think you could be happy here?"

"I will admit, I do miss sushi," she said, and he laughed.

"I could take you to Knoxville," he said. "Or Nashville. I'm sure one of them has it."

"You've never eaten it, have you?" she asked.

He made a face, and she laughed. "Raw fish," he said. "I catch plenty of it, but I'm not gonna eat it that way."

"We'll see about that," she said, her voice playful.

Then she realized, abruptly, what she was doing.

She was still pissed, dammit. She and Maddy were being threatened by a biker gang, and Drill had a part in it, no matter how inadvertently. Why was she making plans to eat sushi with this man?

She pulled away from his hand, silently cursing herself.

"Don't worry. I'm not going to let you get hurt," he reiterated, putting an arm around her shoulders. "Not you, not my sister. I'm going to fix this. And I'm going to stay here to make sure that nothing else happens."

"Are you going to stay here forever?" Thuy snapped . "Because we're not selling, and we're not moving. I know Maddy. She's digging her feet in, and she's angry at you because you let this happen. I don't even think she'd sell if I threatened to leave — and if she's staying, I'm staying, no matter what. So how are you going to stop them?"

"I'm going to talk to Catfish."

She made a noise of frustration, a frustrated, choking growl. "I know what these people are like," she said. "Unless motorcycle clubs are a lot nicer out here in Tennessee than they are in the rest of the world, just reasoning with them and asking them to back off isn't going to do *shit*. They respond to one thing: strength. How are you going to get them to back down?"

"If I have to beat Catfish down, I will," Drill said vehemently. "I'll do whatever I have to, to keep you safe. I will *always* protect you, and do what's best for you. Do you understand that?"

Thuy swallowed. His blue eyes blazed incandescently. He was holding her, staring at her.

"You said before, to that guy from the library," she said, her voice shaking a little. "You said I was yours. Why'd you do that?"

She saw his throat work as he swallowed. "Dammit, Thuy. *You know why.*"

"Swear to God, I don't," she whispered.

He sighed. Then he leaned forward, his lips pressing against hers. "Because I want you to be," he said against her mouth. "I have never felt like this about anyone. Ever."

She hadn't, either. That, almost more than the bikers, scared the hell out of her.

She didn't want, couldn't think about it right now. Instead, she leaned into him, her mouth moving, silencing him. She made a soft little cry of pleasure as he slanted his mouth over hers, meeting her, matching her intensity. She ran her hands up his chest, then linked them around his neck. They were still side-by-side on the couch, but she twisted, pressing her chest against his, trying to get as close to him as possible.

His mouth opened, his tongue licking at the seam of her mouth for entrance. His hands moved lower, cupping her hips. She opened her mouth, her tongue moving against his.

More. I want more this time.

More pressure, more passion, more physicality.

Less thinking.

They were in the cabin, she realized. Privacy. Maddy would not be coming to interrupt.

She felt heat that had nothing to do with the wood-burning stove seep through her system. She pulled away just long enough to tug off her sweater. She wasn't wearing a bra underneath.

She stood there, half-naked, and waited.

He took her in with his eyes, studying her like she was a puzzle he was dying to solve. He reached for her almost reverently. "Thuy," he breathed.

He covered her breasts with his palms, his hands rough from working with engines and riding his bike. The slight abrasion against her excited nipples made her arch her back and gasp, pressing harder against him.

He groaned, leaning down and resting his head against her neck, then pressing hard suction against her wildly beating pulse. She leaned against him, her knees buckling.

He lifted her like she didn't weigh anything, wrapping her legs around his waist. He kissed her, long and hard, and she moaned softly against his onslaught.

More, more, more. She clawed at his back, all but begging him without words to take it deeper, be rougher, simply do more.

After what felt like both an eternity and not enough time at all, he nudged her down, placing her on her feet.

"I can't," he said, simply.

She blinked. "What?"

"We can't," he corrected. "We can't have sex tonight."

"What?" She couldn't help it. She whimpered with need, embar-

rassing herself. "Why *not?*" She rubbed up against him. "Your body seems to be on board with the plan."

"Oh, God, baby... you're making it really hard for me to do the right thing here," he said, and she could see sweat on his forehead, feel the slight tremor run through his body as his hands stroked down her sides.

"I can feel that." Her own body felt like it was on fire. She kissed him, hard, and he kissed her back, then pulled away, his breathing hard and ragged.

"Damn it, Thuy. I just punched out a member of my own club," he said. "They're going to be pissed. And they still want half this farm. I have to fix all this, and I'm not sure if anybody else is going to come tonight for retribution. I want to make sure you and Maddy are safe tonight, then I'll deal with Catfish tomorrow."

The words were like a bucket of ice water poured on her head.

He needed to protect Maddy.

They needed to protect Maddy, dammit. Not screw around and leave Maddy to fend for herself.

She pulled back, taking a step away from him. "Of course, you're right," she said, guilt swamping her. "God. I don't... I forgot. I can't believe I forgot."

"Hey, come here," Drill said, pulling her to him, cradling her against his chest. "Remember what I said? I've never wanted anyone the way I want you. Don't beat yourself up over this."

She struggled for a moment, wriggling, but his warmth and his body enveloped her, and she finally sighed, succumbing to it. She felt his heart beat, still fast and uneven, beneath her ear.

"I don't know if I've felt this way before," she admitted softly.

"Next time," he said, and she felt him kissing the top of her head, stroking her still naked back, "when I've got this fixed... I'm not gonna stop until I'm buried deep inside you, and you're screaming my name with pleasure. Got it?"

She quivered. "Not fair," she muttered, and felt as well as heard him laugh. "But until then..."

"Until then," he said, with a reluctant sigh, "I guess I'd better get you back on up to the house."

She tugged on her sweater, then turned to him. The expression on his brutally handsome face was mixed: regret, hunger, sorrow. And a sweetness, an intensity, that she couldn't remember seeing aimed at her ever.

"Next time," he reiterated, his eyes glowing.

She swallowed hard, then headed back through the cold, back up to the farmhouse. She was getting in over her head with Drill, and she knew it.

Just like she was pretty sure she wasn't going to do anything to stop it.

CHAPTER THIRTY-SIX

Drill slept lightly all that night. The cabin's bed was surprisingly comfortable, but he still jumped at every noise, the shotgun close at hand. He texted Catfish at dawn, telling him to meet him at the Dragon as soon as possible. Which was why he was rolling into the mostly-empty bar at nine o'clock in the morning. He saw Catfish's motorcycle there, a custom chopper that was comprised of mostly stolen parts, gleaming in the cold December sunshine. There were a few other bikes there, too, as well as a rusty pick-up and a beat-up old Plymouth. He walked in to find the bartender serving beers to a few hung-over members. Music was playing low on the jukebox. Drill stalked past the few people there, ignoring their greetings. He went right back to the office, opening the door forcefully.

"What the hell, Catfish?"

Catfish looked up, as did Dirty Dave. Catfish quirked an eyebrow at him. "Good morning to you, too, sunshine," he drawled sarcastically.

"What's he doing here?" Drill said, nodding at Dave. "I told you I wanted to talk to you."

"We've been making some plans for that half of the ranch you'll be selling," Dave said. "Figured you'd want to be here for that. We need to talk about how you're gonna sell it, as well."

"Get out." Drill's voice dripped with venom.

Dave's smile was slow and smug. "Now, now. No need to get all touchy."

"Get. Out."

Dave grimaced. "You gettin' cold feet, son?"

"I'm not your goddamn son, and get out before I throw you out." Drill clenched his jaw so tight he thought he'd crumble his own molars.

"Stay, Dave," Catfish said, his dark eyes glinting with anger. "What's the problem, Drill?"

"You told me that you wouldn't send anyone after my sister until Christmas," he said. "You said I'd have until then to convince them on my own!"

Dave's laugh sounded like a rusty spring. "Convince them?" he asked. "You should just tell 'em! Jesus, how soft are you?"

Drill grabbed the man by his collar. "How fucking soft do I seem now?" he said, shaking the man.

Dave's eyes bulged as the collar tightened.

"Enough!" Catfish shoved at Drill, and Drill released the older man. Dave backed away, staring at Drill warily and coughing slightly. "You weren't getting the job done."

Drill glared at Catfish. "You're the one saying I need to sell and give my half over to the club," he spat out. "Why? So guys like this asshole can skim a bunch? So I can see *my* money go to a bunch of guys who are willing to turn tail at the first opportunity? What the *hell* do you think I owe to this club?"

Catfish's eyes widened.

"Do you honestly think Darrell Winston would've given his wife's cash to the club, if he hadn't been outsmarted by those damned kids of his?" Drill pushed. "Hell, no, he wouldn't. He would've kept every red cent!"

"You're no damned Darrell Winston, boy," Dirty Dave said sharply.

"Damned right I'm not," Drill shot back. "Because Darrell Winston *went state's evidence*. You really going to play the Saint Darrell of the Wraiths card on me right now?"

"Dave, get out," Catfish said, sounding both irritated and tired.

"This asshole..." Dave protested.

Catfish didn't have to say another word. He glared at Dave, then looked at the door.

Dave grimaced at Drill, but did as he was told, shutting the door behind him with a slam.

"Okay. Maybe I shouldn't have sent Sledge and Nick," Catfish said slowly.

"Goddamned right you shouldn't," Drill ground out.

"I'm in a corner," Catfish said, surprising Drill. "The club is coming apart at the seams, and I'm holding it together by the skin of my goddamned teeth, Drill. I need your help with this, and you're dragging your feet."

Drill folded his arms across his chest. "Are we going to go under if we don't have this money? Is that what you're saying?"

Catfish's expression grew cagey. "Not *under*, exactly. But we're losing ground. We've got to make a statement. Having the money will..."

"I don't want to sell," Drill interrupted. "I don't want to give the money to the club."

Catfish grimaced. "Dammit, Drill. I thought we were brothers."

Drill felt some sadness of his own. They had been like brothers, for years. "We are," Drill said. "Which is why you ordering me to give up what's mine is so wrong to me. And threatening pregnant women? What's next? We gonna start mugging old people and shaking down kids for milk money, for God's sake? You know I don't like this kind of shit. I wouldn't do it when Razor's psycho ass was here, and I won't do it for you."

"You're just saying that because she was your sister," Catfish said, scowling.

"The fact that you think I am tells me how wrong I am about you."

Catfish huffed out an impatient breath. "We need to present a united front," Catfish said. "Listen... maybe I crossed a line, telling you to give your cash over to the club. But I didn't think you'd have a problem with it."

"I have a problem with Dirty Dave getting his hands on it," Drill said.

"Fair enough," Catfish said. "The guy's called Dirty for a reason. But if you just walk with the money, that's gonna be a problem. People are gonna think they can do whatever the hell they want. They're going to think we're broken. And that's gonna be the end of the Wraiths."

Catfish sat down, leaning back, studying Drill intently.

"Do you know why the Wraiths were as powerful as they were before, when Razor ran the place?"

"Because Razor was scary as fuck," Drill said. "He wasn't worth crossing."

"We don't have that," Catfish said somberly. "I'm president, but I need them to know that they can't cross *me*."

"And you think that if I don't give up my half of the farm, that means I'm… what? Showing that you're weak or something?"

"Not if I show that it's got my blessing," Catfish said. "But I'm not going to do that. Not unless you give me something."

Drill froze. This was his opportunity. "What do you want?"

"You know what I want," Catfish said quietly. "You need to become Vice President. Show them that we've got muscle on our side. Show them that we've still got the old guard."

Drill felt his chest compress.

Being VP. That meant he'd be bound to the club, and everything it did. He'd know about the killings, if more happened — and he got the feeling, based on Catfish's comments, that they were headed in that direction. He'd be more intricately involved in all the club's affairs. There was no way he'd be able to see his sister once he took this on: even if she somehow was willing to associate with him, knowing what he was involved in, he wouldn't want her tainted with what he would become.

And Thuy. He felt himself compress, like a ten-ton weight dropped on his chest. There was no way he could be with her. No chance in hell they would be able to be together for the long term... and for the first time, he realized, that was exactly what he wanted. He wanted the long term, with her.

He didn't want this. Goddamn it, he *didn't want this.*

"If I take the job," Drill said slowly, "then the farmhouse stuff — that's all off the table? You'll leave it alone?"

"Sure," Catfish said easily. He held his hand out.

Drill sighed, closing his eyes for a moment.

It'll keep them safe.

If he cut this deal, he might not be able to see Maddy and Thuy again, but they wouldn't have to worry about being run off of the farm. The club wouldn't have any reason to go after them. He would be miserable — but they would be free.

He reached out and shook his old friend's hand, even as it felt like his heart was breaking.

"Then I'll take the job."

CHAPTER THIRTY-SEVEN

Thuy went down to the Piggly Wiggly — a name that always made her giggle — the next day. She wasn't scheduled to work, and Kevin was taking care of the cows. She and Maddy decided to make Christmas cookies, since it was right around the corner. Maddy had turned her on to the tradition when they were in the dorms, all those years ago, and it would help keep Thuy's mind off of what Drill was up to.

Last night had shaken her severely… both the incident with the bikers, and her near-miss having sex with him. Which *he* had been the one to stop, she thought, feeling embarrassment burn through her. What was she thinking?

Her body squirmed. *You weren't thinking.*

There was going to be a next time: she was sure of it. The question was, what was she going to do?

Make cookies, that's what you're going to do. Repress. Was it healthy? Nah. But right now, she really didn't care. She'd had more changes and emotional upheaval in the past month than she had in the past ten years, and right now, she had hit her limit. So right now, she was going to shut that shit down and eat some feelings, dammit. *Procrasti-baking!*

She walked down the baking aisle, picking up parchment paper, putting a bag of sugar and a bag of flour in the small cart. She grabbed a few packages of chocolate chips as well, as well as dried and crystallized ginger. Then she headed for the dairy case. Butter. She needed a lot of butter. She might as well grab ice cream for good measure, making a mental note to hit the freezer as well.

As she was grabbing boxes of butter, a woman's voice interrupted her. "You're the girl that lives at the Blount house, aren't you?"

Thuy looked over, blinking. She didn't recognize the woman, but she supposed it was a small enough town that the lady might've been at the memorial service. Maybe the woman recognized Thuy from there? Or was it just because Thuy was a recognizable stranger? "Um, yes," Thuy said finally.

The woman was middle-aged, perhaps in her early fifties. Her skin tone was winter-pale, like copier paper. Her hair was a uniform blonde that suggested box color, and her face was fully made up and a little bit tight, though that was probably from her ponytail. She dressed in fully coordinating cotton-candy pink. Her face looked a bit foxlike, with a pointed nose and even more pointed bright gaze. Her smile was predatory, and Thuy instinctively took a step back.

"It's such a tragedy," the woman said, her drawl rich and slow. "Old Man Blount was all alone there, at the end."

Thuy wasn't sure how to answer that. "I didn't really know him," she finally said.

"But you know his daughter," the woman said leadingly. "You live with her, don't you?"

"She's my best friend," Thuy replied.

"Oh, yes, of course," the woman said, with a tone that suggested she didn't buy it for a minute. "And how long have you two been… *living together?*"

"We've been together on and off for ten years," she said, deliberately letting the woman believe whatever the hell she wanted.

The woman all but drooled at the information. "And you're going to be raising that baby of hers together?"

Thuy tilted her head, studying the woman. "I'm sorry. Remind me again: how is this your business?"

The woman jolted as if she'd been pinched. "I knew the Blount family," she finally spluttered. "I knew Old Man Blount when he was younger. And I knew his wife, Maisey."

Thuy shrugged. "So?"

"So, I know that they would both be heartbroken at how those kids of theirs turned out," the woman said, with a firm nod of her head. "First that trash, no-good thug son of theirs joining the biker gang, and then their daughter — well, I imagine Maisey's heart would just *break* at how she..."

She stopped, as if she suddenly realized what she was saying.

"What you're saying is, Maddy's mother was just as homophobic as you are?" Thuy said, with a small, razor-sharp smile. "And judgmental about what might have driven her son to those extremes? Which, I might add, you know nothing about?"

The woman focused on her defense of Drill. "That kid is a hell-raiser," she said. "Never was any good!"

"Oh, shut the fuck up, Karen," Thuy snapped.

Now the woman gasped. "How did you know my name is Karen?"

Thuy blinked. "Is it? Really?" She burst out laughing in surprise. Sometimes, the universe just handed you one. "It's a figure of... never mind. We're done talking."

Karen's face went splotchy with anger. "You don't know *anything*."

"No, Karen, *you* don't know anything," another woman chimed in. Thuy looked over to see an attractive, middle-aged black woman standing there, lips pursed in disapproval, shaking her head. "Leave this poor girl alone. You're just stirring up trouble and looking for gossip, anyway."

Karen stood up straighter. "Daisy Payton, I was just trying to have a *civil* conversation and this girl cussed at me!"

The woman, Daisy, shook her head. "Bless your heart, Karen. I know you well enough to imagine what you did to provoke it. I'm just surprised it's taken this long for someone to actually do it to your face."

Karen spluttered. "She's living in sin with that Blount girl! And has the... the *gall* to tell me that that biker brother isn't trash!"

"Throwing stones is a dangerous hobby, Karen," Daisy warned. "Especially talking trash when your own house isn't clean."

Karen glared. "I've got nothing to hide."

"Really?" Daisy leaned against her own cart, looking amused. "Where was your husband last Saturday? And — wait for it — where were *you*?"

Daisy's mouth fell open. Then her pale face quickly turned as red as Santa's suit. Without another word, she turned, abandoning her cart, and rushed away.

"Lord grant me patience," Daisy said, shaking her head. "That woman is a *trial*."

Thuy looked at her avenger, Daisy. The woman looked to be a young middle-age, with glowing dark umber skin and burgundy lipstick. Her hair was cut in a stylish bob, matching the sophistication of her business suit. "Thanks for that," Thuy said gratefully.

Daisy held out her hand, and Thuy shook it. "Don't worry. I just didn't want you to think that all of us in Green Valley are like her," she said, dismay evident in her tone. "Close-minded idiot. And like so many close-minded people, she can't seem to be close-mouthed along with it."

Thuy laughed. That was a good description.

"I'm Daisy Payton. I own Daisy's Nut House."

Thuy grinned, pleased. "You make the best doughnuts I've ever eaten in my life," she said honestly.

"Thank you! That's sweet." Daisy smiled, her eyes twinkling. "You and Maddy stop by when I'm around, and I'll buy you a coffee to go with. When's she due?"

"February-ish," Thuy said.

"We can put up a sign-up sheet at the Nut House," Daisy said. "People will make you meals, drop 'em off so you aren't staying up all night *and* trying to keep yourselves fed. We've done it for pregnant moms before."

"That's amazing," Thuy said. "Although I think we still have casseroles from the funeral in the freezer."

"It's the south, honey. We love a good casserole. And we take care of our neighbors," Daisy said, with emphasis. "You need anything, you reach out, okay?"

Thuy nodded. She bit her lip. "Can I ask you a question?"

"Sure."

"About Drill..." Thuy hesitated, then plunged forward. "That's Maddy's brother. Was he really that bad?"

Daisy looked at her with surprise. "I'll be honest — I didn't know the Blounts that well. Sometimes I think that old man had an allergy to anything that brought pleasure, so once his wife died, he stopped going to the Nut House, stopped bringing those kids. I'd heard he was hard on the kids, but it was just gossip," Daisy mused, then frowned. "And he fell in with those bikers. They're a bad crowd. So yeah, I'd say he was trouble."

Thuy nodded, feeling miserable.

"He's probably still trouble," Daisy murmured. "If you were wondering."

Thuy swallowed, then shrugged.

Daisy stared at her for a second. "You're not with Maddy, are you? Not romantically, I mean."

"No," Thuy said. "Although people shouldn't care even if I was. She's my best friend, and I'm here to help her out for as long as she needs me."

"You're good people," Daisy said. "A bit of advice?"

"Shoot."

"Don't fall for troublemakers," Daisy said, her voice tinged with sadness. "They'll break your heart every time. That's probably really personal, and I don't know you, so I don't want to get in your business. But trust me. My daughter fell in love with the wrong type, and it... it ended badly."

Daisy looked sad, and Thuy didn't want to press her further. She nodded. "Thanks again, Daisy."

With a little wave, Daisy went back to her shopping. Thuy picked up the rest of the ingredients, heading to the cashier, her enthusiasm for dessert making suddenly waning. She wasn't sure if there was enough sugar in the world to get her mind off of this.

Don't fall for troublemakers. They'll break your heart every time.

Thuy sighed. But what did you do if it was too late?

CHAPTER THIRTY-EIGHT

Drill knew he shouldn't, but he found himself gravitating back to the farmhouse. He told Catfish he needed the night off, that he'd make the vice president announcement the next day. Told Catfish it had to do with a woman. Catfish had been indulgent; after all, he'd gotten what he wanted, at least in part. Having Drill as vice prez might not be as helpful as the cash, but the important thing was, it'd keep the club together.

Drill felt the weight of a thousand bricks on his shoulders. For Catfish, keeping the club together was like keeping family together. He'd never felt betrayed by the club, never wavered in his faith. And he'd fight tooth and nail to keep the club together and protected from all comers.

There was no escape for it for Drill now, he realized. Not if he wanted to keep Maddy and Thuy safe.

He had to tell them. He wasn't going to be able to see them again, but they'd be in the clear. That was the best he could do.

He knocked, then walked in the front door and was instantly assailed by delicious smells. He sniffed deep, letting the scent envelop him. "Man, what is that?"

"Cookies," Maddy called out, leaning back with a grin and a full sheet tray of them. "Christmas cookies."

His stomach growled. "I haven't had Christmas cookies…"

Since Mom died.

He felt a little clench of grief. So much of their lives had gone sideways after the accident that had taken their mother. That's when his father had gone from strict to demanding, just as Maddy had said. It was when all warmth and comfort had left their home. It eased a knot inside him, to know that Maddy was bringing back some of that warmth and comfort.

Maddy disappeared back into the kitchen. Thuy walked out with a tray of chocolate chip cookies. "Wanna try?" she teased, a small smile playing around her lips. "It's… tasty."

His body tightened. She was teasing him. Deliberately taunting him, her eyes alight with mischief. And God, did he want to take her up on her unspoken offer.

Instead, he picked up one of the cookies, still warm from the oven. He took a bite, melting chocolate oozing, the cookie perfectly crisp on the outside but still somehow chewy. "Delicious," he purred, his eyes never leaving Thuy's.

She blushed. His smile widened.

"C'mon. We made some BLTs," she said, backing down a little.

"Good. I'm really… hungry," he teased.

She nudged him. Fortunately, Maddy hadn't watched any of this exchange. It was probably — no, definitely — stupid of him to get something started that he shouldn't finish. He didn't know when he'd be able to see either of them again, if ever. Maddy would understand, he felt sure. She'd been through this once before, when he'd left at sixteen. But Thuy… if he slept with her, and then left her...

She'd never forgive him. *Nor should she.* Because he'd be an asshole for it.

He cleared his throat, trying to get his head right. He walked to the kitchen. There was a plate full of sandwiches in the middle. He sat at one end, Maddy at the other, and Thuy sat between them.

Maddy's eyes were wary. "Did you get everything cleared up at the club?" she asked. "Are we still in trouble? Should I be expecting… I don't know. Anything?"

"No," Drill said quickly, grabbing a sandwich from the pile. "I got everything cleared up."

"How?" Thuy asked suspiciously.

Of course she'd ask. She'd know that it wouldn't be easy, better than Maddy, better than anyone.

"The new president and I go way back," he found himself hedging. "I pointed out that the old vice president wouldn't have knuckled under and given away cash he had coming to him. And I threatened to rough up one of our captains." He sighed. "Catfish knows that the more division we show, the weaker the club is. We can't afford that. It's even worse than him losing out on the money."

Maddy bought it, hook, line, and sinker. Thuy still looked unconvinced.

He should tell them now. The deal he'd cut with Catfish, the price he was paying to ensure they were safe. But he wanted to enjoy some normalcy, some comfort. Just for one more night, he told himself, as his heart ached in his chest.

This was all he was going to get.

"How was your day?" he asked instead, biting into his sandwich.

Maddy's eyes twinkled. "You should ask Thuy," she said with a grin. "She told Karen Smith to go fuck herself at the Piggly Wiggly."

He choked. When he recovered, he turned to Thuy. "You *what?*"

"I said to shut the fuck up, actually," Thuy said, a little sheepishly. "It was utterly self-indulgent, I guess… but in my defense, she was being rude as hell."

"You know that woman can be rude, Teddy," Maddy agreed, looking at Drill. "Although it's usually, you know, Southern rude. All innuendo and passive-aggression."

"Yeah, well, I'm from Oakland," Thuy muttered. "I believe in *aggressive* aggression."

"Do you miss it?" Drill asked.

Thuy looked at him, surprised. "What? Oakland?"

"You always hear all this bad stuff about it," he said. "And you had a rough childhood there."

"In part of it, yeah," Thuy said. "But I also — I mean, you realize your sister and I *lived* there? Before all this happened? And after we graduated from college?"

He shook his head.

"There are different parts of the city. It's not just one big, bad place," Thuy said thoughtfully. "Even the poorer areas have pockets of beauty and lots of cool things. I loved living there."

He heard the wistfulness in her voice. Maddy must've as well. She fidgeted with her napkin.

"I'm sorry, Thuy," Maddy said. "I know how much you've given up to be here."

Thuy looked at her friend, with a small laugh. "Not this again. Hey, did I tell you I met the woman who runs Daisy's Nut House? And that she's awesome?"

Drill let them talk, liking the easy back-and-forth of their conversation. He helped clear away the dishes, then helped himself to more cookies: chocolate chip, some truly impressive ginger snaps, even some toffee with chocolate and almonds.

Drill knew that it was getting late. He just didn't want to leave.

This could be your last time. He wanted, craved, this warmth, this sense of family. He hadn't had this sense of belonging, even in the Wraiths, since childhood. He did not want to go.

"Are you going to stay in the cabin tonight?" Maddy asked, yawning widely. "In case, you know… something happens?"

"It shouldn't," he admitted. Still — just because Catfish was on board didn't mean that Sledgehammer or someone else wouldn't do something stupid, he rationalized. "But if it'll make you feel better, I can definitely stay in the cabin one more night."

"Thanks," Maddy said. "Well, I think I'm gonna watch a DVD in my room. Or see if I can stream Netflix from my phone."

"Good luck with that," Thuy said with feeling, and Maddy laughed. Then Maddy disappeared up the stairs, leaving Thuy with Drill.

He ought to leave Thuy alone. Drill damned well *knew* he ought to leave her alone.

"Want to come to the cabin with me?" he heard himself ask instead.

Then he held his breath.

This was wrong. They didn't have a future. He'd guaranteed that. And if he slept with her, then walked away — she'd hate him. Hell, he'd hate himself.

She sidled up to him. It looked like she was thinking hard. Then she nodded, like she'd made a decision.

"Yes," she said quietly. "No matter what… yes, I want to go down to the cabin with you."

He understood what she was saying, and his heart slammed against his ribcage. He swallowed hard.

Then he took her hand, and led her out the door.

CHAPTER THIRTY-NINE

Thuy walked hand-in-hand with Drill down to the cabin. She felt hyper-aware of her senses: the smell of woodfire from a chimney, the feel of cold on her cheeks. The way the moonlight shone on the metal roof of the cabin. The strength and warmth of Drill's palm against her own. She swallowed hard. This was a big step.

She knew what it meant, to agree to come with him to the cabin. She wasn't holding off any more. She knew that what she felt about him was serious. She'd defended him at the grocery store, against that horrid woman, because her protectiveness had been triggered. That's what she did for the people she loved.

And she couldn't deny it anymore. Somehow, against all odds and better judgment, she'd fallen in love with Drill.

There was still something to his story that wasn't clicking, and she was pretty sure he was putting himself in some kind of danger to keep Maddy and herself out of it. She would have to ask him. But the fact that he would risk himself rather than let them stay in harm's way was yet another reason why she'd fallen for him. When was the last time a man had even inconvenienced himself for her, much less actually put himself in jeopardy?

She walked into the small cabin, shifting her weight as he lit the fire again. Without a word, she climbed the stairs to the loft. The loft's ceiling was slanted with the roof, but she was short enough that she didn't have to duck her head unless she went to the edges. She went straight to the bed.

She heard Drill's creaking steps behind her. He was silhouetted by the light of the stove on the lower story. She stood in the dark, her breathing shallow with need. Then she sat down on the edge of the bed, taking off her boots and socks. She was wearing a pair of jeans and a sweater, her usual clothes. She wished she'd thought to pack some sexy underwear, but they'd just have to make do.

He stared at her, just standing there at the top of the stairs. "God, you're beautiful," he said in a low, reverent breath.

She felt warm all over. No one had ever looked at her that way. Or made her feel as beautiful as he claimed. It soaked her like a hot tub, warming her and soothing her and still turning her on.

She patted the bed next to her.

He surprised her by kneeling in front of her. He was tall enough that they were nearly the same height. He leaned in, his mouth brushing against her forehead, then moving down. He kissed her eyebrows, her closed eyelids. Her nose. Then he captured her mouth, and she sighed in gratitude, opening to his searching tongue as he framed her face with his hands. She kissed him slowly, deeply, with feeling. He tasted like chocolate and toffee and something utterly masculine that was just *him*, and she clenched her hands in his shirt, tugging him closer to her.

He made a low noise of approval, tugging off his leather jacket and tossing it to the floor behind him. His hands went to her sweater, smoothing up the skin below it. He found her bra, cupping her breasts, then reaching behind and undoing the latch. She pulled away enough for him to pull the sweater off of her head, then slide the bra from her arms. Now, he leaned down, pressing hot kisses from her jaw to her neck to her clavicle — then he leaned down, taking her nipple into his hot, wet mouth.

She cried out, arching her back, pressing deeper into his greedy lips. He licked around the aureole, and she felt herself go wet in a rush. He cupped the other, circling it with his thumb as he worked her steadily with his mouth.

"Drill," she breathed, her hips squirming, her nerve endings going absolutely haywire.

He released her, blowing softly against the dampness of her skin. She wriggled. She could make out the grin on his face in the dim light.

"God *damn*, woman," he murmured, his breath hot against her skin. "You're even sexier than I imagined. And I've been fantasizing a lot."

"Me, too," she admitted. She tugged at his shirt. "Your turn."

He smirked, then pulled it over his head.

Holy. Shit.

The guy was *ripped*. Talk about arm porn. She suddenly wished she'd turned on the light. She could see his pecs, clearly defined, and a six-pack that made her want to cry. If she wasn't turned on before — and she was — she would be now. Doubly so, in fact.

She ran her fingernails down his chest, watching as he closed his eyes like a big cat, leaning against her, making the contact rougher. She wanted to feel that chest against her own, so she pressed against him, her thighs on either side of his hips.

She stroked her fingers lower. Holy God, he had that V cut that led down to what felt like a sizable hardness. Her fingertips traced his happy trail...

"Hold on a sec," he said gruffly, pulling away. She let out a whimper of disappointment. He smiled... then undid his pants.

"I can approve of this," she whispered back, and was gratified to hear him laugh.

"You're gonna need to be patient." His drawl was strong now, she noticed. She wondered if passion amplified it. If so, he was going to sound *really* Southern, if she had anything to do with it. He untied his boots, taking them off, and got rid of the jeans. "There. Poor guy was strangling in there."

She chuckled. The "poor guy" in question was tenting his boxers like a fence post. She reached for him, but only got one good stroke before he groaned and dodged.

"I don't know who you've been with," he said, "but for me, it's ladies first."

She liked the sound of that, too. So much, that she let him undo her jeans, pulling them down her legs along with her panties. She felt self-conscious for a moment, wondering if he'd be happy with what he saw.

He looked mesmerized. Then he gently nudged her back on the bed, her knees still on the edge, her legs still dangling over the side.

When he kissed her stomach, she shivered. His hands smoothed along her thighs, caressing her, bringing her flesh to life. She felt her skin prickle with awareness as his mouth moved lower, circling her belly button, moving inexorably lower. Kissing first one leg, then the other, as his fingers gently parted the curls between. Until he found the spot, the right spot, one so few men ever seemed to be able to find. He pressed gently, then more insistently, adding a swirl.

She gasped, lifting her hips to meet his pressure. Then he leaned down, taking the nub into his mouth and twirling it with his tongue.

She cried out. He sucked on it, putting her legs over his shoulders as he moved more insistently, making noises that said he was enjoying what he was doing as much as she was enjoying having it done to her. She panted, breathing short and choppy, and she clutched the quilt spasmodically as he continued working her.

She felt the clutching precursor to her orgasm and whispered "Drill!" as she came. His acknowledgment was increased pressure... and then, as it started to recede, he plunged his fingers in, moving them with slow certainty.

She almost screamed with the pleasure of it.

She was still breathing hard when he pulled the covers aside and placed her underneath them. Then he tugged off his boxers and went to his jeans, pulling out his wallet and retrieving a condom. She hadn't even thought about it, and she always thought about it. She was both embarrassed and relieved that at least one of them had remembered.

She was still wet and felt pliable, almost melting with the after-shocks of her afterglow. She slid her body next to his. He smiled at her tenderly, and she watched as he rolled the condom on.

"How do you like it?" he asked, as he fitted the latex to himself. "On top? Underneath? From behind?"

"I don't suppose you have more than one of those?" she asked.

He grinned. "I might have one more."

"On top, to start, then," she said. Being a smaller person, it was easy to feel overwhelmed and crushed by missionary. "Then… maybe, we see where it goes from there?"

He didn't answer. He simply lifted her like she weighed nothing, and then adjusted the quilt around her so she wouldn't get cold. She laughed a little. Like she could feel cold after the last two orgasms he'd given her.

He was a big guy — tall, and muscular — and his cock was proportionate. She positioned herself over him, feeling excitement start to well in her again. Slowly, she lowered herself on him, gasping softly as she felt him inexorably fill her. It felt so good. So *damned* good.

"Oh my God, Thuy," he groaned, when she finally had him fully seated inside her. "Christ, you feel good."

She couldn't answer, because she was too busy feeling the same way. She lifted herself, then lowered. She felt him flex inside her, and moaned in response.

He lifted himself to a sitting position, and it amazed her. He wrapped her legs around his waist. It drove him deeper inside her, and she shifted, gyrating her hips as she repositioned. The consequent brush against a spot inside her had her shuddering from the sheer pleasure it presented. She experimented, shifting more.

The motions must've been driving him crazy, too. He held her hips, pulling her taut against him, swirling her around him. He leaned down, taking her breast into his mouth. The jolt from that, combined with the rush from where they were joined below, drove her crazy. She started pumping against him, holding him tight with her thighs. His cock swelled inside her, stroking her… slamming into her with intent, until she could only hold on, clawing at him, begging him for more. Their mouths fused. She bounced against him, their stomachs sliding against each other, his cock huge and insistent.

The orgasm blindsided her. She cried out, screaming his name, clenching against him so hard she thought she'd blackout. She could feel him grow, then shudder inside her, as he pulled her taut against his hips. They sat like that for a second, clutching each other like they never wanted to let go.

Reluctantly, she got off of him. He went and took care of the condom. When he climbed back up the stairs, gloriously naked, she felt sleepy and sated. And deeply, crazily, stupidly in love.

"What should we do with that other condom?" she asked, with a small grin.

He laughed. "Ask me again in twenty minutes," he said gruffly, then climbed into bed, spooning against her. His skin was hot against hers, and she shimmied back, feeling enveloped by his warmth.

She didn't mean to fall asleep. She meant to ask him about what had really happened with the Wraiths. She knew they ought to discuss how he was planning on getting out. And even if she was a little hesitant, she needed to tell him how she felt — and ask what they might want to do about it, if he felt the same.

Then she could ask about — and then demonstrate — how they could use that second condom.

But instead, she fell asleep. And to her dismay, she woke up in the cold cabin, completely alone.

CHAPTER FORTY

Drill got up early the next day. He had wanted to kiss Thuy very badly — kiss her awake, so they could use the last condom — but he knew that if she woke, and they'd made love, he wouldn't want to leave. And he had to leave.

Today was his first day as vice president of the Wraiths. He had shit he'd need to do. He'd have to explain to her why he'd taken the job — and why he'd left — some other time. Right now, he was holding the memory of her warmth, her passion, like it was the last good memory he was going to have for a while.

Probably because it was.

He rode down country roads to the outskirts of town. Catfish rented a house out there, by the woods. He used to live in an apartment like Drill did, and he could've lived closer to the Dragon, but he took advantage of the larger president's cut of their takes, and got himself a nice place with "some privacy." Some of the members joked it was so Catfish could drag bodies out to the woods and bury them if he needed to. Catfish didn't do anything to dissuade people of this notion, so their laughter afterward was usually a little nervous.

Since Drill had helped him move his crappy ass furniture to the place, he knew exactly where Catfish lived. And since Catfish didn't get his ass out of bed before nine at the earliest — usually because the Wraiths ran their business late — he knew that he'd catch Catfish without worrying about dealing with any of the other Wraiths.

He knocked on the door. "C'mon, Catfish, open up. I know you're home."

He waited, frowning, then knocked again. He heard movement. Then the door opened. Catfish was there, in sweatpants, holding a gun.

"*Jesus*!" Drill held up his hands reflexively.

"Oh, it's you." Catfish rolled his eyes. "What the hell are you doing here this early?"

"Needed to talk to you," he said. "I should've said something yesterday, but I was pissed… and Dave was there, and the other guys. I didn't want them overhearing."

Catfish looked irritated. He shot a glance back at his bedroom door, which was closed. Drill realized immediately that he might've been interrupting something.

Too bad. He'd forgone morning sex. Catfish could give him a few minutes.

Sighing, Catfish stepped aside, letting Drill walk in. The house was nice, all things considered. It was neat as a pin; Catfish hated mess. He often got on new prospects for being "fucking slobs" at the Dragon, but with a group of guys, there was only so far you could get with that.

"So, talk," Catfish said. "But don't get comfortable. You're not staying long."

"Wasn't planning to," Drill said, as Catfish put the gun away in a drawer. "It's about the farm."

"What about it? Change your mind about investing in the club, or you keeping it all to yourself?" Catfish shook his head. "Selfish bastard," he said, but he sounded half-joking.

Drill felt his stomach fall. "I'm not… I told you, I wasn't giving my half of the sale to the club," Drill said. "That didn't mean I was taking it."

Catfish's grin fell. "What are you talking about?"

"I'm letting Maddy keep the farm."

"Tell me you're shitting me right now." Catfish's voice was stern.

"That's why I came over here," Drill said. "It occurred to me that some of the members of the club might not understand. I need to guarantee their safety."

"Are you *shitting* me right now?" Catfish yelled. "Listen, if you sold the house, and kept the money, some of the guys might mumble, but frankly, most of them would do the same damned thing. But leaving it to your *sister*?" A vein bulged in Catfish's forehead. "You *don't have family other than the Wraiths,* God damn it!" he roared. "We're your brothers! Does that mean *nothing* to you?"

"Of course, it means something!" Drill yelled back. "But that doesn't mean I'm going to threaten my goddamned pregnant little sister and force her off her land! You knew her, remember? When we were younger? Doesn't that mean anything to *you*?"

"Other people stopped meaning a goddamned thing to me when I got old enough to see how shitty the world was gonna treat me," Catfish said, his eyes blazing with recrimination. "When I joined the Wraiths, *they became my world.*" He paused a beat, looking at Drill with undisguised disgust. "I thought you felt the same."

"I did," Drill said. "Then Lube died. Remember that?"

Catfish grimaced.

"That was fucked up. And we let it happen. And kept letting shit happen. Kept giving Razor a pass," Drill pressed.

"We did what we had to do," Catfish said. "What we were ordered to do. What was *needed*."

"Lube wasn't the only one. He was just the first one I really let sink in," Drill said. "And then there was that shit with the other clubs. Razor's scheme. Darrell going state's."

"You think I don't *know* that?" Catfish snapped. "Why the fuck do you think I've been putting in all this work? I've been trying to fix things!"

"You sent Burro and Nick to go through my goddamned phone, Catfish."

Catfish didn't look sorry. "I had to know I could trust you." For a second, he looked rebellious — but also very, very alone.

"I'll help you," Drill said, even though the words cost him. "But I'm not going to do it at the expense of Maddy, or her kid. That's fucked up. Even for us."

Catfish's eyes narrowed. "Sledgehammer said something to me," Catfish said slowly. "About the other one. The Asian chick."

Drill felt his nerves prickle. "What about her?"

"He said you were real possessive." Catfish glared at him. "Tell me: you banging her? Is that what this is all about?"

Drill thought about lying, but Catfish would put it together. The man was wickedly smart, which is how he'd wound up on top. "My relationship with her has nothing to do with this," Drill said, through gritted teeth.

Catfish goggled. "Your *relationship* with her?" he repeated. "Christ. This gets better and better." The words were sour. He shook his head.

"I need to make sure they stay safe," Drill continued.

"You want to keep them safe?" Catfish said. "Then you make goddamned sure they have no connection to you, understand? You spread the word that your sister bought you out, with plenty of cash, even if it's a lie, so the guys think you got something out of the deal. You ignore her if you see her on the street. And you don't dip your dick in that Asian chick again. You do, and the whole crew is going to know that you went soft." Catfish rubbed at his temples. "And that's gonna fuck us both."

Drill felt cold seep through him, right into his bones. He knew, logically, that this was the only possible outcome.

"No attempts on them, for anything," Drill said. "I'll steer clear, I'll spread the lie. But you have to help me make sure that Sledgehammer doesn't try anything stupid. Or Timothy fucking King," he growled. "You know how he is with women."

"If I give them any protection, it's just painting a target on them," Catfish said, his tone gentling a little. "You know that. I'll keep 'em busy, but you've *got* to stay away from them."

Drill swallowed. "All right."

Catfish looked back at the bedroom door. "Believe it or not... I feel for you. And I'm sorry." He sighed. "Can't always have what we want, man."

Drill nodded, then headed for the door.

"We're introducing you as vice prez tonight," Catfish called after him. "Official meeting, all the members. Don't be late."

Drill nodded. He'd figure out some way to tell Thuy, and Maddy.

And then, he told himself, he'd walk away.

CHAPTER FORTY-ONE

Thuy went in to the library, still feeling confused about Drill's disappearing act.

It wasn't like they had a relationship, for God's sake, she scolded herself. He hadn't made her any promises. For all she knew, he'd gotten what he wanted, and she'd had a hell of a ride, herself.

She would be disappointed if that was the case, but she really hadn't pegged Drill for a nail-and-bail.

And what are you going to do about it? He has his own life. And he's still a part of the damned Wraiths, for all you know. What, exactly, is going on there, anyway?

After an hour of nice and mindless shelving, her mind still roiled over thoughts of Drill, their night together — what was going to happen to all of them moving forward. She needed to talk to him. She *would* talk to him, she decided. Preferably face to face.

"Um, Thuy?" Naomi Winters said, interrupting her thoughts. She looked puzzled. "Could you come to the back office?"

"Sure." Thuy put the book she was shelving away, straightening the row reflexively. Then she followed Naomi.

When she got to the office, there were three large boxes. Julianne was staring at them. "Do you know what these are?" she said, her words crisp.

"They're addressed to the library, care of you," Naomi added.

"They're... oh!" Thuy felt her heart lighten a little. "They must be the YA books!"

"What YA books?" Naomi asked.

"You placed an order?" Julianne said, sounding aghast. "You don't have authority for that!"

"No, no," Thuy said quickly. She picked up a pair of scissors and held them open, cutting the tape. She opened the box. Sure enough, there was a wide selection of YA novels inside. She laughed with happiness, the first good thing to happen that morning. "See? They're donations!"

"For us?" Julianne looked at the box like it held snakes. "From whom?"

"I put out a request on my social media accounts," Thuy said, all but petting the glossy covers. She pulled out some titles. Fantasy, sci-fi, adventure, romance, issue books. This was a nice little cross-section. She couldn't wait to see what was in the others. "I saw another rural library do the same thing, although that was school related. But our YA selection was sort of anemic, I thought we could use a boost. Oh!"

She opened the second box. This one held a wide variety of comic books, graphic novels, and manga. She suppressed a squeal. "Ginny's going to love this," she predicted. "Oh, there's that middle-grade series that..."

"These are misprints," Julianne said. "They're backward. And they're *comic books*."

"That's manga. Japanese comic books. Although they're in English, of course," Thuy enthused. "The kids love 'em."

"We do *not* carry comic books."

Thuy stopped in the process of opening the third box. "Sorry?"

"You should have asked me first," Julianne said sharply. She looked overwhelmed. "These... this... you should have asked!"

"But they're donations," Thuy said. "Most of them from the

authors themselves." She glanced at the first box. "There are bestsellers here, and some award winners. Diverse representation. The graphic novels, too..."

Julianne just looked overwhelmed and upset. "I put in orders for what I feel is appropriate," she said. "Now there are these... these *books* that I have not vetted, including comic books which we simply do *not* carry, and... and... three whole boxes! Where would we put them all? Thank God it wasn't more!"

Thuy winced.

Julianne must've caught the small expression, because her eyes widened behind her glasses. "Are there... you don't mean you're expecting *more?*"

"Let me check something." Thuy pulled out her phone, opening her Twitter account. She saw that she had more than her usual number of mentions, and quickly opened it up.

It's so great that you're doing this! Sending books tomorrow!

Do you have a wishlist?

I'll be sending a selection!

Sent! Sent! Sent!

Thuy gulped, putting her phone away. "There are going to be more," she said slowly. "I'm not sure how many but... I think... maybe a lot?"

Julianne looked gobsmacked.

Naomi opened the third box as they talked. "Oh! I meant to read this one. The Brooklyn Brujas series, right? It looked good. And *The Hate U Give!*" She was all but clapping her hands over it. "We've had requests!"

Now Julianne was staring at Naomi, who didn't seem to notice.

"We barely have enough room as is," Julianne finally said, as if this were the deciding factor. "Where will we put a lot of new ones?"

Naomi paged through *Labyrinth Lost*. Thuy bit her lip, unsure, but then ventured forward. "There are some books that are old in the children's section. I mean, the binding's falling apart," she said, in case Julianne was afraid she was simply targeting classics because of their age. "If we've got these books coming in for free, it makes more sense than paying to try and repair old or damaged books."

Julianne tapped her chin. She was thinking about it, at least.

"And," Thuy said, feeling braver, "we can always put more shelves where the card catalogs are. We don't actually need them, since the system is computerized."

Now Julianne's back went straight as a yardstick. "Those card catalogs have been with the library since its inception," she said. "They were built by some of the town's founding fathers. Did you know that? By Green Valley's own carpenters!"

Uh-oh. Touchy subject. "I'm sure we can still find someplace," Thuy said, backing off a little.

But Julianne was triggered. She crossed her arms. "I really wish you had discussed this with me first," she said. "I know you're from a big city, and you're used to doing things a different way. Maybe you feel like we're quaint, or backward, or that you can just march in and make all the changes you want..."

"But I didn't!" Thuy protested. "I just asked some friends for some books. I thought it would help the teens. That's all!"

"I'm afraid," Julianne cleared her throat, then surveyed Thuy over the lenses of her glasses, "that I'm not sure you're a good fit here."

Thuy froze.

Are you freaking kidding me?

Taking a moment and a deep breath, Thuy waited until she was under control again before asking her next question. "Are you firing me, Julianne?"

Naomi snapped out of her reading. "Wait. What?"

"I am not firing you." The "yet" was heavily implied. "But you know you're here in a probationary capacity. I'm simply saying I'm not sure how well you mesh with our existing library organization."

Thuy felt tears stinging at her eyes. First Drill's rejection this morning. Now, this.

"We have traditions here. We've tried to keep up with the times, but not at the expense of our heritage. I firmly believe in the good of our institution," Julianne said, and it was all Thuy could do not to simply start shouting. Which would do no one any good. "If I don't feel that you can uphold our traditions, then I can't in good conscience keep you on. We'll see how it goes, but..."

"I see." Thuy nodded, then turned and went to the restroom. She splashed cold water on her face.

It should've been a good day. Making love with Drill last night; the books coming in. Instead, she'd been shut down harshly, *twice*.

She wondered painfully if there was any way it could get worse.

CHAPTER FORTY-TWO

"All right. Shut up, everybody! Shut up!" Burro stood in front of the crowd at the Dragon. Everybody there either wore a Wraith's patch, or was a recruit. Catfish stood in front as well, at the bar. His clothes were clean and... not exactly stylish, but definitely crisp, a far cry from some of the more ragged and scrappy clothes the other bikers wore. Catfish looked sharp, always. Now that he was president, he used that to stand out, to show that he wasn't fucking around.

He certainly wasn't fucking around now.

"You guys elected me as your president," Catfish said, his voice carrying over the now-quiet group of bikers. "It's been a tough year for all of us. I know we haven't been bringing in the hauls that we used to, but that's changing soon. We're going to be getting new suppliers, and setting up new runs. We're collecting on more loans, and making more. Gambling's gonna get expanded."

There was a ragged cheer at this, and some laughter. Catfish's cool stare silenced them.

"But I'm gonna need you guys to pull your weight," he said, his voice firm and edged with authority. "You don't, you're out. And trust me, that's not an option you want."

They nodded. This was talk they were familiar with.

"Ever since the shit that went down," Catfish said, obliquely referencing Razor and Darrell, "we've been running low on leaders, fighting amongst ourselves. That. Stops. *Now.*"

More nods. Drill could feel the confidence flowing off of Catfish, and the membership was responding. It was why Catfish was a good choice for president.

"I've chosen Drill to be our vice president," Catfish said. "Timothy King's our new enforcer. Dirty Dave is still gonna be our treasurer. Burro and Sledgehammer, you two are new captains. We'll be cycling in some new recruits to full-fledged members in the next few months, if you prove yourselves," he added, looking at a few youngsters who were nudging each other and grinning. "In the meantime, we're running at a full slate and we're going to make the Wraiths better than they were before. Got me?"

There was a ragged cheer. Catfish nodded, his smile small and satisfied.

"Good." He gestured to Dirty Dave to follow him, and he retreated to the back office.

Drill went to follow him, but immediately felt a hand on his shoulder. He turned to see Sledgehammer standing there, with a smug expression.

"See that?" he said. "I'm a captain now. So, you can't fuck with me."

"Now why would I want to do that?" Drill said, remembering his conversation that morning with Catfish.

"Because… you told me…" Sledgehammer looked confused. "The girl, remember? The Chinese chick?"

Drill fought not to roll his eyes. *Vietnamese chick, you idiot.* "Yeah, I remember. And I know that Catfish said I could be the one to warn her. Not you."

Sledgehammer frowned. "But… wait. I thought he told *me* to do it."

"They're staying in my old farmhouse. I talked to Catfish and he agreed if anybody's gonna get the point across to them, it's me." At least, that was the story he'd decided to roll with. It was that, or kill Sledge, because the guy was too dense to get anything else.

Sledgehammer looked like he was working it over in his mind. His eyes narrowed. "That doesn't…"

"Look, who's got seniority here? You're a captain. Big fucking deal," Drill said, with a sneer. "I'm VP, asshole. So if I want something — or *someone*," he ground out, "I get it. Got it?"

Sledgehammer looked like something finally clicked. "Oh, so *you* wanted to play with her, huh?" he said, with a raucous laugh. "Can't blame you. Would've gotten a piece of that myself, if I had the chance."

Now Drill felt perfectly fine with killing the son of a bitch. He forced himself not to go with the impulse.

He looked over to see Timothy King and his pack of jackals, crowded around a table. They were drinking. Tim was preening. He motioned to Drill to come over.

Drill ignored him. This meeting was painful enough as it was. The last thing he needed was Timothy fucking King, acting like Drill needed to hop when he said jump.

It took several minutes, but unfortunately, Tim made his way to where Drill was standing. "So you're vice president," Tim said. "Congratulations."

He said it in a term reserved for "screw you." Drill took it as such, but still nodded, saluting with his beer bottle.

"Now that I'm enforcer," Tim continued, looking self-important, "I'm going to be keeping a close eye out. Since we lost Razor, and even Repo, the reputation of the Wraiths has gone to shit. Too many restrictions gone loose, too many guys thinking they can do whatever the hell they want."

"You do that," Drill said, drinking some more of his beer. Man, this guy was annoying.

Tim waited until Drill was looking at him again before speaking. "Just so you know," he said slowly. "I'm not going to let *anybody* get away with *anything*. Catfish wants a tight fucking ship, and that's what I'm gonna deliver."

"Good for you." But Drill heard the implied threat in Tim's words. What, exactly, did the little shit think he had on Drill?

And what was he planning on doing in retaliation?

Drill deliberately turned his back on Tim, cutting the conversation short. He could all but feel the younger man's irritation and insult, and sensed when he walked away.

"Another beer," Drill said to the bartender.

He needed to warn the girls — maybe get them to talk to the police, just in case. Then, as long as he could keep Sledgehammer in line and Tim off his back, they should stay safe.

He just needed to stay away from them, he reminded himself.

Especially Thuy.

He closed his eyes.

Especially Thuy. For once in his life, he had to make the right decision.

CHAPTER FORTY-THREE

Thuy drove home that night, feeling like the day had lasted a week. She couldn't wait to get back to the farmhouse, devour her body weight's worth of Christmas cookies, and talk to Maddy about all the crappy things that had happened that day. Maybe not about Drill — or at least, not specifically. Maddy already knew something was afoot when Thuy had shame-walked from the cabin to the farmhouse that morning, but she'd simply smiled and offered to make coffee. Thuy wouldn't share the dirty details, since after all, she'd slept with Maddy's brother. But at least she knew Maddy wouldn't judge her. If anything, Maddy would probably want to kick Drill's ass for his disappearing act that morning.

More pressing, Thuy wanted to talk to her about possibly losing the library job. They needed an additional source of income, and Thuy had wanted to be employed full-time by the time the baby arrived. Now, she wasn't even looking at part-time, if Julianne's outburst of shock and temper were any indication. At least that's what it felt like.

Should've looked at that stocking job at the Piggly Wiggly. Maybe it wasn't too late. She'd check the job listings again on her phone.

When she pulled in, her headlights reflected off an unfamiliar vehicle. This time, it was a white four-door, a Kia or something. Thuy wasn't good with cars.

"Oh, what fresh hell is this?" Thuy muttered, grabbing her bear spray. Were bikers driving midsized sedans now?

She rushed into the house. "Maddy? Maddy, where are you!"

She stopped in her tracks.

Maddy was on the couch, her lips locked with…

"*David?*" Thuy yelped. "What are *you* doing here?"

They jumped apart like shrapnel. Maddy's hair was mussed, and she was out of breath. The guy she'd been so avidly making out with had cocoa brown hair in need of a haircut, tanned skin, and rumpled clothes. Other than looking tired, happy, and maybe a bit determined, he looked just like he did the last time Thuy saw him.

"Thuy," Maddy said, wiping her mouth, her cheeks turning red. "Um… I wasn't expecting you home so soon."

"Apparently not," Thuy said, feeling floored. She turned to David. "Dude. I thought you were in Australia, studying… I don't know, special Australian farming or kangaroo ranching or something."

While your girlfriend was over here pregnant with your child, asshole.

"I was," he said. "But I was miserable. I have been since I left Maddy."

"And yet, you still left," Thuy muttered. "Four frickin' months ago…"

"It's my fault. Not that he left," Maddy quickly added. "But that he came back. I, um, have been emailing him. Every day, just about, since we got here."

"You have?" Thuy stared at her. "When?"

"When you were at work, or at night. Sometimes a couple of times a day," Maddy admitted. "I just… I missed him. And after I blew up at him the first time, we finally started communicating. I think we worked through some important things."

"I finally listened," David emphasized. "And, hopefully, stopped being such an asshole."

Thuy tucked the bear spray back in her purse, then crossed her arms. "So what are you doing back?"

"I dropped out of the program I was in, in Melbourne," he said. "I'm going to be with Maddy now. I'm going to take care of her." He smiled slowly. "She's agreed to marry me."

"*What?*" Thuy felt like someone had knocked the wind out of her. She glanced at Maddy. "Seriously?"

Maddy nodded. "I never stopped loving him," she said softly.

Thuy looked back and forth between them. Then her eyes narrowed. "Funny you're agreeing to marry her now," she said slowly. "When she's suddenly inherited a farm, and all."

"Thuy!" Maddy snapped, sounding scandalized.

David held up a hand. "It's all right. I earned that," he said, and he sounded sad. He turned to Maddy. "She's right to be suspicious, and she's only looking out for you."

Then he turned back to Thuy. "If anything, I have to thank you. I owe you for taking care of Maddy while I still had my head up my ass."

Thuy felt anger and frustration bubble through her. Why today? Of all days?

"I'm buying half the farm," David added. "I want Maddy to know I'm all in. I'm just as invested as she is — I'm dumping in all my savings, and even my parents are kicking in some. We'll be in this together."

Thuy goggled at him. This was definitely unexpected. And, she hated to admit, encouraging.

Maybe he *had* gotten his head out of his ass.

"Let me talk to her," Maddy said to David.

He nodded, leaning down and kissing Maddy on the cheek. "I'm gonna go unpack upstairs," he said. Thuy noticed the roller bag she'd somehow missed by the front door. He lugged it up the stairway.

Thuy sat by Maddy, quiet. "Are you sure?" she finally asked. "I'll back your play — you know that. But are you *sure?*"

Maddy sighed. "It's hard to trust. And part of me is still angry, and we're going to have to work through that," she said. "But we've been talking for the past month. We still love each other. He's going to learn to be more flexible. So am I," she added. "And we're going to be parents. This baby will know his father."

Thuy sighed. "If he leaves again, I get to kill him."

"If he leaves again," Maddy said, "you can help me hide the body."

They laughed, but it was tinged with tears. Maddy hugged her tight. "He said he's going to spend his life making it up to me," she said. "I don't know if that's just the reconciliation talking, but he sounded like he meant it."

"They always sound like they mean it," Thuy said, thinking of Drill.

Maddy must've picked up on the vibe. "There's something I want to tell you," she said. "Even though David is here, and he's staying, nothing has changed for me. I will always, *always* want you close by." She took a deep breath. "But I know it's selfish. I've said it before: I don't expect or want you to give up your job and your whole life, just for me."

Thuy blinked. "You're kicking me out?"

"No! No," Maddy said quickly. "Are you kidding? You've been my lifeline. You're like my sister. I would never kick you out!"

"Then… what?" Thuy felt lost.

A tear tracked down Maddy's cheek. "I just… I know this isn't necessarily a life you ever would've chosen for yourself. I know that you stayed because you felt like you owed me — which totally isn't true, how many times do I have to tell that? — and if it weren't for me, and the baby, you'd probably still be in the Bay Area. Enjoying high-speed Wi-Fi and A's games," she added, with a laugh.

Thuy felt her throat choke with tears, and quickly swallowed them away. "I don't know what to say," she said.

Or how to feel.

"You are always gonna be a part of my life," Maddy said seriously, with a firm nod. "You can't get rid of me. We're friends *for life*. Savvy?"

Thuy nodded, and Maddy crushed her in another hug.

"I'm just saying, don't sacrifice your life for me," Maddy said. "You can visit whenever you want. You can stay whenever you want. My home will *always* be your home, whenever you need or want one." She paused. "But think carefully about what *you* want."

Thuy nodded. "I'll, um, stay in the cabin tonight," she said softly. "Give you two time to, uh, get reacquainted. Loudly, if you want."

Maddy blushed, then laughed. "I have to say, I'm glad you volunteered. I might've suggested it myself otherwise."

"You're *sure?*" Thuy asked again.

"I love him," Maddy said simply. "When you're in love..." She let the sentence peter off, shrugging helplessly.

Thuy sighed.

I know those feels.

"I'll just, um, grab some cookies and head out, then," Thuy said, with one more hug. Then she grabbed a Tupperware full of a selection of sweets and tromped down to the cabin.

When she shut the door behind her, she held it together long enough to fire up the woodstove and munch a few cookies, barely tasting them. Then she climbed up to the cold bed, took off her clothes, got under the covers, and cried herself to sleep.

CHAPTER FORTY-FOUR

Drill drove up to the farmhouse. It was midnight. He'd left the Dragon Bar, slipping out as people got drunker and the party celebrating the "promotions" got progressively wilder. He knew he shouldn't, but he couldn't leave things with Thuy the way they were. He could text her, or call her. He tried to argue with himself that he didn't want Catfish to find anything on his phone, but he could always delete the messages.

The thing was, Thuy deserved more than a text saying he couldn't see her again. She deserved better than that. Hell, she deserved better than *him*.

He shut off his engine and walked his bike up the driveway in the dark, not wanting to wake up Maddy. He owed her an explanation, as well, but she'd understand. He'd already walked away from family once before. He'd send her a letter, explaining everything.

But he wanted to see Thuy. He wanted to *feel* her — even if it was only a hug, or one kiss. And even if it was the last time.

He frowned as he noticed a Kia, parked by the house. He wondered absently if Maddy had traded in the Continental or the truck for it – it'd definitely be easier for someone as small as Thuy to drive. He was about to knock on the door when he saw there was smoke coming out of the stovepipe on the cabin. He frowned, wondering if Thuy was waiting for him there. The steps to the loft were steep; he couldn't imagine Maddy risking it.

His body tensed. He parked his bike and went to the door, unlocking it. Only Thuy would lock doors out here, he thought with a grin. Good thing he kept the key.

When he walked in, the fire had burned down, but still crackled a bit. She'd been feeding it. The lights were out. He walked to the steps, wincing as the creaked.

"Drill?" she asked, in a harsh whisper.

"It's me," he whispered back. He moved quietly over to the bed. She was swaddled up in the blankets.

"What happened to you this morning?"

He sighed. "I had to deal with Catfish. I was pretty sure we were in the clear, but after last night, I wanted guarantees that you'd be safe."

She was quiet for a second. "Next time, wake me up and tell me, okay? I felt terrible when I woke up and you weren't there."

He felt his chest clench. Next time. God, what he wouldn't give for a "next time."

She sensed his sadness, and sat up, reaching her arms for him. "Come here."

He hesitated. "Thuy," he said, and his voice was hoarse with regret. "I… we have to talk."

She stiffened. "It's going to be a bad talk, isn't it?" Her voice was small.

"Yeah." He rubbed his face with his hand. "It is."

She took that quietly. "I want you to hold me first."

His body tightened and he was reaching for her before he knew it. He had to force himself to stop before he finally touched her. "Thuy, I don't… this is a bad idea."

"I think I know what you're going to say," she replied, her voice low and even. "But I have had a shitty day. And I'm pretty sure I'm going to lose you. But you're here tonight, and so am I." She paused. "Can you give me one more night, Drill?"

He groaned. He already knew he couldn't, wouldn't, say no to her.

She pulled back the covers, revealing she wasn't wearing anything. Her tight little body was inviting, and she presented herself like a gift. The most precious gift anyone had ever offered him.

"Come here," she murmured, her eyes filled with both passion and pain. "Just come to me."

He was moving, stripping down before his rational mind could catch up. He reached for her. Just enveloping her, smelling the scent of her warm skin as his body smoothed along hers, was the ultimate sense of comfort. It was a relief that he hadn't felt ever. He'd heard church types talk about a "balm for the soul" and he'd thought it was bullshit.

Until her.

He nuzzled her neck, breathing deeply. Then he nipped at her, little love-bites. He felt her pebbled nipples dragging against his torso. He notched himself between her thighs, then cursed himself, getting up. "Condom," he muttered.

She kept her legs parted, smiling.

He got himself covered, then moved back, wondering absently what it'd be like to be inside her bare. But even though he knew he was clean — he was damned careful, and had tests to prove it — he couldn't ask her to trust him like that. Not when he was leaving.

When he put himself back in position, she wrapped her legs around his, arching up to reach his lips. "Is this okay?" he asked, keeping himself propped up on his arms so he wasn't crushing her.

"Yes," she breathed. She rubbed her hips up, stroking his cock along her seam. He could feel the hard knot of her clit against the underside of his shaft, and he shuddered slightly, almost dizzy with the sensation of it. She made a sexy little whimper of need. "Inside me. I want you inside me," she all but chanted.

He inched lower, reaching down, stroking his cock head against her opening. She gasped, panting softly, her legs tightening around him as if she were trying to force him inside her.

"You're so damned wet," he said, as his cock slicked inside her with no resistance. "It feels so good."

She made mewling little sounds, and in the dim light from the lower level, he could see her eyes were shut, her mouth working in a small "o" of pleasure. He pressed hot kisses across her chest, up her throat. He slid in all the way, seating himself deep, then pulled out almost all the way. The stroking sensation was driving him haywire.

It seemed to be doing the same thing to her. She circled her hips, her inner muscles clenching at him. "Drill," she rasped, her hips juddering slightly.

He kept up the slow, relentless rhythm, driving and retreating like ocean waves. He wished it would last longer. *I need more time with her,* he thought, as his body kept pace, joining with her tenderly yet with relentless persistence. *Forever might be enough.*

The ache of loss was brutal, and the only thing that was keeping him from driving mindlessly inside her, losing himself to the pleasure of her body.

"Drill," she cried, her body moving faster, her hips shifting and moving, drawing him deeper. Their bodies pistoned together. His movements turned jerky as he felt his orgasm start to hover, unstoppable.

"Come for me, baby," he pleaded. Then he drove into her, a firm thrust right where her G-spot ought to be.

She let out a yell of pleasure, and he felt her muscles clench around him like a fist as her whole body shuddered. She clawed his shoulders. *"Oh, God, yes!"*

Her body, her words, her damned *sexiness* slammed him into his own orgasm, and he came hard, harder than he could ever remember doing, his vision going black and his ears ringing. His hips jerked forward and he emptied himself into the condom with each thrust.

"Thuy," he hissed, resting his head against her shoulder. He felt her little butterfly kisses, light as whispers, against his neck.

The sense of sorrow was overwhelming.

He pulled out, taking care of the condom in the small trash basket. Then he turned to her.

She was sitting up now, holding a pillow to her, covering her nakedness. Her hair was mussed, her eyes large and dark and troubled. She looked vulnerable — and expectant.

"So," she said, in a tiny but unwavering voice. "I guess you'd better tell me now."

CHAPTER FORTY-FIVE

Thuy braced herself, pulling up the covers over her rapidly cooling skin and clutching the pillow to her like a shield.

This is going to be bad.

She knew from the moment Drill came in that he was stopping whatever was going on between them. It was all over but the shouting — and the details.

Maybe it was masochism. But after her shitty day, she had to know why he was breaking things off.

He took a deep breath, getting under the covers next to her, propping his head up on one muscular arm, his bright blue eyes intent. "You know I talked to Catfish," he said slowly. "I told him you and Maddy were staying on the farm. He thought I was just selling it and keeping the cash. If it looks like I'm letting my sister — who I shouldn't even be calling my sister, you know? — stay in the farmhouse… if it looks like I'm walking away from a small fortune, just so she can be comfortable… especially now that Sledgehammer knows I'm interested in you…" He let out a rough breath. "I'm trying to squash some of the rumors. Tried to make Sledgehammer believe that I just wanted to bully you myself, and that he'd invaded my turf."

She shuddered, thinking of the large, ugly man.

"But I don't know if he'll believe it." Drill sounded worried. "And the rest of the crew needs to be convinced that Maddy paid me off, somehow."

"That shouldn't be too hard, actually," Thuy finally commented. "David came back, and he's buying half the farm."

"Who's David?"

"Her boyfriend. Father of the baby?"

Drill's expression darkened. "He's showing up *now?*"

"And he seems to have gotten his act together," Thuy said, surprised that she was defending the guy. "Anyway, people will see that your sister has her man back, and he comes from money, so at least that should take some pressure off."

She felt a tiny sliver of hope: *does that mean we can still see each other?* Even if it meant sneaking around…

"It'll help," he admitted. "But right now, the leadership of the Wraiths is still shaky. There were too many power struggles. If I show the smallest weakness, somebody's gonna go after it."

He reached out, stroking her cheek.

"You're my weakness," he said, his voice cracking slightly. "I can't have anybody hurt you, Thuy. I just can't."

She felt tears form in the corners of her eyes, and wiped them haphazardly with the back of her hand. "Damn it. *Damn it.* There's no other way? No way to get out of the Wraiths?" She paused. "Is that even something you want?"

"It's definitely something I thought about," he said. "I considered talking to somebody… I mean, I don't want to go state's or anything, like Darrell Winston did. But I know a lot of shit about the club. I've been around a long time. I know where the bodies are buried." He swallowed. "Literally."

She shuddered.

"But a lot of what I know tracks back to Darrell and Razor, not the guys coming up now," he said, with a frown. "And besides, if I tell them that the evidence will be released if anything happens to me, or you guys, I don't know if that will stop them. These guys respond to power. I think they'll see it as cowardly — and push back for it."

Thuy closed her eyes. He was right. She remembered what her father was like, what his crew was like. They didn't respond well to threats like that, either. Because the shit they did was worse than going to prison.

"I don't know what else to do," he said. He sounded as miserable as she felt. "I… I can't see you, not after tonight. I shouldn't have come even now, but I didn't want to leave you hanging. I couldn't just walk away like that."

On one hand, she was glad. She knew it was going to come to this when she'd seen his hangdog expression walking in. She'd slept with him again, with a clear understanding that he was going to walk away.

On the other hand, she was now dealing with the slashing pain… and the aftermath.

"They're probably going to fire me from the library," she said softly.

He looked surprised. "What? Why? You're awesome," he said staunchly.

She hiccupped, a soft, watery little laugh. "How would you even know?"

"You got me reading," he said simply. "I'm getting pretty far in that book you recommended. Even stayed up too late reading it."

She laughed. "That's maybe the best compliment anyone's ever given me," she said. "But I guess they don't see it that way at the Green Valley library. I'm only there in a probation period, and if I don't fit in, they're canning me. And they're kind of pissed at me," she added. "I think I'm going to be fired, maybe before the holidays."

He made a sound of disapproval. "Fuck them."

She smiled. He was supportive. A lot of her ex-boyfriends — who she now realized were tools — would've asked "well, how might you have contributed to the situation?" or brushed off her concerns, or shrugged and said "it is what it is." Drill's superpower was loyalty. It was unfortunately what drew him to the Wraiths, but his unwavering support was something she'd miss.

"And now David's back," she continued. "He's an actual farmer, or wants to be one. That's what he's studied. He's strong, he's the baby's father, and he's devoted to Maddy. Maddy doesn't really need me anymore, either."

She looked at him. *And now you.* He seemed to follow her hint, nodding sadly.

"I'm just wondering," she said slowly, "if there's any reason for me to stay here, in Green Valley. If I don't have a job, I feel like I won't have anything to offer Maddy. I'll just be sponging off of her and David. I quit my old job, but I might be able to get another one on campus, or at a corporate library. I still have the apartment. I could just go back to my old life in Oakland."

She stared at Drill, imploring.

"Or… I could stay," she said softly. "If there's any sort of chance."

With you.

He closed his eyes for a moment, his expression filled with longing. She almost reached for him, wanting to hold him tight. Hold him always.

Then he opened his eyes, which were filled with regret and loss.

"Maybe," he said, "going back would be best."

And just like that, her heart broke as she watched him put on his clothes mechanically, send her one last longing look, and walk away, closing the door softly behind him.

CHAPTER FORTY-SIX

Drill had spent the better part of the weekend sullenly drunk, passing out at the Dragon. He didn't initially mean to. He just wanted to drown his sorrows. People kept buying him drinks, thinking he was celebrating his promotion to Vice President. They didn't realize they were buying a dead man drinks at his own wake. He could see the rest of his life stretching out like this, surrounded by "family" that didn't really give a damn about him or each other. Guys like Timothy King, and Burro, and Sledgehammer. Guys he didn't come up with. Some of the kids showed some promise. He wished he could send them away.

I hate this. I hate this.

Catfish seemed proud, as close to happy as he could get any more, between the strain and struggle of keeping it all together, and the paranoia that it might all be taken away. "I told you it'd work out," Catfish had said, clapping his hand on Drill's shoulder. And it seemed to be, for Catfish.

Now, it was Tuesday night. Christmas Eve. At least, it would be for people who celebrated it. He'd heard that there would be drinking at the Dragon, but that was typical for any Tuesday. A few guys had old ladies and little kids, and they might be excused to get presents and shit, but it was more likely they'd stick with the club. Sometimes the strippers wore Santa hats, he remembered.

He stayed home.

He knew Catfish would be pissed, but he couldn't spend one more night there. Especially not when he pictured Maddy and her boyfriend, and maybe even Thuy, around a fireplace. Unwrapping presents, or drinking cocoa, or eating cookies.

He hadn't realized he missed that. It had been years since he'd really enjoyed the holidays — not since his mother had died. His father hadn't tried to make them particularly festive, it only seemed to remind him of the loss of his wife. He'd known his father loved their mother, incredibly so, and had never gotten over being without her.

Now, for the first time, Drill had an inkling of what that felt like.

I wonder if Thuy's left yet.

Missing her was like a physical pain in his chest. When drinking didn't work, he'd done the only other thing he could think of, to both distract himself and feel the tiniest bit closer to her.

He read.

The book was getting good — he was over halfway — when there was a knock on his door. He frowned, then his heart jolted.

Maybe it's Thuy.

He didn't think about the fact that she didn't know where he lived. He just got up and opened the door.

Instead, it was the kid, Nick, who stood there with a vape pen. As ever, he looked twitchy. "Why aren't you at the bar?" he asked. Whined, really.

"Didn't feel like it." Drill leveled a sharp look. "I also didn't realize I needed to report to *you*, Nick."

Nick cowered a little. "Timothy needs you there."

Drill scoffed. "Don't report to him either."

"They're calling a meeting," Nick said, holding up his hands. "Catfish, I mean. Tim said that there's gonna be, like, a trial."

Drill rubbed his hands over his face. "It's Christmas fucking Eve, Nick. What the hell is he going on about? A trial? For who, for what?"

"I don't know," Nick said, sounding peeved. "He just wanted me to round up all the captains and members and stuff. He didn't say anything else."

Knowing Tim, the asshole wanted to put on a big show of his authority, as quickly as possible, to get people to fear him. Drill wanted to tell him to fuck himself, but he knew that Catfish would want him to be part of the business. Also, as vice president, he'd be able to keep Tim in check better than anyone.

"Fine," Drill said, grabbing his jacket.

"Hey," Nick said, noticing the paperback copy on the table. "You still reading that book?"

"Yeah."

"So, what happens to that Kvothe guy?" Nick looked like he was trying hard *not* to seem too interested... and failing miserably.

Drill reluctantly smiled. "I'll tell you when all this shit is over, okay?"

He just hoped Tim's power play didn't take too long. *And this is your future,* he told himself.

Maybe he *would* drink again tonight.

CHAPTER FORTY-SEVEN

It was Tuesday night, what normally would've been teen night, but it was also Christmas Eve. The library had canceled teen night because it was closing early, six o'clock rather than the usual nine o'clock. They'd had a little holiday party for the kids that weekend. Thuy wished that they'd stay open the full shift, though. She wanted to see the kids.

She wanted to say goodbye.

After her talk with Drill, and Maddy, and her interaction with Mrs. MacIntyre, she just didn't see the point in staying. What she was doing was making *no* difference. She was about to get fired. Her best friend didn't need her. And the man she'd fallen in love with was barred from seeing her. There really wasn't any point left in staying.

"Ms. Thuy!"

She looked up from the circulation desk to see Ginny and Jeremy. She smiled. She would miss them. At least she'd get to say goodbye. "Hey, guys," she said easily. "Where's Kevin?"

"Don't know. He got held up." Ginny's eyes gleamed. "Merry Christmas!"

She held out a little decorated gift box.

"Oh!" Thuy was surprised. "You didn't have to get me anything."

"You fixed the computer that had been broken all the time," Jeremy said. "And you're cool. You're easy to talk to."

"Yeah," Ginny agreed. "And it's nothing special. I mean, it's just a little thing. To kind of say 'thanks' and all."

They watched her eagerly. Embarrassed, she opened the box. It had a few little knick-knacks, a painted rock with googly eyes on it that said "LIBRARIANS ROCK", some wrapped chocolates, and…

She pulled out a little piece of cardboard. "Is this… did you make me my own playing card?"

"Yep." Jeremy straightened out, blushing a little, but obviously proud. "You introduced us to *Magic: The Gathering,* so we thought we'd make you your own!"

"See?" Ginny pointed to the stats. "I did the artwork, and Jeremy came up with the description."

Thuy studied the painted card.

MS. THUY, it said. Ginny had done a very good drawing of her, smiling, looking like she was juggling books with magical powers.

Creature: Librarian

Mana color: Blue (Knowledge)

Powers: Seeking and Matching (because she always helps us find the perfect books!)

Thuy felt her eyes prick with tears. "This is so awesome," she said, swallowing hard. "Seriously. I've never gotten anything so cool."

The kids looked pleased. "Got any plans for Christmas?"

Thuy shook her head. "Just, um, hanging with my roomie and her boyfriend. Fiancé," she quickly corrected.

Ginny's eyes widened. "Father of the baby?" she blurted out, then her cheeks turned red. "Sorry! Sorry. That was rude."

"No, it's fine," Thuy said, clearing her throat. "I, um, I'm not sure how much longer I'll be staying around, actually."

"What? Why?" Jeremy quickly protested.

Thuy felt misery bubble up from her chest. "It's complicated," she said.

"I wish you'd stay," Ginny said quietly. "You really listen to us. You've made teen night fun, and you help during study hours."

"You got me started on Python coding," Jeremy added. "And Kevin really liked the book you recommended."

"All the kids like the books you recommend," Ginny said. "Do you have to go?"

Thuy sighed. "I... It might be for the best."

Ginny looked frustrated. "Now the library's going to go back to the frickin' stone age."

"Ginny!" Jeremy chastised, looking at Thuy. *Like I've never heard "fricking" before,* Thuy thought with a smile.

"No, Jeremy. They didn't like us hanging out here. They treat the middle-graders like babies, and they never got the good books for us," Ginny said sharply. "It just feels like they're missing out, and they don't even *care*."

Jeremy shook his head. "It is what it is," he said, sounding older and more cynical than his years.

"Excuse me?"

She looked up. "Yes?"

It was Jim Thompson, the man she'd run into the very first day she'd stepped into the library. The one she'd helped on the computer. "Miss... Thuy, is it?"

She nodded, pleased that he'd gotten her name right. Seems like she was starting to be recognized by some of the regulars, at least.

Too bad she wouldn't be around to enjoy it.

He held out his hand. "I just wanted to thank you."

"Thank me?" she said, automatically shaking his hand. "For what?"

"I got the job." He stood straighter, his eyes alight with gratitude. "After filling in that stupid... sorry, the long form on that computer, they called me and I finally got the job. And I would've given up, if it weren't for you."

Thuy swallowed hard. "You're very welcome."

"I might need to look up a few things. They said they'd send me the employee manual over email. Is that something I can print out here?"

"Absolutely," she assured him.

"Oh, good." He looked relieved. "Thanks, again, Miss Thuy."

She nodded as he walked away.

Libraries were so much more than just a building full of books. Especially in a small town like this, where the broadband was limited and people didn't have the electronic access that was so often taken for granted in cities. These were good kids. Good *people*. They just needed some resources, and some guidance. And somebody that was willing to help them get and use the stuff that was out there. Someone who was willing to set up programs, and advocate for them. There was a lot that could be done.

Thuy straightened her shoulders. She hadn't gotten fired, not yet, but Julianne had been watching her like a vulture, waiting for a corpse to die. And worse, *Thuy had rolled over*. She'd been cautious, she'd kept her mouth shut.

Well, if she was going to get fired, she might as well get fired on Christmas Eve. Because she wasn't going to just sit there like a lump anymore. This library could be doing a hell of a lot more, and if they wanted to ignore the needs of their people out of the excuse they were "upholding tradition" and harkening back to a better time... nope. Thuy was going to say her piece. Respectfully, but clearly. And loudly.

She stepped into the back office. Sabrina Owens was quietly loading books on a cart.

"Can you watch the desk, Sabrina?" Thuy asked. "I need to talk to Julianne."

Sabrina nodded. She was painfully shy, and didn't talk much, but she was good at her job. She moved to cover circulation.

Thuy walked to Julianne's office, rapping sharply on the door. Julianne looked up from her paperwork.

"I was just going to go home," Julianne said. "My grandkids are coming over tomorrow, and we've got finishing touches to do for their gifts. Is this important?"

"Yes. I'll try not to take up too much of your time," Thuy said, then stopped hedging. "But if I'm going to get fired, I want to talk now."

Julianne's eyes widened. "Fired?"

"Or quit," Thuy said.

The surprise was evident. Julianne sighed, then gestured to the chair opposite her desk.

"Well then," she said. "I guess you'd better have a seat."

CHAPTER FORTY-EIGHT

Drill arrived at the bar, and it was crowded. When he walked in, the mood was far from festive. Guys were giving him looks that were either skeptical or disappointed.

What the *hell* was going on?

He followed Nick, walking past people, headed for the back office. Timothy King stopped him with a hand on his chest. "That's far enough."

"Fuck off," Drill said tiredly. "Where's Catfish?"

Catfish appeared by his side. "I told you," he muttered, barely over a whisper. It was ignored by the rest of the group, who were muttering between themselves. "I fucking *told* you."

"As enforcer," Tim said, with puffed-up self-importance, "it's my job to make sure that the club's rules and laws are being followed. Drill, it's been brought to my attention that you're turning your back on your brotherhood, and I'm here to shut that down."

Drill's eyes narrowed. "So it's me, huh?"

Of course. The little shit wanted the VP position so badly. Actually, he wanted *president*, but right now, Catfish was bulletproof. If Tim could get one step closer to Catfish's job, he'd take it — and wait until he could make his move for the top spot.

"Is it true that you hit one of your brothers when he was carrying out an assignment given to him by the president of this club?" Tim sounded like he was trying to be on *Law & Order*. He sounded like an idiot.

"You mean, did I hit Sledgehammer? Yeah." Drill shrugged. "Fuck. Sledgehammer hit Burro last Saturday night, I don't see you dragging his ass up here."

"He was cheating at poker!" Sledgehammer yelped. Burro grumbled, raising a fist.

"Sledge was *on assignment*," Timothy pointed out, undeterred. "You threatened him. And you told Nick to ignore a direct command from Catfish."

There was mumbling. Drill felt sweat trickle down his back. *Shit.*

Catfish was right. This was a problem.

He had to distract them from Maddy and Thuy, *now*. "Catfish and I discussed it," he said. "And I was made V.P. after it, so it isn't that big a deal."

"So, who's prez now, him or you?" Tim said.

"He is," Drill said quickly. He wasn't jumping on that landmine. But he looked over to see Catfish grimace.

Shit, shit, shit. Now Tim was setting it up as a challenge to Catfish's authority. Which meant Catfish had to let this play out, no matter what happened to Drill.

"What, exactly, is your problem?" Drill said, getting in Tim's face.

Tim shoved him back a step. "My *problem*," Tim said, his eyes bulging slightly, "is that you seem to be losing faith and losing focus. We're your *brothers*. You don't have any family but us. But instead, you let your *sister*," and he practically spat the word out, "keep that family farm of yours. When we all know damned well you should be getting cash for that shit."

"You've gone soft!" somebody — Burro? — yelled out.

Drill felt adrenaline start to flood his system. He needed to get a grip on this situation, and fast. "She's paying me. Buying me out," he said. "Her husband's back in the picture, and he's got cash. The fuck do I want with a farm? And selling it and shit, that takes time. This is easier."

"So when do we see the money?" Dirty Dave said, all but drooling.

"Who says you see any of it?" Drill shot back. "What the *hell* is this? And don't tell me any of you would just hand over a bunch of cash if you fell into it."

"Yeah we would," Tim lied. "Because we're *brothers*."

"Bullshit," Drill said.

"Maybe it's not about your sister at all," Tim said, after a beat. "Maybe it's that little piece of ass that's staying with her. Sledge said that you claimed her."

Oh, hell. And there it was.

"She's going to be leaving town. At least, that's what I hear," Drill said, with what he hoped was a shrug. "I hit that shit, but I didn't want her to stay."

Liar.

"But you punched a club member over her," Tim pointed out.

"She was mine. I wasn't interested in sharing."

"Don't want to share your cash. Don't want to share your woman. Seems like you're getting really selfish, *brother*," Tim mocked.

"Seems like wanting to show off how important you are has blown up your head, *brother*," Drill said. "Throw a fucking clip-on tie on you, and you'd be a full-on mall cop."

Tim turned an ugly red, especially when some of the members started laughing.

"So you're telling me that you don't give a shit about either your sister or the Asian chick?"

Drill shrugged. "Not remotely." His voice was steady and cold.

Tim's smile was slow and vicious.

"Then you won't mind if we burn that farmhouse down."

"What?"

"You don't need it," Tim said. "You said so."

He was bluffing. Wasn't he? Drill looked at Catfish, who shrugged as though it was out of his hands.

"But… the money," Drill said, hoping to throw them off. "How the fuck am I supposed to get the money if you burn the house down? They'll just move away, and we won't be able to sell it for anything!"

"You shouldn't be keeping stuff from the club," Tim said piously. "And if the guy's as rich as you say he is, maybe we can shake him down and get the cash another way. I'm sure holding onto his wife until we get the cash is good enough, don't you think?" He paused. "Or do you *care* about her? Huh?"

"What the fuck is wrong with you?" Drill shouted. "You're willing to kidnap a pregnant woman now? On Christmas fucking Eve? *What is wrong with you?*"

"You!" Tim shouted back. "Standing in the way. Acting like you're better than the rest of us, just because you've been here so long. Well, you've gone *soft*. If the Wraiths are going to get back on top, then we have to be *tougher*. Like Razor was." His smile had a tinge of crazy, one that unfortunately Drill found familiar.

Look who wants to be the next Razor. He'd seen it coming. Catfish was going to have his hands full.

"So, we're going to the farmhouse. Now. And we're gonna have a little bonfire," Tim said.

Drill looked at Catfish.

Catfish sighed. Then he nodded. "Okay," he said. "Let's go."

"Catfish!" Drill yelled over the commotion of people heading for the door. "*Curtis.* Fuck, man. I helped you become president. And you're going to do me like this? You're gonna let this happen?"

"I tried to fucking warn you," Catfish said, in a low voice. "You put me in a bad spot. And he's right: we need to be tougher. If we aren't… we're going to get taken over." He looked pained, and angered. "I'm *not* gonna lose the Wraiths, man. You can be on board… or you'll be an example."

"It's like that?"

Catfish nodded. "It's like that."

Drill clenched his teeth. "Fine."

Then he turned, and punched Tim in the throat.

It was chaos from there. Drill punched harder, striking out, but too many of the others surrounded him, grabbing his arms. He caught hits to his stomach, his ribs. He struggled, kicking and biting, lashing out.

Then somebody hit him hard with something heavy, right at the back of his head, and everything went black.

CHAPTER FORTY-NINE

Thuy sat in the chair opposite Julianne. She noticed the books that were shelved throughout Julianne's office— a leather-bound set of Encyclopedia Britannica, brown bindings with blue bands and gold lettering. There were framed photos of the library throughout the years. Obviously, there was a lot of history here.

"I didn't realize I needed to discuss asking for donations with you," Thuy said. "I see that I should have asked for your input. But since they were donations, similar to drives I've contributed to over the years, it genuinely didn't occur to me that it would be a problem."

Julianne nodded. "I can see you were trying to be helpful. But you see, you haven't been here that long. You don't know what the needs of the community are, and you... well, you don't know how we do things here." She steepled her fingertips together, looking at Thuy through her glasses with a thoughtful expression. "Naomi has been here for years. She's taken Sabrina under her wing. They've grown up in this town, and they know the patrons. They know what books circulate and what books don't. We have lots of elderly readers, people who grew up with Rex Stout and the Perry Mason mysteries. We have children who love story hour. We have poetry readers. We have our craft night on Tuesday. I know that you're just trying to be helpful, but... well. We're not a café. We're not some hip spot for people to 'hang out'. We offer treasured reads, and valuable services, and I take what we do very seriously."

"I take what we do very seriously, as well," Thuy countered. "And I may not be from this town, but I think you're doing them a disservice by only catering to what you think they want, and what they've always had."

Julianne's eyes went wide. "Excuse me?"

"It's not just the kids," Thuy said. "Although they're a good start. You've got a whole, well, crop of teenagers in this town. A lot of them will be working farms, but a lot more of them will be going into cities for work. Shouldn't they learn more about the world outside? Diverse reads would help with that, and there are so many that are coming out now. It would also help with the kids who are already here, ones who aren't seeing themselves represented in books that are on the shelves. Aren't they patrons, too?"

"Of course they are," Julianne said, looking troubled.

"And I know you don't want people getting 'caught' in the internet, but the fact is, the internet is a big part of people's lives. Even in a small town like this," Thuy said. "People pay bills online. They find jobs online, like Jim Thompson. They do research and get their news and entertainment online, when they can. For people who live out on the farms, the ones who have slow internet service, coming in to stream shows or Youtube is a big deal."

"So you'd have them come to the library to watch T.V." Julianne sneered. "Surrounded by books, you'd have them..."

"It's not just shows and movies," Thuy said. "Although what if it was? Is watching a movie on Netflix, if they have an account, worse than reading a novel? We loan DVDs, after all."

"We're a *library*," Julianne said sharply. "Do you want people to stop reading? Is that why you think comic books are a good idea, for goodness sake?"

"Comic books are an art form!" Thuy felt her head throb a little. She'd seen old school librarians like this before. "Graphic novels are addressing more and more complex topics, and they can be diverse.

They're also very attractive for kids who might not otherwise be drawn to reading!"

Julianne looked unconvinced.

"Or take eBooks…"

"It's not the same thing as real books," Julianne quickly interrupted. "People here like the *feel* of a real book. The smell of it. That's the kind of tradition I'm talking about."

"Oh? And how much of your budget is dedicated to large print?" Thuy countered. "You've got an elderly population whose eyesight is deteriorating. With eBooks, they can adjust font size automatically. And if they have internet, even slow connection, they don't have to come in to check out or return books. They can do it in the comfort of their own homes, even on sleepless nights, without worrying about transportation or library hours."

Julianne fidgeted with a pen. "They like coming here," she said, her chin raising a bit. But she looked away for a second, uncertain.

"And nobody's stopping them," Thuy pressed. She felt like a Pentecostal minister at this point, all but singing her case. "It's about *choices*. It's about giving more resources and more information and more options. I know that your budget's tight. It's a war for funding, especially in rural public libraries. I studied it, and I've seen it," she said. Then she swallowed. "When I was a kid, I lived in a… well, let's say it wasn't an affluent neighborhood."

She thought about the tagging, the needles, and used condoms and empty beer cans that littered the sidewalks and bushes. "Not affluent" was the understatement of the year.

"There was a library in walking distance in one of the places we lived. It was my sanctuary," Thuy said quietly. "From the time I learned to read, the library was the place I could escape. I felt Sarah Crewe's nobility in *The Little Princess*, as well as admiring Tasha Tudor's gorgeous illustrations. I rode dragons in Anne McCaffrey's books. I went to the restaurant at the end of the universe with Douglas Adams. I read romances and mysteries and thrillers." She swallowed for a second, feeling emotions welling up inside. "When we moved, I found the nearest library, even though it was two bus transfers away. I went there, and I found non-fiction: cookbooks and how to knit and how to stay healthy, even when we didn't have health insurance. Most importantly, librarians helped me figure out how to prepare for the SATs, get into college, and get my life back."

Julianne had fallen silent. Thuy regretted sharing so much, but she'd gone this far. She had to continue.

"I know you feel like I'm just this young nobody, tromping into your nice library, thinking she knows better than the people who have been here for years," Thuy said sincerely. "I promise, I wasn't trying to. I'm just reaching out to *my* resources, to help with *yours*. To help the teens. And, if I stayed, I would've helped the elderly population, as well."

"How?"

Thuy thought about it. "It would depend on funding," she said. "And what you were willing to do. But I'd volunteer time, or work it into a shift, to help teach computer stuff. Like using Office, or Photoshop. I'd look at our intra-library lending options. Do you have a collective, between the other rural libraries, or maybe the larger libraries in cities like Knoxville or Nashville?"

Julianne shook her head. "There hasn't been much need," she said, but looked troubled. "Or interest."

"That might be because people aren't aware they can ask for books from other places," Thuy said. "That would open up so many more resources, for everyone involved. And I'd look at fundraisers. There are a lot of books in the collection that could use updating. We could donate older books to assisted living facilities, places that would love more books to read."

Julianne was quiet for a long moment. "You've given this a lot of thought."

"I love libraries," Thuy said. "I respect your position here, and I know how hard you all work. I would've liked to have worked on it, too, because I like the people here, and I think there's a lot I could contribute."

"I haven't fired you."

"Yet." Thuy grimaced. "But you might be right. The things I'm suggesting, my mindset — it clashes with what you're used to, and I'm sorry for that. But also not sorry. I stand up for what I believe in."

"I see that." Julianne's mouth curved into a small smile. "You know, I make some people nervous."

Thuy thought about her family. Her past. "It takes a lot to make me nervous."

"Did you say you were going to quit?" Julianne said. "Or are you just considering that course of action?"

"I may be leaving town, after all," Thuy said. "For a number of reasons."

"I'll give what we've talked about a lot of thought over the holiday," Julianne said. "And I'll give you our decision about your employment when you come back next week. Is that all right?"

Thuy shrugged. "I'll know by then if I'm going to leave, anyway."

"It was good talking with you."

Thuy felt lighter, grateful that she'd cleared the air and spoken her mind. She held out her hand, and Julianne shook it.

"You're a good librarian," Julianne said, with a firm nod.

Thuy nodded. "So are you."

The older woman grinned. Thuy walked out the door, headed back to the farmhouse, feeling a little better than she had. Even if she was leaving, at least she'd made a difference — and an impression.

CHAPTER FIFTY

Drill came to in the back of a truck bed, sore as hell. It took him a minute to realize where they'd gone. They'd taken him to the farmhouse.

They're going to burn the place down.

He realized he'd been bound and gagged. Struggling, he sat up, looking over the side of the bed.

There were a lot of bikers that had traveled from the bar out to the remote location. It must've sounded like Sturgis, with all these motorcycles. Obviously, a few people had brought trucks, since he'd been dragged out in one of them.

They were making him an example. They were "teaching him a lesson."

In that moment, he could've killed them all.

Timothy King stood on the porch. "Anybody there? Come out, come out!"

Drill let out a low growl of menace.

Tim knocked on the door. "I see lights on. Anybody home?"

Drill could only think of Maddy, probably terrified, unable to move quickly, worried about the child inside her. Even with the shotgun, she was horribly outnumbered. He prayed that she got out when the trouble began.

But what if she didn't?

"We cut the phone lines, darlin'," Tim yelled, winking at the bikers around him. Some of them laughed, rubbing their hands together against the cold. "I know reception out here sucks. And it'll be a while before the police could get here anyway, so — I hate to say it, but unless you want to go up like a tinderbox, you probably want to get that fat ass of yours out here."

The laughter around them grew a little more nervous, and Drill saw several of the bikers warily exchange glances. *We're not really gonna burn up a pregnant woman in her own house, are we?*

But peer pressure was at the wheel tonight, as was stupidity. And Catfish, God damn it, was doing nothing to pull the brakes on this thing.

"Start pulling out rags, boys," Tim ordered. Then he looked at Catfish. "I mean… that's the order, right? We're burning the joint down?"

Catfish shrugged. "We're all alibied up: we were all at the Dragon last night," he said. "And yeah, Drill needs to be taught a lesson. Nobody's bigger than the club. We're about the Wraiths," he yelled. "We protect the club *at all costs.*"

There was a cheer from the members. Then several guys went to one of the trucks, pulling out gas cans and rags and bottles. They were going to stuff rags under the eaves, he realized. Maybe throw a few Molotov cocktails, just to give the guys a fun, interactive experience.

Please, Maddy, he prayed. *Please, please, don't be in there.*

He struggled to break his bonds, but his feet and hands were tied tight, practically cutting off circulation. He shifted on his back. He couldn't yell, couldn't do much of anything.

From that position, he could see the barn. He squinted. Was that… movement?

It was. He saw a head peer out, then disappear into the darkness. A man. One who nodded at him.

He assumed it was Maddy's boyfriend. At least, he hoped it was. If the guy was up there, then he probably had Maddy hidden. Now, he just hoped that the idiots would stop with the farmhouse, and not burn all the outbuildings.

Wait. Where's Thuy?

He squirmed again, raising himself, looking desperately for the Chevy.

"So you're awake." Burro's gap-toothed smile was wide and cruel. "Look! Drill decided to show up for the party after all!"

"Bring him here, then," Tim said from in front of the house.

A few of the members dragged Drill out of the truck bed, letting him drop from the tailgate to the ground. He groaned as the pain resonated from the fall. Then they dragged him to a standing position, his feet trailing behind as they got him to the front. "On your feet!" Burro said, kicking at him.

Drill stood as best he could. He glared at Tim.

"Ah, don't be like that," Tim said insolently. "It's not my fault you're in this mess. You got sloppy. I cut my family off. I know where my loyalty lies. So does every other man here."

"Or he will," Catfish said meaningfully, his solemn gaze sweeping the crowd. The men nodded, some looking nervous.

"Apparently you need a bigger reminder, so we're just going to burn your family's house. Your sister'll go away, and that'll be that." Tim smiled viciously. "And you have the honor of torching the place yourself. To show that you finally understand the lesson. Got it?"

Drill felt himself sag. He nodded.

"Good boy," Tim said, patting him on the head like a dog. *Like a goddamned dog.* "Cut his hands free."

Drill waited until Burro's knife cut through the bungee cord that had him bound. He waited until Burro had his knife put away, and that the man was heading for the truck to get a tiki torch.

He waited just long enough. Then he lunged for Tim.

Tim was ready for him, but he still wasn't quick enough — or big enough. Drill heard the satisfying crunch of Tim's nose breaking. Drill hit him again and again, kneeling over him, until various members dragged him off.

"My *nose!*" Tim sounded like a squealing pig. "He broke my goddamned nose!"

Drill drove his head into another guy's face, kicked out with both his legs. He was damned sure going to take out as many guys as he could this time. He noticed that not everybody was as enthused to get into the mix with the club's muscle, even if his feet were still bound.

"Take him *down*," Catfish ordered.

Drill put up his fists, but he was vastly outnumbered. They might kill him now, he realized. Catfish might have had enough of his rebellion. At this rate, he couldn't be trusted; he would never be a trusted Wraith.

He was a liability.

"Should we kill him?" Tim said, pinching his nose. "We should kill him! That fucker broke my nose!"

Shit.

"Not here," Catfish said firmly. "But he'll be dealt with."

Like that, his friend Curtis vanished, and Catfish, president of the Wraiths, was fully realized. He'd sacrificed his soul to keep his perceived "family" together — a family that no longer included Drill.

"Come on, then," Drill said, his hands up. "Come get some."

And they descended on him like locusts, a cloud of fists, boots, and mayhem.

CHAPTER FIFTY-ONE

Thuy knew immediately that something was wrong. As she drove closer to the farmhouse, she could hear the commotion. She saw a crowd of people in the headlights of the truck, and immediately killed the beams before they noticed she wasn't one of them.

This wasn't a party. This was a riot. What the hell was happening?

It was the Wraiths. It had to be.

Was Maddy all right? Thuy's heart pounded. Where was David? And where the hell was Drill?

Fear pulsed through her veins. She pulled out her phone before anyone noticed she'd pulled up.

No bars. *Damn it!* Her mind raced.

Should she pull away? Drive to where there might be phone reception? Go back downtown and find the police station? She didn't even know what was happening, and if anything was wrong with Maddy, it could take over an hour to get anyone out there, between her hunting for the cops and actually getting them out to the farm.

She needed to see what they were doing here. But if she walked out there, she'd get surrounded — and taken. Then she'd be no use to anyone, especially if Maddy was in trouble.

"Yeah! Kick his ass!" She heard a man's voice yell out. "Fuckin' Drill! Thinks he's too good for us! Fuckin' pussy!"

Her chest clenched, and she felt her breathing speed up.

They were beating up Drill.

Her heart was racing. She looked around. There were lights on in the house, and it looked like guys were stuffing rags up under some of the shingles of the house, up in the eaves, under the porch.

They were trying to burn the house down.

By the time she left and got help, they'd have burned it all to the ground. And Drill might be dead.

Oh God. Oh God. Oh God.

They had Drill, were beating him. They might have Maddy. They were going to burn down the farm. She couldn't call the police, didn't have a weapon. She was one woman in a truck.

No. Fuck that. Think, dammit.

She wasn't just one woman in a truck. She was born to one of the most dangerous men in the country, and she'd seen shit that most people couldn't even imagine in their worst nightmares. She'd survived worse things than a bunch of drunk, stupid bikers in a small town. She wasn't going to let them tear down her friend's dreams and hurt or possibly kill the people she loved.

Fuck. That.

She blinked.

Her father. Her past.

For once in her whole godforsaken life, it might actually work to her advantage.

Fury and purpose driving her, she felt the yelling of the crowd seem to diminish, time slowing to a crawl. She felt cold, a numbness that had nothing to do with the bite in the air. She squirmed out of the truck's window, climbing onto the roof of the cab. It put her up high, out of reach of the sprawling gang below.

They finally noticed her. "Hey, look what we've got here! The other chick!"

The truck got swarmed.

They were catcalling her, baiting her. She reached in her bag, gripped the bear spray. It wouldn't be enough to fend off all the men surrounding the vehicle, but it would buy her time if she needed it.

I won't need it, she thought, with icy calm.

"Come on, cutie," the guy who had accosted her outside the library said, his leering grin wide. "Come see your boyfriend!"

She looked over to see Drill on the ground. He was squirming slightly, obviously in a great deal of pain.

A lot of the bikes and several other trucks had their lights on, illuminating the scene. The bikers started shaking the truck, pushing on the frame, causing her to fall to one knee to keep her balance. She glared at them.

"Who's your leader?" she shouted. "Who's in fucking charge here?"

They laughed at her. "It sure as hell isn't you!" someone yelled.

She'd have to take her chances, then. She took off her coat, and they started cheering.

"Strip! Strip! Strip!"

She pulled up her sweater, and turned slightly.

"Who here recognizes this?" she shouted. "Come on, you can't all be this fucking stupid. *Who knows this mark?"*

Someone was climbing up in the truck bed, getting ready to grab her. She pulled out the bear spray, but kept the sweater up.

"Tell me somebody fucking recognizes this!" she shouted. "What kind of club are you? Seriously, are you just a bunch of redneck hicks or what? *Nobody recognizes this symbol?"*

There was a guy with a gap in his teeth whose eyes narrowed as he got a good look. "What the... holy shit!" he squeaked. The other guys were still jeering at her, but that guy started backing away, his hands up. "I never touched you. I never fucking touched you!" he said quickly. "I had *nothin'* to do with this!"

Thuy's smile felt feral. *Finally.* After all these years, and all that trauma, her childhood was finally going to do something good in her life.

"What are you talking about?" Sledgehammer asked the guy, who was wide-eyed with fear.

"That's a brand. Fucking Red Dagger. Don't you know anything?"

There was a murmur that ran through the crowd, electrifying it. "Red Dagger?" A few more men backed off.

They'd heard of it, all right.

"A brand?" Sledgehammer repeated, sounding unsure.

"That's how you know it's not fake. It's not like a damned tattoo. That gets *done* to you, man. Red-hot iron shit." The gap-toothed man shook his head. "Okay, party's over. If Red Dagger's into this, I am out of it. This ain't worth it."

A man with dark brown skin and surprisingly light eyes stepped through the crowd, followed closely by a blond man who held a rag to his nose. Blood had seeped through it. Obviously, he had broken it. The black man's jacket had the patch: CATFISH.

This was the guy Drill was talking about. The man in charge.

"You're with Red Dagger?" he asked. His voice was one of quiet authority, a deep baritone. He looked calm, while the blond guy looked irritated.

"So fucking what?" the blond said, although his voice was muffled and sounded like he had a bad cold. "We'll take her out with Drill..."

Catfish turned and hit the blond guy right in the stomach. He fell to his knees, coughing.

"Thought you were a librarian," Catfish said, hazel eyes narrowed as he turned back to Thuy. "Did Drill know you're with that crew?"

She nodded. "I'm just out here trying to live my life, but my dad's the leader, and my brother's one of their best. I make a call, and they're out here." She paused a beat. "I go missing, and they're *definitely* out here. Pissed. And looking for payback."

Catfish swore under his breath.

"These people — Maddy, Drill — they're under my protection. The Red Dagger's protection," she said, making sure her voice carried. "You really, *really* don't want to fuck with me."

"Who is the Red Dagger?" Sledgehammer asked, looking both confused and frustrated.

"Support club," Catfish said, shaking his head. "They make the Black Pistons look like saints, though. Anybody who follows the national scene knows about them, although last I heard, they were headed toward Detroit." He narrowed his eyes. "They headed for the south, librarian lady? Maybe Tennessee?"

"Not to my knowledge," she said, her voice sounding level and unaffected. She sincerely doubted it — her father hated the humidity. Of course, they didn't know that, or need to know it.

"So why are you here? Hiding out?"

She shrugged. "My father didn't have anything for me to do."

"Yeah, right," the blond said, with a nervous guffaw. "Short little thing like you? What're you gonna do, stab my ankles?"

"My father is Long Nguyen," she said sharply. "He's about five foot two. And I have watched him kill people in ways that would make you shit your pants."

Silence fell over the crowd. The blond stared at her. "Are you kidding me?"

"*Shut up.*" Catfish's irritation was clear. "Don't you know anything? A support club like Red Dagger moves in, and shit goes down. All local clubs, all territories, get threatened. Or wiped out. Didn't you hear about Tempe, and the Bronze Skulls?"

Finally, it got through. Blond guy's eyes went wide. "That was them?"

She nodded.

Catfish sighed. "We didn't know," he said, with the smoothness of a politician. His eyes glittered in the light of dozens of high beams. "We'll leave the farm alone, and your people."

"But Drill!" the blond protested.

"... is under protection." Catfish raised his voice. "Drill is cut out of the brotherhood. He's no longer a Wraith. Nobody here touches him — nobody harms him. But nobody helps him, either. You do either one of those things, you'll find out what happens to traitors."

"He needs to be banished," the blond whined. "If you're out of the club, you're off our turf!"

Catfish looked at her.

"My. Protection." Her voice brooked no argument.

Catfish sighed. "He's cut out. It'll have to do. We don't need the shit."

The group that had been so drunkenly enthusiastic now looked chastened.

"Come on. We're riding out." Catfish turned to Thuy, nodding his head as if he were tipping a hat. "We won't be seeing you."

"Be sure of it," she replied. She nodded back.

The blond looked irate, but also scared. He followed.

Thuy stayed on top of the cab, riding an adrenaline wave, watching the parade of motorcycles and trucks roll down the dusty driveway. When the last light had disappeared onto the main road, she carefully climbed down, her muscles shivering violently as the rush left her system and relief flooded in. She made it to the ground, and bolted over to Drill.

He looked terrible in the porch light. Both eyes were swollen shut, and his mouth was a bloody scrawl. His puffed cheeks were one big bruise.

"Thuy?" he mumbled.

"I'm here," she said, tears of residual fear and concern falling down her cheeks and hitting his skin.

"I'm sorry," he slurred. "I did everything I could to keep you safe. I didn't want this to happen."

"It's okay. We're okay," she said, and gently kissed his shoulder. The world smelled like gasoline and booze and car exhaust. Thank God she'd been able to talk sense into them before they burned the place down.

He coughed, and then made a pained sound. She had to get him out of here.

Maddy and David emerged from the barn. David held the shotgun. "They're all gone?" David asked, scanning the road.

"Yes. And I think they'll stay gone," Thuy said. "In the meantime: can I borrow your rental car? It has GPS, right? I'm taking him to the hospital in Knoxville."

CHAPTER FIFTY-TWO

Drill didn't remember much of the rest of that night. He spent Christmas day itself drugged to the gills, barely registering his sister and Thuy hovering over him. It was the day after Christmas now. He could see out of his eyes, although his face still hurt like a motherfucker. He could tell he'd cracked some ribs, and his body was sore all over. Still, they hadn't broken his nose, unlike Timothy King. He grinned at the thought, then winced as his split lip tore slightly.

Tim had deserved that, and more. Catfish was going to have his hands full with that asshole.

Not my problem any more. He remembered Thuy's shouted declarations from that night. He hadn't been able to see what was going on, but he knew that she'd managed to back down the entire Wraith crowd with her bravado — and threats of her powerful family. The Wraiths were too fragile to take on a support club like Red Dagger. Catfish knew better, even if Tim didn't, and he'd keep the rest in line.

As for being cut out of the Wraiths? As far as Drill was concerned, he couldn't have gotten a better Christmas present.

"You awake?"

Drill looked over to see Thuy walking over with a cup of coffee and a plastic cup of apple juice. "Hope that coffee's for me," he croaked.

She shook her head, popping a straw in the cup. "Juice it up, buddy," she said. "Trust me. You're not going to want hot beverages on that lip for a little while."

He drank the juice gratefully, realizing that his throat was parched. "How are you?" he asked.

"Better than you look and probably feel," Thuy joked, but her eyes were dark with concern. She put the coffee down on the nearby tray, then pulled up a chair and took his hand. The feel of her soft skin and small palm in his large, rough hand was like being touched by heaven. He stroked the back of her hand with his thumb.

"I'm so sorry," he said. "I just wanted to keep you safe. I didn't want to drag you into all of this shit. They almost burned down the house. They could've hurt Maddy. They could've hurt you..."

"Shhh." She got up and sat on the bed next to him, looking at him intently. "We didn't get hurt. You could've gotten *killed,* do you realize that? You did everything you could."

"I never should've joined up," he said bitterly.

She sighed. "You were sixteen years old, and they were what you needed at the time," she said, her voice gentle and soothing. "Besides, you know what I'm figuring out?"

"What?"

"If you hadn't joined, then Maddy might not have gone to Berkeley. She wouldn't have David, or me. She wouldn't have the baby she's so eagerly expecting." Thuy smiled at him. "And I wouldn't have found you."

He swallowed hard, and it had nothing to do with the dryness of his throat.

"And I hated my childhood, and my family. I hated what they did to me," she continued. "But it wound up saving my life, and yours. I wouldn't wish it on anyone, but I'm making peace with it. What happened to us makes us who we are."

He thought about it. She was right. His father's cruelty was a result of his own harsh upbringing. And as much as he hated the thought, he'd go through anything if it meant getting a chance with Thuy.

"Are you going to catch any fallout?" he asked. "Using the Red Dagger's name, I mean."

She sighed. "I thought about that later," she admitted. "I don't think it will be a problem. It's not like they're going to catch wind of it. But even if they did… when they branded me, my father told me that I'd always be a part of the club. That I couldn't escape it. If anything, it would be a big 'I told you so' moment for him." She paused. "And up till now, he could've killed me at any time — it's not like he didn't know where I was. So I think I'm good."

He held her hand, squeezing it. He didn't like the thought of her being scared, living with the potential that her father might kill her at any time. It made him want to tuck her against him, put her someplace safe, and stay with her forever. Not that she needed protection, as was evident with her run in with the Wraiths. But still, he wanted to *be* with her.

Which brought up his next problem.

"Are you still thinking of moving back?" he asked. "To Oakland, I mean?"

She shook her head.

He frowned. "It's not just to protect Maddy and me, is it? Keeping us 'under your protection' and all that?"

She chuckled. "You know, Maddy asked the same thing?" she said, shaking her head. "No. I'm staying because I like it here. I might not have a job at the library, but I could still volunteer or something, or work on book drives for the school. I could always get a job somewhere else, or work remotely. And I can still help Maddy, even if it's just watching the baby so she can get some sleep."

Drill stroked her hand, covering it with his other hand. "Does that mean you'll give us another chance?" he asked quietly.

She took a deep breath, then put his hands up to her face, kissing his bruised and battered knuckles. "I was leaving because I thought we didn't have a chance," she said. "If you're willing, if you're ready to commit…"

"Are you kidding? I'm all in," he said eagerly, interrupting her. "The only reason I thought you should go was because I thought you'd be safer. Well, and because I thought you were too good for me. And that you might not be happy here."

"And now?"

He grimaced. "I'll be honest. I'm too fucking selfish."

She laughed.

"I'll make it up to you," he said. "I'll learn to make the fancy food you like, or take you to the city. And I'll do everything to make sure I'm good enough for you."

"You don't have to do anything," she said. "You're just what I need."

They smiled at each other. He tugged her so she was next to him on the bed, even though his cracked ribs protested. He coughed a little, then settled her in.

"So what are you going to do now?" she asked.

"Now that my career in a motorcycle club is finished?" He mulled it over. "I was going to talk to Maddy. Technically, if I decided to work the farm, too, it'd belong to both Maddy and me. I need to talk it over with her, but I think I could help with the farming. It'd be good financially. She could focus more on the marketing and the specialty produce, and David and I can work the land more for the larger crops or for livestock. There are decisions we can make."

"Sounds like a good plan," Thuy enthused, nuzzling his shoulder.

He cuddled her. He'd never been a cuddler before, but he could see himself getting used to it.

"You know," Thuy said slowly. "If you're going to work on the farm, you might want to, um, live there. Like in the cabin."

He smiled at her, her words warming his chest. "Only if you're there with me," he said, his voice a low rumble. "I know, that's stupid fast, but..."

"I fell in love with you stupid fast," Thuy said with a smile. "If you're in, I'm in."

He kissed her. Gently, but with a deep promise of more.

"I love you," he said against her lips. "And if you let me, I'm not going to let you go."

She kissed him back. “Damn right you’re not,” she replied, and he laughed.

CHAPTER FIFTY-THREE

Thuy went back to the library after more than a week of being away. She hadn't been scheduled, and after her little talk with Julianne, she wasn't sure she was going to be scheduled in the future. But Naomi had called her, asking her to cover a shift, and she'd complied.

Drill was back now, settled in the cabin, convalescing. She had an early shift, and she was going to go home and make him some home-made pho. She already had the broth going in the crockpot she'd gotten from Maddy for Christmas, for just such usage.

"Thuy? Can you come back here for a moment?" Julianne said.

Thuy sighed. They hadn't opened for business yet, so she doubted it would take long. And she didn't think that Julianne would fire her when she was covering Naomi's shift. Who else would man the desk? Still, she was nervous as she accompanied Julianne to her office.

"I wanted you to know, I've been doing a lot of thinking since our talk," Julianne said, gesturing to the same seat Thuy had occupied then. "I've been here so long… it's meant so much to me. I was threat-ened by the changes you wanted to make, and you're right: I didn't think that you understood what it meant to be a librarian here. To care about this place, and this community."

Thuy didn't know what to say to that, so she stayed silent.

Julianne sighed. "But the more I thought about it, the more I realized... you're right. This isn't about keeping things the same as they were, necessarily. Tradition is a good thing, one I value. But change is both good and needed, especially when things could be done to improve the lives of the people of Green Valley. People I care about very much."

Thuy nodded.

"That said, I did a lot of soul-searching, and I can't help but feel that the library's role and vision is dictated by its head librarian," Julianne said solemnly. "The head librarian sets the tone, makes the choices, that guide the institution into the future."

Thuy felt her heart fall a little. So, even if she agreed that change might be necessary, ultimately, she was the head librarian. And what the head librarian stated was law. Which meant Thuy and her rebellious notions didn't fit.

Okay. Fine. She had other options, and she'd readied herself for this outcome, even if it was disappointing to her.

"That's why I'll be retiring this month," Julianne said. "And recommending that you be hired as my replacement, as head librarian."

"*What*?" Thuy said, blinking. She was sure she hadn't heard that correctly.

"You understand what it will take to bring the library into the future," Julianne said, nodding briskly. "Just look how you are with the teens. You engage with them. You know how to fix the computers. You're connected on social media with authors. Your vision for how to help rural communities shows that you genuinely care, that you're not looking down your nose from some city-dweller's derisive perspective. You want to help." Julianne's voice broke a little. "You're going to love them, just like I do. I know the library will be in good hands."

Thuy's eyes stung, and her heart warmed. "But Naomi, or Sabrina..." she protested. "They've been here so much longer than I have."

"They're not technically librarians," Julianne said. "Besides, they don't have your particular expertise or training. They'll follow your lead. And you'll do a great job."

"Thank you," Thuy said. "I'll be happy to accept."

"And I'll be happy to spend more time with my grandkids," Julianne said, her eyes bright, her whole posture more loose-limbed and less tense. "It'll be strange, not coming into the library."

"No one's stopping you from coming as often as you like," Thuy pointed out. "You're always going to be welcome here, you know."

"I know. And I'm excited to see what happens in the future."

Thuy thought about it — about transforming the library, and getting closer to the community. About spending time with Maddy, watching as her farm and her family grew, being a part of that growth. And she thought about Drill, and their future.

"I'm excited to see what happens, as well," Thuy murmured. In fact, she couldn't wait.

EPILOGUE

Drill sank into the cabin's bed, groaning a little. It had been a long day on the farm. Now that it was March, they were getting fully ready for planting. He'd worked most of the day on getting the tractor tuned up, and helping David with getting the cold frames set up for Maddy's planned produce. He'd taken a break at lunch to spend some time with Maddy and his nephew, Cole. The kid was a pistol, with Maddy's blue eyes and David's dark hair. He always looked serious. Maddy said when he got a little older, he'd smile more. He was still less than a month old and looked about the size of a large loaf of bread. Still, the kid was amazing. Drill had never given much thought to a family of his own, but seeing Cole, he definitely warmed to the idea.

Especially when Thuy was holding a baby, Drill thought, and smiled.

He glanced at the clock. It was nearly ten, but it was Tuesday. Tuesday was teen night at the library, and Thuy always stayed late to lock up. Nonetheless, after their dust up with the Wraiths, when Thuy wasn't on the farm, he was a little nervous. They hadn't given Thuy, Maddy, or himself any more trouble since the incident, but he was always on the lookout for a potential breakout. So far, Catfish had ignored him, and the other bikers had given Thuy a wide berth out of respect for her family and crew. Her bluff had worked like a charm.

He yawned, stretching slightly, loosening his tight muscles. He ought to be reading the book on permaculture David had given him. It had taken him a little while — and a private talk — to warm up to the guy, but he had to admit, David was turning into a doting father, and he treated Maddy like a queen. *Which he damned well ought to,* Drill thought with a nod. And David was an unconventional farmer, but he'd probably do well. Still, he was really bookish, and Drill had spent enough time on a farm to just *know* shit.

It would be an interesting summer, and an even more interesting harvest. They'd see how it turned out.

Still, he didn't feel like lying in bed and reading a textbook. He'd finally finished reading *The Name of the Wind* after the New Year, and then he'd gotten sidetracked by Cole's birth and helping Thuy move their stuff from Oakland, and then getting rid of his apartment and moving in with Thuy here in the cabin. Now, he was starting *A Wise Man's Fear,* the sequel.

He couldn't believe it, but he was *excited* about reading a book.

It was all because of Thuy. She'd changed his life. And he couldn't thank her enough.

He heard her open the door. "Hey, baby," she called up to the loft. "Mmmm. It's nice and toasty in here."

He'd built up the fire before he went to bed, knowing that's how she liked to come home. "It's even more comfy in bed," he called back, in his best tempting voice.

She laughed. He heard her putting her stuff down, settling in. She climbed up, her dark eyes alight with amusement. "You *do* look cozy," she remarked.

He grinned, resting his book on the nightstand. "Have fun with the kids?"

"More teens than ever were there tonight," she said with a happy smile. He loved the way she glowed, talking about them. "The middle-graders did a St. Patrick's thing, and there was a decent *Magic: The Gathering* showing. But the book club is gaining speed, too. They read

An Ember in the Ashes and talked about parallels to modern politics and Roman history. I'm so proud of them."

"Have I mentioned how much I love you?" he asked, responding to the emotion in her voice.

She looked taken aback. Then she stared at him, glowing. "I always love hearing it," she said. "Almost as much as I love you."

They stood like that for a moment, grinning at each other, just happy in each other's company.

"So," she continued, "the grant the library got — it's covering a lot of things I hadn't even realized. We're going to be opening the Native American art and cultural exhibit, we'll have some money for a remodel, even another position. And I was able to get new shelves for the YA books we got. The teens, and the adults, are thrilled."

She undressed as she talked, unselfconsciously. She stripped out of her blouse, tossing it in the laundry basket, then shimmied out of her skirt and stockings. She was just in her bra and underwear.

Drill felt his mouth water, book forgotten.

"What about you?" she asked, with a small smile. "Do anything interesting while I was gone?"

"Not as interesting as I'm about to be doing," he said, his voice rough and low. "C'mere."

She laughed again, her eyes twinkling. "Why, Drill," she said, with a fake Southern accent, "I do believe you're trying to seduce me."

"No try about it," he said, and kissed her.

ABOUT THE AUTHOR

Cathy Yardley is an award-winning author of romance, chick lit, and urban fantasy, who has sold over 1.2 million copies worldwide. She writes fun, geeky, and diverse characters who believe that underdogs can make good and sometimes being a little wrong is just right. She spends her time writing in the wilds of East Seattle, riding herd on her two dogs, one son, and one husband.

Website: http://www.cathyyardley.com
Facebook: https://www.facebook.com/CathyYardleyAuthor/
Goodreads: https://www.goodreads.com/author/show/6777.Cathy_-Yardley
Twitter: @cathyyardley
Instagram: cathyyardley

Find Smartypants Romance online:
Website: www.smartypantsromance.com
Facebook: www.facebook.com/smartypantsromance/
Goodreads: www.goodreads.com/smartypantsromance
Twitter: @smartypantsrom
Instagram: @smartypantsromance